To Jenny
With love,
Sarah

OUT THERE

OUT THERE

a novel

SARAH STARK

LeafStormPress

SANTA FE, NEW MEXICO

LEAF STORM PRESS
Post Office Box 4670
Santa Fe, New Mexico 87502
LeafStormPress.com

Leaf Storm logo is a trademark of Leaf Storm Press LLC.
For information about special discounts for bulk purchases, please email LeafStormPress@gmail.com.
Author photo by Laurie Allegretti

ISBN 978-0-9914105-0-7
Library of Congress Control Number: 2014931471

First edition
Printed in the United States of America
Set in Caslon
Designed by Ian Shimkoviak and Alan Hebel, thebookdesigners.com

Publisher's Cataloging-in-Publication Data
(Provided by Quality Books, Inc.)

Stark, Sarah.
Out there : a novel / Sarah Stark. -- First edition.
pages cm
LCCN 2014931471
ISBN 978-0-9914105-0-7

1. García Márquez, Gabriel, 1928---Fiction.
2. García Márquez, Gabriel, 1928- Cien años de soledad--Fiction. 3. Soldiers--United States--Fiction.
4. Indians of North America--Fiction. 5. Iraq War, 2003-2011--Fiction. 6. Post-traumatic stress disorder--Fiction. 7. Mexico--Fiction. 8. Adventure stories.
I. Title.

PS3619.T3738O98 2014   813'.6
                              QBI14-600033

To my parents,
Susan and Richard Stark,
and for
Reuben Paul Santos (1982-2009)

I was too young to know that I would go on living,
Human and nostalgic,
Remembering without bitterness,
Multiplying all that is good,
Softness in my heart.

—JEFFERSON LONG SOLDIER

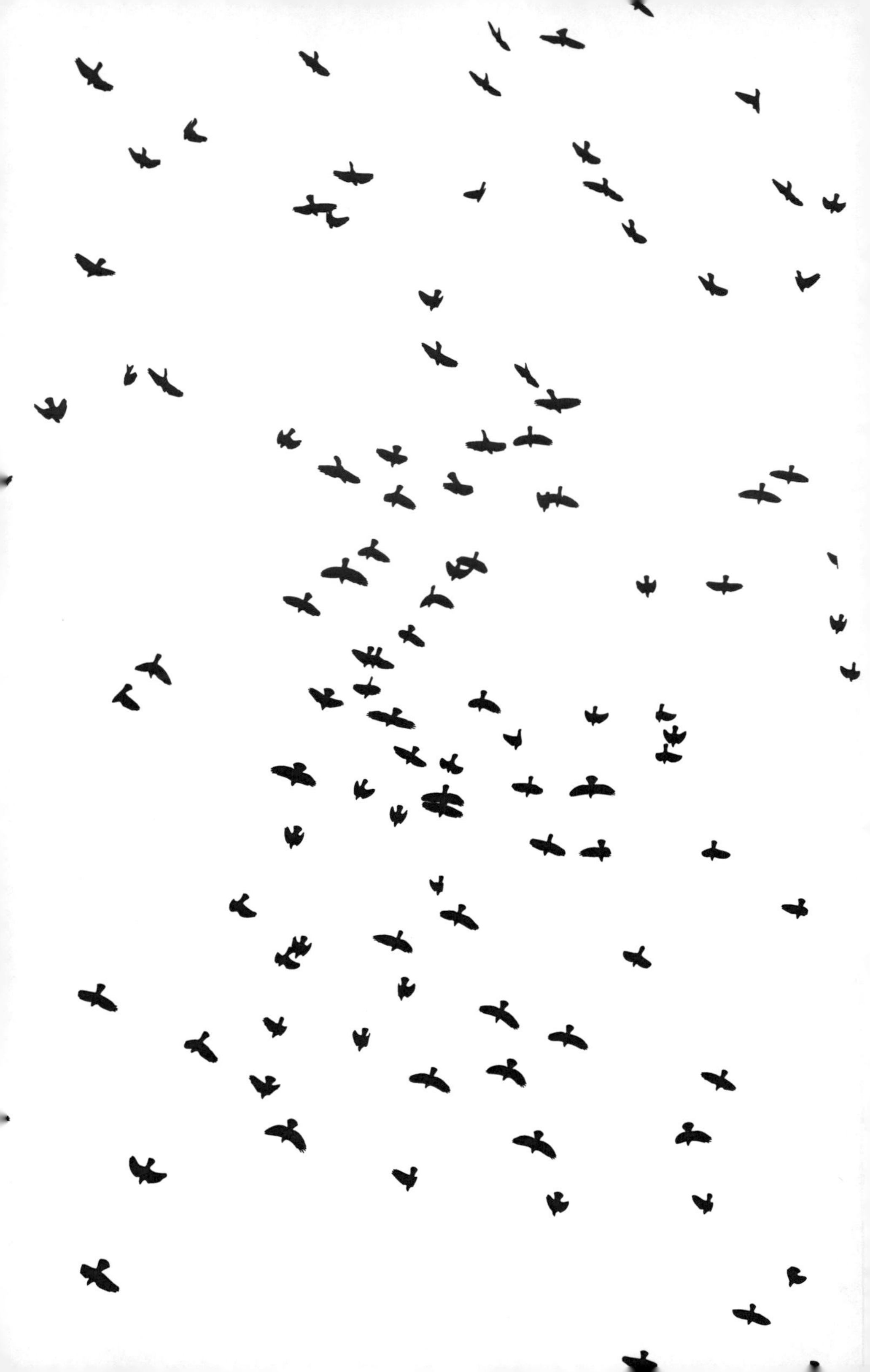

JEFFERSON FELT FOR the book at his chest—still there—and walked on his own two feet up the ramp and down the wide hall past the A gates, more fortunate than so many others. The New Mexican light was bright; he remembered his old friend now as it seared his dream state back into the present. All these tourists streaming past with their rolling suitcases. He remembered them as he put one foot in front of the other, these ladies from Dallas and Chicago and Atlanta in search of turquoise and silver and framed art for their foyers. These executives out west for their annual meeting in the desert, a chance to ride a horse and smell a mountain and taste the sky. Past the burrito stand he walked, almost skipping, his beautiful beaded high-tops honoring each new step. He paused now to adjust the headband he'd carefully finger-crocheted over the long days of his journey home, using the plastic bags that had held his sandwiches, his magazines, his gum.

It was not a matter of hoping it was safe out. It was not a matter of being careful or identifying the exit signs or saying his prayers or dodging bullets. There were most definitely snipers in the airport, explosive tumbleweeds on the highway, insurgents in stolen minivans, undercover extremists buying lattes in front of him and single mothers wired for explosives behind. A whole non-war-zone world on the brink of apocalypse.

He had thought a lot about reentry over the previous weeks, each time with less than satisfactory results. It seemed impossible that his return home could be how he'd imagined it. In the movies there always seemed to be white and black and Chinese little brothers and sisters standing beside their parents, wearing new clothes and waving flags. Happy tears, a small-town band playing "America the Beautiful." The media behind the rope, with their cameras and lights and microphones, vying to interview the beaming soldier. Jefferson had replayed this little film clip in his head over and over, curled up into a ball on his bunk as he struggled to find a more realistic vision of what his return to the Albuquerque International Sunport might actually look like. Nothing had come to him.

He walked past that same old Navajo woman selling roasted piñons from her wooden cart. She'd been right there when he left, three and a half years before. She smiled at Jefferson now through those same tight lips, those same slanted eyes. Like that woman in the famous painting. The . . . the . . . what was it? Lisa. The *Mona* Lisa! *Mona*. What an angelic name that was. *Mona Lisa*. Jefferson thought of the old piñon woman as New Mexico's own Grandmother Mona Lisa. He nodded at the unsmiling smiling old woman, and gave her his own version of the unsmiling smile, a smile meant to express how beautiful he thought her, how humble and good, and then he continued his light-footed walk to what he imagined to be the absolute midpoint of the atrium that stood at the intersection of Concourse A and Concourse B. He thumped his duffel and backpack onto the ground, checked the book at his chest again—still there. Then he turned to gaze down the straightaway with its moving sidewalk—about the length of a nice sprint, maybe a two hundred yard dash—that led to the security barrier, to the free world, to Esco and Cousin Nigel and home.

OUT THERE

Here was his moment of reentry. Here was his moment—before all these good travelers, before God and the angels and the possible terrorists hiding behind plastic plants and the beautiful Grandmother Mona Lisa of New Mexico and the tired traveling families and the businessmen—to do it as close as he could to how it should be done. It was not meant to be a big moment, not in the sense of trumpets and snare drums. It was not meant to be loud. Jefferson felt that if it had a color, the moment would be white. From the sky would float thousands of tiny white flowers, and there would be soft flutes and clarinets, heard as if from far away. And the deep-rooted trees that had survived along with him would reach up into the blue sky and offer prayers of thanksgiving with their rustling branches. A quietness would accompany him. For here he was, Jefferson Long Soldier of Santa Fe, returning home unscathed.

He straightened his spine and his legs, swept his arms slowly out and over his head, stared at his outstretched fingers on each side, pointing to the heavens beyond the skylights. Hallelujah Jesus and Joseph and the Wise Men, he thought. Hallelujah O Blessed Lady of Guadalupe. Thanksgiving to God for this beautiful day. Thanksgiving to God for this moment of quiet before all these good people. Thanksgiving to God for all that is to come.

He prayed for inspiration and pulled up his sweatpants to just above his shins and took a deep breath. He smiled down at the beautiful beadwork at the top of his high-tops, giving thanks for the time he'd been granted, time to hand-stitch each of those tiny little beads to the tough canvas, and he adjusted his headband one last time. He unzipped his backpack and pulled out his harmonica—the closest thing he had to a flute—and latched his drumsticks to his belt. Closing his eyes, he blew a few chords, chords he was happy to hear, chords that vibrated with precisely the sad, scared, thankful way he was feeling. As he hummed through the harmonica, Jefferson tried to think of just the right line for this moment, something between a prayer and a declaration, something that would remind listeners where he had been, that would celebrate his return, that would mourn the losses. If he really focused, if he breathed deeply while he sang, perhaps his hands would stop shaking. The shaking was normal, he'd been told, but Jefferson was hoping for a reentry celebration without it.

But his mind was jumbling everything up, and his headband kept sliding over his right eye, making it very difficult, frankly, to concentrate, and the long straightaway before him was looking more and more like a football field's length, or two or three, much, much more than a sprint. God, it was a long way down there to the outside world.

What had he been trying to remember?

Jefferson saw through the narrow slits of his eyes that a small crowd had formed around him as he played the harmonica. He thought of the notes he played as homecoming notes, notes that would express both celebration and sadness.

But what was he going to chant?

He felt for the book, considering whether he might take it out and consult it in plain view. This would be the easy answer, but he had vowed to keep the book safe and therefore secret for at least the first few days. He couldn't risk exposing it to a world such as this, where danger and the possibility of misunderstanding lurked in the most unexpected places. So even though Jefferson could not remember the name of his favorite character, the man who had survived twenty years of war in García Márquez's novel, even though every single word of the novel that had saved his life had fled, Jefferson refused to take the book out of its hiding place.

Something must have been wrong with his brain.

The crowd was medium-sized by then, and the faces turned upon him seemed concerned, sympathetic. So he finished the little melody and made his body still. Surely now was the perfect time to express what he needed to express. Maybe these people didn't even know themselves why they had stopped, why they stepped closer to listen. That was fine. How could they understand how important it was that he tell them where he'd been?

Now that he'd had time to think, he knew the line he would chant. It was his own words mixed with García Márquez's words, a chant in the spirit of García Márquez. Jefferson knew GGM would approve. And so he opened his mouth and began filling his lungs with air. In. And. Out. With the first big breath, he opened his eyes and saw that the crowd now numbered nearly fifty people. With the second breath he filled his gut and the back of his lower rib cage and began to bellow the words in the deepest voice he could summon up:

I am Jefferson Long Soldier, and I am returned from WA-AR.

He sang slowly, a whale underwater, desperate to reach the open sea. When he arrived at the word *war*, he divided it into two syllables, taking a quick intense breath between the first, *wa*, and the second, *ar*. He held the *ar* for as long as he had breath in his lungs. Then, seeing the crowd to be eager, he repeated the line, thinking of a follow-on line as he sang:

I am Jefferson Long Soldier, and I am returned from WA-AR.

The crowd forming around him tingled with compassion, and though there were no tiny white flowers yet, he imagined they might begin snowing down once he stepped out of the terminal.

The follow-on line was one he'd loved since the first time he came across it. It was what the guy in the novel said when he returned from twenty years of civil war and had to answer for himself. Jefferson was a little distracted because he could not remember the name of the soldier, the one about whom García Márquez had written so many beautiful lines. Where had the guy been? everyone wanted to know when he returned. He'd been "out there," the guy in the novel had replied. *Out there,* an incomprehensible faraway place. As in, *You cannot understand where I have been.* Jefferson stared out into the sea of compassionate and confused faces and filled his lungs once more, hoping in this final breath for one last moment of quiet and reflection at the center of the crowd.

Where have I be-een? You say, where have I be-een?
And I tell you I have been out—there . . .
I have been out there . . .

As he sang, Jefferson divided *been* into two syllables—*be-een*—just as he had *wa-ar,* for it was like this, he imagined, that monks of long ago had chanted in windowless stone passages in Scotland and England and Spain, places he'd never seen but which he imagined as full of grit and sacrifice and darkness and faith. He imagined these ancient prayerful men to be his brothers, and he thought of them as he sang out to the onlookers at the airport, chanting as he imagined ancient men of God had done, men who chanted to believe in something large and bright. Closing his eyes and arching his spine and tilting his head back, Jefferson chanted louder, forcing the air out of him and up toward the high ceiling, trying to find some measure of peace.

I have been out there . . .

He breathed life into the end of the line, this time searching for hope.

Out there . . .

And once more, this time his breath a prayer for understanding.

Out . . . there . . .

When he had expelled all the air from his belly, and felt as if the meditation had come to its natural conclusion—announcing his solemn and yet, he hoped, gracious return to the not-at-war world—Jefferson hoisted his duffel and backpack onto his shoulders, scanned the crowd, and bowed his head to them. Deciding against playing the harmonica again, he returned it to his pocket and set off down the straightaway.

OUT THERE

The onlookers watched the honey-eyed, brown-skinned young man go, wondering. Such lovely eyes. So young. Lucky to be alive, though. And they kept wondering long after that moment, in the sad, disconnected way in which we all try to imagine the tragedies of strangers.

WAY UP THERE, at the end of the straightaway, Jefferson could make out the low, stocky shape of his grandmother, Esco, and, next to her, his mammoth cousin Nigel. Hazy both—but, he could tell, solid and hopeful as always. A lone red balloon bobbed between them, whooping silently, "Welcome home! Welcome home!" along with all the other things they meant to tell him—that they loved him, for instance, and that they'd feared this moment might never arrive. No Josephina, though. Maybe she would surprise him later.

Between him and them stood that crazy contraption that had always given him the shakes. A final test. Whose idea was it to create a spinning door, a door that denied passage to the uncoordinated, the slow, the anxious, the crippled? What deft entrepreneur had made millions over this faux piece of progress? Jefferson felt a familiar surge of frustration—hatred was too strong a word. Yes, he was able. Yes, he was alert. But did he really have to think so much about his footing, just to pass from one side to another?

Esco and Nigel were both smiling, waving at him hopefully, nearer now but still distorted and blurred through the multiple planes of Plexiglas. He knew what he had to do. He'd been traveling for almost a week now, from the day he left

Iraq, so he'd skipped a few days, and now he felt ungrounded. Unthinkable, to cross this tricky, shifting threshold without placing his hands on the ground.

From her side of the door, Esco had all the clarity she needed. There Jefferson was. He might be jumbled through the glass, but she could see him. He was alive.

But she couldn't understand what was happening. Why had Jefferson stopped and placed his duffel by his feet? Maybe he needed help. Why was he looking over his shoulder?

Jefferson checked behind to see that no one was walking too close, rubbed his hands together, and planted them on the floor in front of him as he kicked his heels up behind him and over his head. He paused for a moment to get just the right bend in his knees, just the right arch in his lower back, for equilibrium, and then began to walk on his hands. God, it was good to be upside down. This would make all the difference, his hands heavy and pulsing now, a heartbeat in his fingertips, the skin deep purple.

He felt a great amassing of himself between his eyebrows and even farther back than that, behind his eyes, back where he imagined they connected to the filaments of his mind, all the mystical wirings of his inner universe. He was one with the orangutans and the spider monkeys and the lemurs, the bats and stalactites who slept all day in the caves of Carlsbad, the icicles on warm days that hung long and drippy from underneath the eaves, all reaching, reaching, reaching for the earth.

Esco, seeing her grandson upside down on the other side of the security barrier, pulled away from Nigel's grasp and rushed the glass doors, yelling, "Come on, honey. Stop doing that! Get up! Come on!" It was as if someone was playing a terrible joke. She was so close to holding her grandson tight, and now this. A security guard near her stood up and began talking excitedly into her phone. *We could have a problem—I need some help down here.* Another guard, from back at the intersection of Concourse A and Concourse B, was running Jefferson's way. What was going on? Why was he on his hands, now that he was so close to home?

But Jefferson had come to the natural end of his pose—dizziness and a feeling of lonely dehydration, was how he usually described the sensation that brought him down—and so he kicked down out of it and smiled a big smile at the uniformed man who had rushed up to him, yelling "Move it along! Move it along!" Why was he holding on to Jefferson's triceps so hard, pushing him along, making him walk—after all that—through the regular glass door off to the far right, the door usually reserved for people in wheelchairs? Hadn't the man ever realized some people needed a little extra grounding to get through a revolving door?

The guard pushed him through the door, and Jefferson lugged his duffel the final paces to his family. Esco was wearing her favorite mauve tracksuit, the one that had always made him cringe at the way it accentuated her thick middle. But her hair was cut short as always, wiry in its health, and her skin glistened. Nigel swayed from side to side on in-turned ankles that nevertheless appeared to be holding steady under their burden. He was as big as ever.

It was true that Jefferson had left the jurisdiction of the US Army, officially and in good standing, at 8:15 that morning at Fort Drum, but only now, as he crossed the security threshold in Albuquerque, did he know he'd truly made it. He felt tired suddenly, much more so than he'd realized before the chanting and the walk down the long hall and the handstand and, even before that, all the packing and planning. But there was some relief, even if it was not the instantaneous happiness he'd hoped might descend like a miracle upon him. The smile on his lips was only partially forced, he realized, and he was able to find a few words, more words in fact than he had spoken in many days.

"Esco," he said, embracing her. "Nigel—" He held the large arm of his cousin, beginning to weep. And he found that he could say nothing more; he could only hold them and let them hold him in return.

Now that he was living the moment, though, Jefferson felt that something about it wasn't right. Esco was there, and that was right. Nigel was there, and that too was right. The Sandias welcomed him out to the east, and though he could not see them, Jefferson sensed the Jemez Mountains up in the north. The distant plateaus and red rocky mountains and wide-open sky all participated in his return, listening and watching and recording. So too the birds of the high desert and the lizards and the burrowing rodents of the ground. Jefferson's body, unscathed, was there as well. But some large, unidentified piece of his spirit—he didn't know where it was, or how long it had been missing—had remained behind.

This was the part of the homecoming that was not right; not all of Jefferson had come home.

Outside, a plane scudded down the runway and took to the sky, and he thought of all those other soldiers returning home. Survivors from San Francisco and Waco and Charlottesville and Birmingham, Las Cruces and Española and Abiquiu and Los Alamos, each one leaving a plane and walking through an airport and hugging and being hugged. Each one returning home.

"Let's go home," said Esco, curling her small arm into the crook of Jefferson's elbow as she had since he was a teenager. Nigel picked up his duffel, and the three of them moved as one through the airport and out into the familiar solace of the high desert.

WHEN THAT HORRIBLE thing happened to Ramon's throat on the forty-seventh day, Jefferson wrote it down on a piece of paper and folded it inside the cover of the book, thinking it would be his tribute; there, he would keep Ramon's memory close to his heart. It was a single line on a blank piece of paper, a lone memory of a solitary loss Jefferson had seen happen right next to him.

Not too long after, the thing that happened to the guy named Adair, from Hollidaysburg, joined the thing that happened to Ramon. Then there was Dudzinski, twenty-two. Then Hazelton, twenty-nine. Then Alton with the corn-husk voice from Nebraska.

Still, it was not a list.

The string of losses on that piece of folded-up paper kept multiplying, but Jefferson would not call it a list. Like an ancient scribe recording by candlelight all that would otherwise be forgotten, Jefferson wrote, memorializing hometowns and the ages of the men and women he had watched die. With few exceptions, these were the only details that stuck with him. Not so much the names—names had always been secondary for him, difficult to remember—and only occasionally a detail about the face or the voice, but rather the places from which these soldiers had come. The trees rooted in the land in those places, the birds that roosted there, according to their own natures. These were the pictures that took up residence in his mind.

OUT THE CAR window, purple mesas and red sky slid past, a welcome celebration for Jefferson's eyes. He knew Esco and Nigel were trying not to ask questions. What parts of him were aching? How could they make it better? The ordinary part of Jefferson's brain had expected this, but so much more of it was spinning. He'd thought something about these two would have changed, but when he looked at them, it was as if he had never left. He'd thought his hands would have stopped twitching by now. He'd thought Nigel would at least have said something about his beaded high-tops. He wondered if he should recite from García Márquez, something simple for the two of them, something that might help, but decided against it when he noticed the deep wrinkles in his grandmother's forehead. Maybe she had changed a little, after all. He was sure those wrinkles hadn't been there before.

She reached out to him with her right hand. "Oh my boy. Oh my boy—it *is* you. Is it really *you?*"

Her hands were as soft and hardworking as he remembered, patting his shoulder and then tucking short hair behind her ear, correcting the steering wheel as it veered right. She couldn't stop saying it. "You were gone for so long, honey. Gone a long, long time. Is it really *you?*"

15

"Looks like it, Esco, sweet old woman," he said when she stopped talking. She seemed tired. He held on to her hand as she drove, smelling her lavender conditioner. He wanted to tell her stories about the guys he'd met, and explain why he hadn't come home once in more than three years, but his mind was jumping along the highway.

What he really wanted to talk about was the puppy, how he'd dreamed of her on the last leg of the flight. He was hoping Esco could drive straight to the animal shelter on the way home. The pup could help him unpack, witness his struggles with sympathetic eyes and ears. Jefferson imagined reading to the pup after everyone else had gone to bed, maybe a little García Márquez, maybe a little of the list. And then the pup would be with him when he woke up on his first new day home. But Jefferson didn't know what time it was as they continued on up the highway toward Santa Fe—he couldn't even say what day it was—so he decided to hold the dream inside just a little longer.

Nigel thrust his head into the gap between the two front seats, not sure what to say but wanting to be a part of it all. Little Jefferson was home. True, he looked a bit beefy. The beaded high-tops were a nice touch—Little Jefferson always did have a certain flair—but what was with that plastic headband cocked catawampus across his forehead? And there'd been some commotion down at the end of the straightaway at the airport—Nigel could see the other passengers hanging back, staring, as Jefferson approached the security barrier—even before the hand-walking that had almost gotten them all arrested. But Jefferson was alive, and now they were in the car, headed home, and it was all going to be okay.

Darkness was coming as they began the climb up La Bajada Hill, a little more than halfway home. Esco and Nigel would do just about anything for him, Jefferson told himself.

He wished he could sink his hands into the earth right now, let the blood run heavy into his head, but that was impossible in the car, so instead he closed his eyes and prayed. As Esco gunned the Corolla up the long rise, he visualized his fingers gripping the stones by the road, his feet waving to the ravens.

Nigel tapped him on the shoulder. "You prayin', cousin?" His big head was too close.

"Sorta," Jefferson replied, his eyes slits.

Nigel got the message, withdrawing his head and sitting back.

Jefferson closed his eyes and summoned back the place where his hands traveled through the rough scrabble along the highway, thought about needing a dog and wanting a dog and how Esco and Nigel had to understand this.

The Corolla crested the top of La Bajada Hill, and Jefferson knew the timing would not get any better. Esco and Nigel might be tired and ready to get home, but at that moment they were also the least likely people in the world to say no to anything his heart desired.

He cleared his throat. "Do you think we could stop at the animal shelter on the way home, Esco? I'm hoping to get a dog a puppy, really. I'm thinking a sweet puppy with an old soul to keep me company now that I'm home. You know, to listen." Jefferson stopped, not knowing what else to say.

Esco seemed to force a smile, and Nigel said, "We can do whatever you need us to, cousin," and so they drove to the animal shelter. It was twenty-five minutes before closing time, and there were background investigations and forty-eight-hour waits and fees to be paid. But the volunteer on duty had lost her lover in Vietnam, and she looked upon Jefferson with a pure and heroic love as he explained his need for a dog, and escorted him through the kennels until he settled on the pup of his visions, a gray-eyed blue heeler that had some oddly comforting measure of hound in her bold voice.

He named her Remedios the Pup, after Remedios the

Beauty in *One Hundred Years*, who was said to be wise beyond her years and of a beauty so intense as to drive men to insanity. Nigel, not understanding the reference, said of the pup, "Well, she is a very pretty girl," and Esco just clicked her tongue in approval.

Once they got home, Jefferson nestled Remedios in soft towels on his bed. No one slept much that night because of her various needs and insecurities. Esco stationed herself on a cot at Jefferson's feet, and Nigel slept in his sleeping bag on the floor. They were not taking any chances with Jefferson's safety, they told him. Though they were sure he was okay and the pup would be his guardian angel, they'd still sleep better right there with him.

OVER THE NEXT few days Esco found herself unable to settle. She stood behind the counter as Jefferson ate his tofu breakfast burritos, filling small bowls with cashews and Cheetos and raisins, dusting the tile mosaic of Our Lady of Guadalupe over the stove, sitting on her stool with her book, pretending to read but unable to track the words along the page. She had so many questions she wasn't brave enough to ask out loud. When would he tell her how he really was? When would the stories from over there begin to come out of him? And what was he carrying strapped to his chest, under his shirt? She'd noticed the bulk of it when they hugged at the airport, but she hadn't said anything, waiting for a better time.

And what had happened to his voice? Aside from a few words of greeting at the airport and his request to stop by the animal shelter on the ride home, she had only heard Jefferson baby-talking to little Remedios the Pup and singing late at night in the bathroom. He hadn't mentioned the new turquoise paint on the kitchen cabinets. And had he forgotten the garden behind the house? She'd thought he would go straight back there.

Jefferson found himself wanting to recite again—that dry anxiety forming in his throat, that thirst for the words—but he took another bite of his burrito instead. The night before, he'd taken the book out in the bathroom before getting into bed and sung a few favorite lines in what he imagined to be a whisper. Esco had given him an odd look when he'd jumped—cannonball style—into his old bed, but he ignored it. He'd tell her all about García Márquez and the novel later, when he felt more connected to his surroundings. When he'd spent some time in the backyard, maybe, clipping back the chamisa and rosemary bushes he was sure had grown wild while he was away. When he'd caught the scent of piñon and begun to remember this place he had called home for so long. Airplane travel created a problem for people like him, who needed time to adjust to the land. It was too much to be in one sandy country at the beginning of the month, in another sandy country by the middle of the month, with ten days in between at a military base in New York near Lake Ontario.

In the bathroom he'd looked in the mirror at the vaguely familiar outline of skin and bones and cartilage. For several minutes he'd whisper-chanted his own version of the line from the novel—*I have the tired look of a vegetarian. I look like a tired vegetarian*—laughing to his reflection. That idea always struck him right in the funny bone. What did GGM have against vegetarians?

His skin looked tired, as did his eyes, which made sense. A pretty woman in the army had told him that war was terrible for your complexion and your eyes. "Unless you like looking wise." She laughed. "They say every death you witness adds ten years." She'd been wrong, though, Jefferson thought, sitting down on the tile floor. He looked old, but he didn't look ancient. After that he'd begun again with another tribute to GGM, another riff on a line that he loved for its humor in the face of sadness. *All the politicians are the same. The only difference is, some go to church at eight o'clock and some go at eleven.* Oh, how he loved that line, and in the cozy pink-tiled bathroom of his home, he found it had just the cadence to calm his brain. Just this one line, he thought to himself as he chanted. Just this one line. And he had gone on to chant it for fifteen minutes with his head propped against the wall next to the tub, like he'd done in middle school when he'd wanted to listen to Coldplay in privacy. Even chanting very softly, he liked the natural way his voice paused after the first two syllables of *politicians* before belting out the final two syllables more quickly and in a lower register—*PO-LI-ti-shuns*. After singsonging the entire line for all those minutes, Jefferson became so attached to this word that he chanted it for an additional three minutes.

Though he loved the sound of the word *politicians*, it brought up the difficult topic of politics. Jefferson didn't understand why anyone spent energy on politics. In the range of all human activity, politics seemed so dishonest and low. He imagined the good things all those politicians could have done with their lives if only they'd chosen other paths. If he found himself in a conversation that turned political, he just threw his hands down on the nearest level patch of sand and kicked his heels high overhead. This tended to kill the conversation.

He was trying to remember what the next line had been when Esco, still standing across the kitchen counter but now staring at his chest, said, "What was that you were singing last night in the bathroom? Sounded nice—a song, maybe?"

"Oh, that," he said. "You heard that?"

She gave him the be-serious look.

"More like chanting," he said.

She just stared.

"I'm serious—you know me, I'm no singer, Esco."

But her curled lip said she was in no mood for his funny talk. "And what's that you've got under your shirt?" she said.

Jefferson returned his grandmother's penetrating gaze with a pinched-eyebrow look of his own. Though he wanted to move toward honesty and openness, he didn't have the energy now. To allow himself to heal, he needed to take his time when it came to discussing difficult issues. And the book strapped to his chest? García Márquez's godlike words? Words that had been a blanket of comfort ever since the night Ramon from Las Cruces was shot in the throat, two feet from Jefferson in an overturned humvee? That was his own private business, and it was sacred. For all her spirituality, all her love of books, Esco would not understand his need to have GGM's words strapped to him, so close.

"Under my shirt? It's nothing, really," he said, trying to reassure his grandmother, not deceive her. He rubbed the book reflexively through his shirt, and grabbed a handful of Cheetos. "Sure is good to be home, Esco. Sure is good to be home."

Esco was hearing an echo. Ever since Jefferson walked through that door at the airport, his words had come at her as if in a dream. His voice sounded faraway and hollow, like her mother and grandmother's voices when they visited in the night. The boy was heavy, too, as if he'd stuffed himself with white bread and soda over there. She noticed a tightness in his jaw—he must have been grinding his teeth—and his eyes seemed to pulse to a brooding, uneasy drumbeat. Though his body bore no visible wounds, it was clear that his soul was sick.

She didn't believe that he had nothing under his shirt—she could see the outline of something stiff and rectangular—but she was too tired to pursue it. All she wanted now was to sit on her stool in the kitchen, watching him eat his food. She too had trouble envisioning the future, what Jefferson would do now that he was home. But she was older than he was—a lot older—and she'd had plenty of practice in waiting. Most things in life resolved themselves in time.

"Go see your cousin," she said finally. "He really missed you."

JEFFERSON WALKED WITH the pup the two blocks to Nigel's, past the Old Man Ramirez rental shacks and the old woman's adobe with its boarded-up windows and the plastic tulips in pots on the porch. She might be dead by now, but the same concrete blocks were still stacked by the mailbox. Passing Brae Street, he thought of Josephina. She was probably home right now, probably married. It was stupid even to think about it, so he kept on. He cut through the chamisa and scrag grass of the vacant lot and headed straight for the shed in the corner of Nigel's backyard.

Auntie Linda, Nigel's mother and the much-older sister of Jefferson's own mother, was probably still asleep in the house. Esco had had two daughters, both wild as jackrabbits. Unlike Jefferson's mom, Linda had stayed around, but in her fifty years she had yet to find a job that mixed well with her hard late-night habits. Nigel's dad Jorge, a kind-hearted loner who worked for one of the museums, had stayed around too.

Jefferson could see Nigel in the entrance to the shed, his bulky body filling half the doorway, spilling over the upturned concrete blocks that served as his stool. In addition to the shell of a Ford Pacer, the shed housed tin cans full of nails and screws, a stack of old tires, an electric train set, and a ten-speed's seat and handlebars. Throughout the neighborhood Nigel was known as a fixer. At the moment he was fiddling with his old motorbike, and he didn't look up.

Jefferson ducked through the doorway and positioned himself in Nigel's line of sight. From the old CD player on the windowsill floated the screechings of the Bee Gees. He could have sworn the Gibbs brothers had been belting out the same track the last time he'd visited Nigel's shed. Nigel had loved the Bee Gees since sixth grade, when "Stayin' Alive" was the first 45 he ever played on his portable record player. Smokey Robinson and certain Johnny Cash tunes also held special places in his heart.

"Wuzzup, Nigel? Looking good." Jefferson indicated the motorbike, which had been an on-again, off-again project for Nigel as long as he could remember. It too had begun as handlebars and a seat.

Nigel smiled broadly. "Can't complain," he said. "My bike's almost done, you're home safe and sound . . . *stayin' aliiii-iiiii-iiii-iiive* . . ."

Jefferson bowed.

Nigel paused, but when they finally came, his words were as expected. "So, you think you're gonna be okay after a while? You look pretty good to me." He chuckled to himself as he tightened a screw. "Life pretty much back to normal, you think?"

"Right. Life back to normal."

From around the corner came the deep rumble of a Harley—Manny-Down-the-Street, Jefferson guessed, still fixing bikes out of his garage. He looked for the metal folding chair that had at one time been his, but it was nowhere to be seen. He knew the Pacer was off-limits, as were the stacked tires, so he crossed his ankles and sat in the dirt.

The two had never been big talkers, but there were things Jefferson needed to share if Nigel was going to understand the New Jefferson. It would take time. For now he would let Nigel believe that all was well, that his transition back home would be smooth. Jefferson wanted to believe this too, but the shakiness in his hands and the way he'd jumped just now when Nigel dropped his wrench on top of the metal toolbox made him doubt it.

"Esco make you your favorite breakfast?" Nigel asked.

"Yup. Tasted so good. I don't know what was up with the army's tofu, man, but I couldn't get it down. Practically had to start eating meat, I'm telling you."

"Doesn't look like you skipped many meals to me, cousin."

"You're one to talk, big guy."

At this Nigel lumbered up from his stool, an elephant trying to be a yogi in his loose sweatpants and a threadbare tent of a T-shirt. His beaming face seemed the size of Jupiter up close. The Gibbs brothers were still screaming from the windowsill as Nigel took his place in front of the car. Holding an imaginary microphone and staring with theatrical menace first at Jefferson and next out and up, as if to a broader crowd, he proclaimed, "If you got it, flaunt it, baby. If you got it . . . flaunt it." He swiveled his fat hips and rolled his giant shoulders, closed his eyes and nodded his chin to the beat, singing along about a mother or a brother. Staying alive.

It's good to be home. That seemed to be the thought of the day, but Jefferson felt he was beginning to say it too much, to think it too much, so he held the sentiment inside. He wasn't even sure what it meant. He was glad not to have to go out on any details today. He was glad he didn't have to report to anyone about anything. He was glad that he could eat out of the refrigerator. And yet. He'd had months to prepare for his return, months of anticipating his first day home, and now that it was upon him, none of it felt quite right.

He grasped at the book. Still there.

He stared down at the dirt and tried to think of the perfect line for this moment. There had to be one. All those lines about women waiting for their sons and husbands and lovers to come home from war, only to find them unrecognizable . . . Nigel wasn't a literary kind of guy, and he certainly wasn't a woman, but he'd probably appreciate one of those. But nothing came to Jefferson. He clutched at the book. It would make all this anxiety go away—and it would make Nigel so happy—if he could only rip the novel out from under his T-shirt and look for the words he needed there, but instead he reached for a piece of string in the dirt and wove it absentmindedly in and out of his fingers.

"There's a jangle in here somewhere," said his cousin. "Driving me crazy."

Jefferson wove the string between his fingers, five rows deep, tighter now than he'd intended. He wanted the whole thing off now, but as he pulled, it gripped.

It's good to be home.

If he thought it enough, would it be true? Perhaps he should start chanting that, as if it were a line from the novel. His hands had begun to tremble again. He wanted to open the book and recite, but his plan had been to wait until noon. Surely he could make it till noon. But even then, not with Nigel around. Not yet. He couldn't expose the book like that. It had to be held close. Protected. Jefferson stroked the outlines of its cover and saw that Nigel was watching him. Perhaps his cousin thought he was crazy, like those guys in the dining hall in Iraq had.

Eventually Jefferson would need to explain.

But first he cleared his throat and began in a middle register, what he liked to think of as G from his long-ago days playing trumpet in middle school band.

It's good to be home.

Oh I say, it is good. To be home.

As he sang, Jefferson imagined himself a raven, flying through the never-ending New Mexican sky. A raven that had just escaped a brush with death would not worry what it was going to do with itself today. It would fly, and it would sing.

Nigel continued working quietly as Jefferson sang, occasionally looking up at his cousin, shaking his head slightly, and smiling. Finally, he spoke.

"What're you gonna do today, Jefferson?"

"No idea. Maybe clean up the yard. It looks terrible."

He'd glanced out the back window this morning. The irises and crocuses were coming up, but the overgrown garden told the larger truth: Jefferson had been away for too long. It would be good to get his hands in the dirt. It would be good to clear away some dead branches. After that, who knew? Maybe he'd get his bike, ride down to the arroyo behind the high school and sit for a while in a sunny spot. He didn't really want to go on campus. He didn't want to see anyone at the high school, though he wouldn't mind running into Ms. Tolan or Coach Shelton. It was the end of track season, he suddenly realized.

"You could go say hey to the C de Bacas," Nigel said, but then seemed to think better of it. "Long as you don't get any big ideas about you know who." Nigel knew about Jefferson's long-standing thing for Josephina.

Jefferson hesitated. "I think I'll just sit here and watch you fiddlin' around, how's that?" he said finally. "No one's expecting me anywhere."

"You're welcome to do that, cousin—but I'm not fiddlin'. This is pure science you're witnessing here. You can stay, but I demand respect, man. Respect—you know what I mean?" He raised one eyebrow at Jefferson and then the other.

Down the street and around the corner, Manny's old pit bull barked, as he always had at anyone walking near his fence. He was joined by the baying of unseen hounds and mixed breeds who seemed to bark and bay whenever the old pit bull did. A Harley gunned its engine, and behind an open window somewhere nearby, a baby was crying.

Jefferson was home, and so much was exactly as he had left it. Yet his hands jittered in his pockets as he walked, and he was certain not all was well inside him.

OUT THERE HE had had many fears, and most were more immediate and tangible than dying a quick and simple death. He was afraid of being maimed, particularly of losing a leg— like Deblanc before he'd died—or of losing an arm or a hand or even the knuckle of one thumb—like Tristan. As he thought about the dangers, and tried to focus on the goodness in life, Jefferson could not help but cling to his wholeness, such as it was. He feared being hit with a grenade, not because it might kill him but because of how he imagined it would hurt. In the same way he feared a bullet being lodged into the meatiest part of his thigh, as he'd seen happen to Henry of Golden, Colorado, before his poor heart eventually stopped. He did not fear so much being killed immediately from a shot to the back of his head—like the nice guy from West Seneca, New York—but he was terrified by the possibility of being shot in the eye or the throat—like poor Ramon—and then *surviving*.

But some of his fears had nothing to do with war. Jefferson feared being kidnapped and suffocated in the trunk of a car. He feared that Esco would fall in the kitchen, and no one would find her in time to help. The thought of a scorpion stinging him on his stomach while he was sleeping paralyzed him, or the idea of rattlesnakes, anywhere, but most often coiled under the driver's seat of the Corolla or behind the Rubbermaid box under Esco's bed. He feared what he imagined his mom's life to be. Out there, he'd been afraid he'd never make it back home. Now that he was home, he feared that time was not passing, that every day was another Monday, that the angels he imagined hovering around him, protecting him, were nothing but delusions.

JEFFERSON SPENT THE morning pulling weeds in the backyard, trying to let the irises' beauty shine through, thinking of his sweet Esco, and remembering how much he'd missed her out there.

Jefferson's grandmother was half Mexican, one-fourth German, and one-fourth Scots-Irish. Her given name was Escolita, but her father had called her Esco as a baby, and the name stuck—when she became a mother, her children had called her Esco, and after that her two grandsons learned the name as well. After her mother's death her father had raised her as a German Scots-Irish American child. She helped him with the family store, sweeping the front steps and the back porch each morning and evening and refilling the bins of onions and potatoes, and when business was slow, he taught her to play the fiddle. By the age of seventeen, Esco had a high school diploma and a growing list of places she wanted to visit: St. Petersburg, London, Paris, Rome. Against her dark brown skin her eyes shone crystal blue.

Jefferson remembered the day it had truly dawned on him that he was in a foreign land without Esco. It had been early in his first tour, and he had just eaten a terrible burrito at a stainless steel table. The first wave of homesickness had broken over him just as he identified the odd taste in the beans as turmeric. He'd yet to find anyone among the food service staff who understood the difference between a jalapeño and a green chile. It would have been smarter to avoid the burrito altogether, but his hunger had made him hopeful. It felt like the kind of late afternoon he'd have spent lounging on the couch with Nigel, watching reruns, a bowl of Cheetos between them, Esco in the kitchen making tamales.

Esco didn't belong in a war zone, but Jefferson wished she were there nonetheless. She had never been to Mexico, and she'd lost her Mexican mother at the age of fourteen, but not before she'd learned how to make tamales and *biscochitos*. Her beans would not have tasted of Indian spices. She would have busied herself at the sink while he ate at the counter. They would have talked about the weather or the unusual mixed-breed dogs roaming the base or nothing at all, as the sun shifted across the strange desert outside.

Afterward he'd sat awhile as a middle-aged Pakistani woman mopped the floor and two others prepared nachos and fries behind the counter. He'd resisted touching the book as long as he could. A few strangers had been making comments about it recently, saying that he was becoming too attached. He'd made it through the previous day without taking the book out until evening, and now it was after midday of the following day.

Jefferson looked around to see if anyone was watching. The mess hall had emptied out, no one left now but the mopper, the cooks, and a handful of guys eating several tables away. No one from his platoon. No one he recognized. And so with anxious hands he pulled the book out from his backpack. The clear packing tape he'd reinforced the cover with was wearing thin, and he knew he'd have to buy more soon and reinforce, especially along the spine. The bottom corner of the cover was curling back on itself, as were the first forty or so pages. He'd lose that corner soon if he didn't reinforce. There wasn't much to be done about the pages. He'd just have to be more careful. Letting the book tumble about in his backpack wasn't helping. Maybe he could figure out a better way to carry it.

He opened the pages and flipped back and forth, even though the ritual felt unlikely to help that day. It couldn't get him the only thing he wanted just now, which was an afternoon at home—his *real* home. To glance over and see the back of Esco's head as she washed dishes in the kitchen, to hear Nigel belting out an Abba tune and swiveling his hips like John Travolta.

He flipped absentmindedly back and forth a few more times and then made himself stop on a section of the novel he hadn't read carefully, that perhaps in fact he had skipped over in his hurry to prepare for English class all those months previous, for its pages remained crisp. He looked down and read the word *Úrsula*.

He read on, pulled by curiosity. Who was this *Úrsula*?

Jefferson sat on the metal chair at the metal table in the middle of an unknown desert and read about Úrsula Iguarán, the salty woman who'd told her infamous full-grown soldier son she'd pull down his pants and spank his bottom if he didn't behave himself. Jefferson read the sentences three times to make sure he had gotten it right, glancing around the nearby tables each time to make sure no one was watching. Esco was the only woman Jefferson knew who'd publicly claim the right to pull down her grandson's pants and give him a spanking.

He read on.

After a few more paragraphs Jefferson felt he was beginning to recognize this old woman in the novel, Úrsula Iguarán, with her sturdy nerves, her love of rearranging furniture, her willingness to discipline her own grandchildren. The familiarity began to cut through his melancholy.

He read on.

He scanned whole sections for her name, each time reading, then flipping through the pages until he caught it again.

Úrsula. She was everywhere, always working or lecturing a family member. Always ready with a meal for whoever happened to be in her kitchen.

By the end of an hour's worth of haphazard reading, he had no doubt. The old woman on the pages was both an ancient family member and a new friend. From that day on, whenever homesickness threatened him, whenever he imagined he might never again return to Santa Fe, Jefferson would flip through the pages until he spotted her name. He'd shake his head as he read about her and he'd feel as if his own grandmother, Esco, was somehow near.

More and more, the thought that the two women would never truly get to know one another gave him a bittersweet pang. He would buy Esco a copy of *One Hundred Years* when he returned home, he decided. He'd earmark or sticky-note a few of his favorite Úrsula passages, passages he could share with Esco—though, knowing his grandmother, there was no need; she would read the novel from cover to cover until she knew it better than he did himself.

The old woman from the novel seemed to have been *born* old, just like Esco. It was difficult to imagine Úrsula Iguarán as the young woman with whom her husband had fallen in love. And Esco? Had she ever been fresh? Jefferson had seen one tattered black-and-white photo of her long ago, a smiling child next to her father and their mule, but it was difficult to connect that young girl to the old woman whose thick ankles swelled out above her socks. She must have been one of those teenage girls with matronly breasts and a face that had always looked wise.

Both women were busy from morning to night, Úrsula with her candy animal business, Esco making tamales and running the store and wiping down the linoleum countertops. Both wore yellow on Sundays, and sneezed when the sun shone too bright in their eyes. They could have been twin sisters separated at birth.

OUT THERE

When Jefferson finally came home from war, Esco upheld what he thought of as her Úrsula Iguarán tradition. She made two trips to Sam's Club in one week, she told him, filling the house with veggie burgers and chips and ice cream. She baked a double batch of *biscochitos*, Jefferson's favorite, even though it was not Christmas. She prepared black bean and zucchini tamales, and she bought a new aluminum patio set with four chairs and an umbrella for the back stoop—so they could watch the sun set in comfort, she said. And in a plastic pot by the front door, she planted an overflowing mass of purple petunias—a symbol, Jefferson thought, of all the worries of which she could not speak.

DAY BY DAY the part of his brain that knew he had nothing to fear became smaller. He was alert in a way he'd never been, his eyes detecting motion to his far left and his far right, his nose sure it caught a whiff of burning flesh and ammonia. Deep within him, his soul cowered at the frightening proximity of life—Esco's simple cooking, Nigel's perpetual tinkering, the familiar sounds of the neighborhood—it all seemed to accentuate his heavy burden. When the sun shone, he could feel its malignant rays inciting cancer in the cells of his skin; when the tyrannical late-spring wind blew cold, he felt small, vulnerable, a paper kite caught in a dust devil.

The part of him that knew how to hide and how to please took over. This made many things simpler, but by the second week, he had an appointment with a doctor at the VA in Albuquerque. He didn't think he was unstable, and he didn't think he had an issue with whatever everyone seemed to be worried about, but he did wonder about his future. At what point would he need to move on from his current status as ex-soldier to whatever role he would establish for himself in the next phase of life? Part-time student? But hadn't he missed all boats headed out for college? Grandmother's assistant? Although he wanted to be there for Esco whenever she needed his help, did unloading boxes and sitting behind the counter selling gum and soda really qualify as a plan? Nigel's assistant? Could he stand the grease and the music—and anyway, did Nigel need any help? Neurosurgeon? Probably not. Tree trimmer?

It wasn't that he hoped for answers. He was smart enough to know there were no answers—at least not yet—to most of the questions jangling in his head. But the idea of a woman whose sole job it was to sit and listen to him talk—that such a woman existed!—was enough to convince him to skip his morning bull session in Nigel's shed and make the one-and-a-half-hour train trip to Albuquerque. He imagined a plush couch facing floor-to-ceiling windows overlooking the Rio Grande Botanic Garden, the only place in Albuquerque, aside from the zoo, he remembered visiting as a child, and though Jefferson knew the doctor's office would not literally be adjacent to the gardens, he nonetheless imagined that green manicured view. That Albuquerque was always greener and warmer than Santa Fe was a known fact.

He knew that the doctor was a woman because of her e-mail:

```
Looking forward to meeting with you next
week, Jefferson.

May 1, at 11:00 a.m. Let me know if you
have any questions before we get together.

Dr. Emily Wesleyan
Raymond G. Murphy VA Medical Center
Building One, 2nd floor
1501 San Pedro Dr. SE | Albuquerque, NM 87108
```

He tried to imagine how the doctor would look and smell and sound. In the end he settled for the most minor of assumptions, what must at a minimum be true of any person who'd agreed to counsel ex-soldiers: that she would be kind.

The Rail Runner wove its way south along the highway through misshapen rocks, breaking out into a fine view of the high Cochiti plateaus and, of course, the Jemez. It was a landscape for the movies, a landscape to be populated with celluloid cowboys and Indians. From the downtown train station he rode the bus up Coal Avenue and over on University and way up Gibson, through a part of Albuquerque he'd never seen before, landing finally at the VA. Building 1 was just there on his right when he got off the bus. It wasn't as serious-looking as the five-story hospital building over to the left, which seemed to be brimming with activity, lots of men and women, some in uniform, but many not, some pushing walkers, some walking just fine. There were trees and grass near Building 1, just as he had hoped, and in the middle of the circular drive a giant flagpole waved the Stars and Stripes as well as the more somber flag of prisoners of war and those missing in action. The soft click-clack of the flags against the pole was a comfort, and the shade of the ponderosas and cottonwoods quieted Jefferson's spirit as he walked beneath them, preparing himself for what was to come.

Inside, the waiting room was occupied by a number of young guys who looked a lot like Jefferson, brown-skinned ex-soldiers, many of them lost in shell-shocked stares or chattering incessantly, compulsively. He signed in and waited until his name was called, and a nurse led him down a hall with pale blue walls and many closed doors, finally ushering him through one of the doors into a room painted a deeper blue. There was no window at all, much less one looking out on the garden of his daydreams, with its greenery, its flitting birds. He took a seat on one of two black metal chairs—he'd been wrong about the plush couch too. Someone was crying on the other side of the wall.

He'd been helping Esco make tamales on Thursday night when he told her about the doctor in Albuquerque. She'd grabbed his wrist across the bar on which the pork and chile mixture, the bowl of masa, the cornhusks, lay, squeezing him in her relief. She looked as if she was about to cry, the space between her eyebrows earnest, but then she spoke instead. "This doctor will help you, Jefferson."

He hadn't known what to make of his grandmother's words. Frankly, he hadn't been aware that he needed help, even though he had called the VA hotline late that one night. Because of that, he guessed, he'd been scheduled to see the doctor right away. He'd thought that his grandmother and Nigel, and even Auntie Linda, who he'd spoken to only once and then briefly from her front stoop, were feeling good about him, were proud of him, were waiting to see what he would do next. They seemed to believe in him as they always had, their faith unshaken that now that he was home from war, he would do good things. It was as if they were thinking—each time they saw him—that here was Jefferson, their sweet, smart youngest boy who'd graduated with honors from Santa Fe High and, on the authority of his own well-informed and intelligent brain, gone off and joined the army. Jefferson had not sensed any worry or judgment from any of them. And he thought he'd done a pretty good job these past few weeks of living up to their expectations. He was okay. The word had become a staple of their conversation.

Are you okay?

Yes, I'm okay.

How are you?

I'm okay.

But the truth, as Jefferson was beginning to suspect, was that he was not okay. That's what he'd told the man on the hotline. He needed someone, maybe a doctor, to help him. He wasn't sure what form the help would take, but he hoped it might be an answer to a question that was getting louder and louder in his mind. *Why?* Could a doctor help him answer this question?

Dr. Wesleyan arrived almost as soon as the nurse had checked his pulse and blood pressure. The door had shut briefly and then opened again, leaving him no real time to prepare. He'd hoped to be able to sing and possibly pray just a bit before beginning his conversation with her. He felt he needed to put himself in a meditative state of remembrance before he could answer the sorts of questions he imagined she might have for him, so he could ask for the help he needed. *Why?* That was the question he needed help answering.

"Hi, I'm Dr. Wesleyan," she said, sticking out her hand.

She was young. So young that Jefferson tried to calculate the minimum number of years required to get through college and then medical school. When he'd come up with the number seven—some people graduated from regular college in three years, he knew—he looked again at Dr. Wesleyan. She must have graduated from high school at age fourteen, he decided.

"Hey, good afternoon. How's it going?" he said finally.

"I'm doing well, thank you. It's Jefferson, right?"

"Yep."

She sat down across from him in the swivel chair. It looked far more comfortable than either of the two metal chairs, but it was clearly labeled "the doctor's chair" in an unlabeled way, so he hadn't thought of sitting in it. He chuckled a little to himself at the thought of this young woman in front of him being a medical doctor. She was probably the same age as he was.

"So what brings you in here today, Jefferson?" she began—a little too quickly, he thought. Wasn't there going to be a warm-up joke or two? Wasn't there going to be a moment for him to get to know her before the serious talk began? But the doctor had jumped straight in, and now she plowed right ahead in what seemed to him a droning singsong, hardly stopping to draw breath.

He thought he'd uttered some sort of answer, and then she'd gone on to ask him about when he'd first gone over to Iraq and where he'd been stationed exactly, the name of his unit, his commanding officer's name, what his title had been, what kind of daily assignments he'd been given—"You know, just a few of the details, to give me a little of the background of your experience." Once she'd recorded all of that, she explained, they could get on to whatever he wanted to talk about.

Jefferson heard all of this, and yet he didn't. He was trying so very hard to concentrate on what she was asking of him—he knew it must be important but his head was beginning to have a strange watery feel to it, a dizziness that the purplish hue of the room's fluorescent lights accentuated. Her words swam at him like the faces of people he had seen in a long-ago dream. And just as Jefferson began to grasp the fact that these words were in fact people he had known, not just ones he'd dreamed, they became butterflies escaping her mouth, lovely free creatures circumnavigating the room. He watched the doctor's eyebrows move up and down, the up-and-down of her lips. And this odd squinting thing she did with her nose—an unattractive little antic in an otherwise soft face. He glanced back at the ceiling, where the butterflies were now disappearing into the metal grate of an air conditioning vent. Suddenly he found himself wondering why he was sitting in this blue room.

"What was the question again?"

"Right, so I know that was a lot to throw at you—but can you just tell me a little about yourself?" She smiled a sweet-seeming smile as she sat, her pen poised over the yellow legal pad that lay on her lap, and for a moment Jefferson wondered if she had practiced the expression in her bathroom medicine cabinet mirror. He wanted to believe that the doctor was on his side, that she could help him answer the question *Why?* But something inside his brain was preventing him from believing it. Jefferson knew this was most likely his own problem, that his lack of trust was due to a problem—a temporary problem, but acute at the moment—with his brain, that it had nothing at all to do with Dr. Wesleyan or her intentions. It was true that she was young and most likely inexperienced, and that she could have used a little work on her bedside manner. She probably worked too hard to have a boyfriend to loosen up her smile. It didn't mean she was an enemy.

"My name is Jefferson Long Soldier," he said, and stopped. As soon as he heard his own voice, the sound of his own name inside that calm, blue room, he felt he could not say any more.

The doctor wrote something on her yellow paper and looked up at him, waiting. "And you were with the Tenth Mountain Division, I see here." She was reading from a piece of paper in her lap. "Light artillery, I see." She looked at him expectantly.

Jefferson stared up at the air conditioning vent, now absent any butterflies, and wondered where they'd all flown. It was possible that the ductwork in this building was connected to all sorts of places, that those butterflies could have ended up, for instance, in locations as varied as New York City or Atlanta or Baton Rouge. Some of the guys in his platoon had been from those places. He looked back at the doctor.

"I was a member of the Tenth Mountain Division out of Fort Drum, New York."

"Right," she said, writing something on her yellow paper again. "Fort Drum."

He knew there had been other parts of the question she asked, but those words had flown so far away from him, he could not possibly remember what they had been. They could have flown all the way to Tucson by now. He stared back at the doctor's face, questioning her. Could she help him? Did she know the answer to the question *Why?*

"And what was your basic job over there?" she said, guiding him onward.

"Right," he said, remembering the question now. "I was a light artillery guy. We called ourselves the Rock Guns."

She asked him a few more questions about the Rock Guns—what his specific assignment within the group had been, how many guys he had worked with, how often that had changed—but none of it struck him as anything he felt able to answer at that moment. He was aware of searching again for the butterflies up at the ceiling and wondering again where they might have gone when he became aware of the doctor's voice again.

"So, anything else you want to say about the guys in your squad or platoon, Jefferson?"

"Nope, not really," he said, standing up to shake out his legs and his hands, which were beginning to tremble a little. He wondered whether the doctor might want to hear about his sweet Remedios, but decided against it for the moment. She was still writing in her yellow tablet, and he guessed she was a busy woman and that probably the half hour was close to gone, so he probably shouldn't bring up any new topics, particularly something that she hadn't initiated, like his dog.

As he stood and watched her write, right there and yet so far away, he wondered what she really thought about talk therapy for veterans. Did she really believe it could help? But he didn't ask because he didn't want to offend her. He wouldn't have told her this, but he hadn't felt much of a connection with her, not like he'd hoped for. He didn't know why he'd held out so much hope for this visit, but he had, somehow envisioning just the right listener for all his troubles. The bus ride from the train station had been interesting, and he always loved a train ride. It had been good to get out of Santa Fe for the day. And there was no reason to make the young doctor feel bad about her job.

Still, Jefferson felt himself making up his mind as he watched the doctor continue to write his few words down on her yellow tablet: his question could not be answered by a doctor like Dr. Wesleyan. He wasn't angry at the army about this. He wasn't angry at Dr. Wesleyan. Instead he tried to think of an appropriate quote. He paused as he began to turn toward the door and racked his brain. What would Gabriel say to this woman?

"Wait a sec," she said, finally noticing that he was leaving. "You're leaving? Well, here's your paperwork. Just schedule your next appointment on the way out, okay?"

Okay. It was the wrong word to say to him. Jefferson—caught in the middle of searching for possible quotes from Gabriel—found he could not let the word lie untouched. To do so would be irresponsible. If he truly wished to heal, Jefferson could not let anyone anywhere—not even this well-meaning young doctor assigned to him by the Department of Veteran Affairs—roll the word *okay* off her tongue at him.

"No," he said now. "You see, I'm not okay."

"Excuse me?"

"You just said, 'Okay?' as if you were asking me a question, so I'm answering. No, I'm not okay."

The doctor seemed in that moment to be the last person in the world who could ever understand him.

"Well, of course not," she said. "And that's why you're here."

The polish of her well-thought-out dark blond waves had required a lot of time with a blow dryer and a brush, he saw now. He imagined her standing in front of the bathroom mirror, putting on makeup. He imagined her as a high school senior in the front row in Honors English, raising her hand for every question.

"You have no idea why I'm here, Dr. Wesleyan."

He felt the bravest thing he could do was stand with his knees locked and let the words sink in. The reason he had come to this doctor's office had now been made clear to him. He stared at the blue wall in front of him and back at the young doctor and then back at the wall again. This was not the place or the person to help him.

"I don't want to be rude or disrespectful to you—I'm sure your intentions are good. But this coming down here on the train and talking to you is not going to work for me."

"No one likes this the first time, Jefferson."

"I'm not coming back, Dr. Wesleyan. I'm leaving now."

She became very passive, as if practicing another technique she had learned in medical school. She told him that she understood, and that if he didn't want to come back, it was certainly his decision to make, but she wondered who he had to talk to back in Santa Fe. She wondered if he wouldn't consider scheduling another appointment next week, just in case he changed his mind. Just in case he needed someone to talk to. And then she said the thing that triggered a whole lot of what was to follow. She said, "Just in case you can't find that perfect person who can listen to your stories."

"But I already know who he is," Jefferson said, realizing the truth of what he was saying as he said it. He did know the perfect person. It was as if the answer, strapped to his chest as it had been all these months, was only now making its presence known. How simple it was! What wonderful sense it made, now that he had realized it! But the doctor did not seem to be traveling along with him in the epiphany. She had a sudden strained look between her eyebrows. She said something about how nice it was that he had someone to talk to, but that he should make a follow-up appointment just in case.

She glanced at the wall clock behind him and began shuffling the papers on her lap. "Time for my next appointment, Jefferson. Best of luck to you, if I don't see you again, though I hope I will." She was dismissing him, no doubt already thinking about the name and rank and job description of the next guy, but Jefferson found he had a bit more to say. He didn't want to give the wrong impression, to make her think he was a guy who didn't care about his own mental health. He wanted the young doctor to realize that he had a plan for his own recovery, a plan taking shape right here in front of her. Maybe something he had to say would help her in her job.

"Jefferson? Is there anything else?" She seemed to be turning a tad impatient, but, as he'd felt so often in war, Jefferson believed it was his job in this moment to share the beauty of what he was experiencing. This mission trumped any minor annoyance. She'd realize in time that the delay had been worthwhile.

"Yes. Actually there is something else," he said. "I want you to know who it is I'm going to talk to about all this."

"Oh, okay. Who is it? Someone I know? Someone I've heard of?"

"That depends," he said. "Have you heard of Gabriel García Márquez?"

"The writer?"

He just raised his eyebrows and nodded.

"Is he even alive?"

"Of course he's alive. The guy's immortal."

"Ha. Very funny. But what do you mean? Do you know him—I mean, personally? Is he like your great-grandfather or something?"

Jefferson felt the woman was finally loosening up a little, so he laughed at this last question, obviously her attempt at a joke. "Very funny. My great-grandfather! You think I'd've signed up for the US Army if my great-grandfather was Gabriel García Márquez? Now *that's* funny!"

He thought then about the story he'd told himself, the story about how GGM had held him as a baby, had brought him birthday presents. He'd daydreamed until it ceased to be fun or even uplifting, and instead began to strike him as a loss. The idea of birthdays made him think of his mom, and the fact that he really had never known her, because one hazy memory of sharing a Welch's soda together did not constitute a relationship. And then there was the fact that he'd never known his father, or either of his grandfathers.

Looking at the blurry outline of his navy sneakers on the floor below him, he did his little wake-up exercise, asking himself, *Where am I? Where am I?* Dr. Wesleyan was smiling patiently, he could see now, and speaking in a soft voice. "Jefferson? Are you okay? Jefferson? Can you hear me?"

"Yes, I can hear you, Dr. Wesleyan. I can hear you just fine."

"Listen, why don't you come back next week, Jefferson, okay? I need to get on with my next appointment, but I think this is all very important, and I really hope to see you then. Okay? We can talk about Gabriel García Márquez. You can bring in a favorite book or something. Okay?"

There was that word again. *Okay? Okay? Okay?* It seemed to be the only thing people could say to him since he'd returned. But what was that the doctor had said about bringing in a favorite book? Now that was a good idea. Genius. Only why wait an entire week—especially since Jefferson knew as well as anyone that he had no intention of taking the train down here again next week—when he could show the doctor right here and now?

He'd begun fiddling the novel loose from its place under his shirt and inside the Ace bandage when the doctor clutched her heart. "Oh my god! What are you doing? Please, Jefferson! Oh my god!" She held her arms out stiffly toward him as she slowly backed away. "Please, Jefferson. Please don't! Oh my god, please!"

The book popped out of the bandage and flew from Jefferson's grip, landing with a *thwump!* on the floor between them.

"Oh my god, what are you doing?" the doctor yelled. "What's that book?"

"*One Hundred Years of Solitude*, the masterpiece of Gabriel García Márquez. I carry it with me. It saved my life."

"You need to leave," said the doctor.

"But I want to share just one quote with you."

The doctor had lost any sense of humor she might have ever had. Eyes bugged out, she stepped back from the book on the floor.

"Don't worry, Dr. Wesleyan. Just one—a short one. I'm not crazy. You'll see," Jefferson said, waving his hand apologetically. He was sorry he'd scared her—that hadn't been his intent—but he was sure that if he could only paraphrase the right line, she would feel much better, and the awkwardness would pass.

The doctor clutched her chest with one hand, breathing hard and heavy as she stared at his knees. "You just about made me have a heart attack. I have other patients. Now!" She pointed to the door.

Seeing that he was out of time, Jefferson stooped to grab the book up off the floor and backed away from the young doctor, who had now moved nearer to him and was standing in a power pose, arms wrapped tight around chest. There seemed to be nothing to lose, so he proceeded to recite the line he had decided in the previous several moments would be the best one in the circumstances, a continuation of his answer to several of Dr. Wesleyan's earlier questions. He recited, half speaking, half singing, in the rhythm he often used, his eyes closed and his gut full, his breath searching for a listener in all the noise. He hoped Dr. Wesleyan was listening.

You ask where I have been and I answer: Out there.

His belly was empty from bellowing out the truth of those words. He refilled his gut and went at it again.

You ask where I have been and I answer: Out there.

In the third breath he saw through the slits in his eyes that the doctor was on her phone, her face that of a crazed feline. Nonetheless he shared the line one more time.

You ask where I have been and I answer: Out there. Out there.

Jefferson continued chanting even as a security officer ushered him roughly by his elbow back down the long blue hall and out through the waiting room, still full of young men who looked like they might have been his brother. By the time he was dumped outside in front of Building 1, the flags fluttering high in the May air above, he could claim the satisfaction of sharing the last word with the famous writer.

THAT AFTERNOON JEFFERSON took the pup and a crow-
bar out to the back corner of the yard, where his mom's old
camper van had sat since 1986, and pried open the passenger
side door. The steel creaked as he'd expected, but there were
no rats or snakes. Anything that had spoiled had long since
turned to dust, so he climbed inside and took a look around,
wondering in part why his curiosity had never taken him this
far before. From this vantage the back of the house looked
almost foreign, the tan stucco mottled with the sinking sunlight, the half-dead elm off to the left. God, did it need to be
pruned. He made a plan to get his old clippers out the next
day and clean up the tree and all the other neglected shrubs in
the yard. It was one of the things Jefferson seemed to be alone
in caring about—the errant twigs and branches sprouting hel-
ter-skelter off the main trunks of trees and bushes. Didn't anyone else in the family see the mess that was going on in the
yard? He tried to envision a covered deck off the back of the
house—a redwood-stained deck with pots of petunias, Esco's
favorite—and how happy that would make her.

He pulled the door closed behind him and crawled into the
back. It was quiet and warm, and he felt he might bring out
a pillow and blanket, a flashlight, and stay out here all night.

How had this not occurred to him before, this ultimate hideout? And though it felt mildly juvenile to be hanging out in his back-yard—he'd always wished his family had been into camping out in the woods, but they hadn't—it also felt undeniably pleasant.

He was in the midst of calculating the dimensions of the deck he might build for his grandmother, how much lumber it might take, and how he might muster up the money, when he saw movement from inside the house and knew she must be home from the store. He'd go inside and tell her. She wouldn't believe it. The van was intact, and he was going to sleep out there, plus he had a great idea for a deck off the back.

Jefferson jumped from the van, opened up the driver's side as well as the sliding door for a little ventilation, and dashed into the house. He could not wait to tell her that he'd found a cost-free solution to his need for a little privacy. It was hard to believe he'd never thought of the van as a refuge before. Here it had been, right here, all that time.

"Hey, Esco!" Jefferson shouted, but she must have gone to the bathroom, because there was no reply. There was no time to waste, so Jefferson pulled down two blankets from the high shelf in the hall closet. He was looking for a flashlight in the kitchen when she found him.

"I didn't realize you were home. How was the meeting? How was the doctor?" Her eyes were so hopeful.

Oh, that, he told her. It was okay.

And then he asked her where he could find a flashlight. The morning's meeting with Dr. Wesleyan seemed to have happened in another lifetime. The train ride home alone had taken almost three hours, counting the bus ride and the wait-ing and the walk back to the neighborhood. Though he felt that in some ways it had gone well, he also knew he would not be returning to her office, and he was not sure which part of the story to share with Esco. She'd become a worrier, and this fact made him uncomfortable and generally complicated their conversations.

"The office walls were blue," he said finally.

"Yeah?"

"Yep, sort of an ocean blue. Dark, but calming."

"So that's it?"

"Pretty much."

Knowing that food would be a good distraction, he began opening cabinets and feigning hunger. Esco hovered a few feet away, pretending to sort mail.

It was impossible to find anything in his grandmother's cabinets. She had a horrible sense of order, and so, as Jefferson thought back to the meeting with the doctor in Albuquerque, he began taking all the spices and cans of food out of the pantry and sorting them into groups on the counter. If someone had asked him, he would have said there were no better words in the entire novel for him to share with the young doctor than the ones he'd chosen. *Out there.* He chuckled to himself, thinking what perfect words, what a gift that he had been able to recall them just before he'd had to leave the office, and he felt himself swell with pride. It was a good example of everyone doing his or her part to make the world a better place. Him, Jefferson Long Soldier, reciting the perfect words to her, Dr. Wesleyan, the words she needed to hear if she was going to put herself out there like that, trying to help ex-soldiers, trying to get in their heads and reshuffle their bad stuff. There had also been a few looks of interest among the veterans in the waiting room as he had continued chanting while being escorted from the office.

He hummed the words again now as he spooned peanut butter onto a rice cake.

You ask where I have been and I answer: Out there. Out there.

Jefferson felt confident that at least one of those guys in the waiting room had benefited from his recitations. He told himself, just as he'd told himself every day in the war zone, that if he'd reached one person, that was enough to make the effort worthwhile.

Esco moved closer to Jefferson, trying to remind him that she was there, she was standing right next to him. Where had his mind traveled now? What was all this garbled humming? And what did he plan to do with that pile of blankets on the couch?

"Are you hungry?" she asked. "I was gonna make dinner in a little bit, but I could start now." She gave a heavy sigh as she surveyed the contents of her cabinets, strewn across the counter, and clucked her tongue. She didn't really mind, though; it wasn't the first time Jefferson had organized her cabinets. In fact, it was one of the things she'd missed when he was at war. She would not have chosen this moment for it, but then again, at least he was home and alive. Let him do it. Busy his brain and his hands with something a little more useful than finger-crocheting and chanting.

Ah, he was a little heavy now, but the skin-and-bones would be back soon enough. That was his nature. She'd probably never stop worrying that Jefferson was undernourished, even now when he was eight pounds pudgy and eating peanut butter. As a baby he'd been underweight and prone to ear infections, and then too, she would always be the grandmother, trying to make amends. Feeding Jefferson had been the best way she knew to try to make things seem okay for him.

He was smiling at her, that goofy smile that was new since he'd returned, almost like he'd had a stroke and was visiting a distant galaxy, and now he smacked another bite of the peanut butter rice cake and told her he could wait for dinner. He just wanted a snack.

"Okay, sweetie. Okay." She took the sponge from the sink and began to wipe down the countertop where the rice cake had crumbled.

Jefferson hoped Esco wasn't upset. Her short round frame bent down and away from him as she wiped the crumbs off the counter, and now she seemed intent on silence. He didn't feel as if he'd been withholding important information, though. She was probably just fine. Grandmother rarely got upset, and when she did, it usually had something to do with the bread order for the store or a dog pooping in her yard, practical things like that. She wasn't the fragile kind of woman who cried or got her feelings hurt. She'd had too much in her life go haywire to afford to cry every time some little thing upset her—or, for that matter, to get in a bad mood. Moodiness and anger were for rich people, Jefferson had always thought.

"I love you, Esco," he said, just after she brushed against his arm with the sponge. "So glad to be home, you know?"

She paused in her cleaning and took a breath as she looked at him. And then it was as if a meteor had hit the earth somewhere far away and shaken Santa Fe in the process. She lunged against his chest, burying her face in his T-shirt and letting out a long string of wails that to him sounded both nocturnal and oceanic. He held on to her head, breathing into her hair and telling her it was okay, it was okay, everything was going to be okay now. When she had sobbed several long minutes without cease, she began to speak into his chest, as if she could only get out the words she needed to say if she did not look at him straight on, a barrage of thoughts and emotions that went on and on, *Oh my grandson, oh my god, you are home you are home, you really did make it home alive, oh my god, oh my god, oh my beloved, my child, my sweet one, you are alive, oh I love you so much, so much you will never know, never know, never know, you are here, here you are, your sweet skin, oh my god, your sweet skin, your sweet hands, oh your eyes, oh your tiny little fingers, when you were a baby, oh my god, I was so worried, I was so worried, I thought you wouldn't survive and I did my best, oh my god, my sweet baby, I did my best.*

Jefferson had always imagined but never witnessed Esco saying things like this. Of course he knew she loved him. Of course he knew she was the reason he'd survived childhood without a mother. Of course he knew she worried. But this

outpouring, this desperate clinging to his chest, this sobbing . . .
She wasn't supposed to be crying, and now that she had flung
herself against his chest, now that she clung to him as if to prove
to herself it was really him, Jefferson knew more than ever that
he had to find a way to heal himself. If that doctor down in
Albuquerque was not the one to help him, then Jefferson had to
find someone else. Esco needed him to be well.

Finally the darkness seemed to have lifted within Esco.
She raised her head, and looked past Jefferson at the pile of
blankets on the couch.

"What is that all about?" she asked.

When he told her in an excited voice that he'd opened up
the van and that it was a perfect hideaway in which to heal,
no visible rats or snakes, and that he planned to start spending time out there, beginning that very night, and that tomorrow he was going to prune all the dead stuff out of the elm
and beautify every chamisa and lilac and rosemary bush in
the yard, and oh, by the way, did she know where his clippers
were? she thought someone had yanked the braided rug, the
rug that had covered the floor under the kitchen table for fifteen years, away from under her feet.

"You can't sleep out in that van," she said.

But he was already gone, halfway through the expanse of
dirt and weeds, humming a tune she couldn't place but that
she'd heard several times as he'd showered lately.

A WEEK LATER, while his grandmother thought he was on his way by train back down to Albuquerque to meet Dr. Wesleyan for the second time, Jefferson watched Nigel read the weekly alternative paper—he liked the classifieds on the back page and the kinky sex column written by the gay guy—as one of the Bee Gees screeched yet again that whether you were a brother or a mother, you'd best be staying alive, staying alive. Piles of projects awaited his cousin's attention: a blender, several kids' bicycles, a footstool missing a foot. Over in the corner a Kawasaki 400 motorbike, rebuilt and repainted burnt orange—a classic from the 1980s, Nigel claimed—leaned against the wall. It was hard to believe, but Nigel actually made enough to pay for his food and entertainment working as a fixer. He charged by the job—small jobs, $25; medium jobs, $65; large jobs, $100—and always had a backlog. Several hours each day he devoted to his own projects; for a while now that project had been that Kawasaki 400, which he'd bought for $50 from the bike's owner's widow.

"You ever hear anything about Josephina?" Jefferson had waited just about as long as he could, and now he finally had to ask.

"You mean Joz?" Nigel raised his eyebrows and curled his upper lip when he said it.

Jefferson nodded.

"She's all messed up, man. I think she's havin' a kid, I don't know really."

Jefferson did his best to show no reaction to this information, instead asking his cousin about the Kawasaki again—when he was going to be finished with it, what he planned to do with it when he was done. As Nigel talked about how he was going to bask in his creative juices, though, Jefferson wasn't really paying attention. Instead he was thinking about Josephina being pregnant and what Nigel meant by the words *messed up* and whether or not he should still drop by her house and say hello. In other words, whether or not he and Josephina had any hope of turning out like José Arcadio and Petra Cotes, in love despite it all.

Nigel flipped through a few more pages of the paper, paused briefly, and then moved on again, finally refolding the whole thing and flipping over to the back page. He read every back-page ad on Wednesday mornings, the day the weekly came out, and now, as Jefferson watched, he began reading from the top left column.

"Listen to this," he said, reading aloud. 'Want some affection? Hug 'n' cuddle therapy sessions.' How 'bout that, cousin? You want some affection?"

Jefferson could hear what Nigel was saying, but something about his cousin's voice seemed very far away now, echoing as if Jefferson's eardrum had been bored through. He was thinking of Josephina. Josephina Maria C de Baca. The girl who'd been his friend since second grade at Kaune Elementary. They'd been in the same class all the way through elementary school. Ms. McIntyre. Ms. Thompson. Mr. Treadway. Ms. Amanda Cisneros. Ms. Otero. They'd held hands for a week during sixth grade on the walk home from school, and Jefferson had never forgotten the tingling, the sensation of his heart momentarily stopping. He'd helped carry the diorama Josephina had constructed on the Great Sphinx of Giza, using bottle caps and Styrofoam curlicues. He knew that she preferred Dr Pepper to any other soda, and that she had alternated between salted peanuts and M&Ms as an after-school snack through most of middle and high school.

"Here's one," Nigel continued. " 'Yoga for Veterans.' How 'bout somma that? Or this—'Potters for Peace. Make a handmade bowl to feed the homeless. This Saturday on the Plaza.' "

But Jefferson was thinking that if he were really honest, he'd have to admit that he'd always thought he would end up with Josephina. That they were meant to be together. It didn't hurt that she lived on Brae Street, one block over from his house on Tesuque Drive. It was true that he hadn't had many real conversations with Josephina since ninth grade, and that since that time she'd spiked her hair in an odd asymmetrical way, and that her new friends called her Joz. It was true that she'd dated a few rough guys who had dropped out of Santa Fe High, one of whom was busy selling weed at the park while another already had a kid with a girl from Española.

Sometimes Josephina had shown up at track meets and watched Jefferson dash the 200. Several times she had invited Jefferson over to tell him about one of the rough guys and how bad he had treated her, but the whole thing was so nauseating to Jefferson that he had started saying he was busy when she came into the store with her mascara running. He was smart enough to know when being in love with a childhood friend was going to bring him nothing but trouble.

"Here's a woman who'll help you write your novel *and* give you a massage. I mean, I think she's a woman. Says her name is Per. I guess that could be a guy, no?" said Nigel, jiggling the newspaper.

Esco had gone to Walmart with her friend Waci on their biweekly outing for toilet paper, paper towels, frozen burritos, candy and canned beans and condiments for the store.

Jefferson needed to be around when she returned, help her unload, but that would be hours from now.

"What about you, Jefferson? What're you gonna do? You unpacked yet? You need me to give you a job?" Nigel could go on all day like this, but already Jefferson's weariness had developed an edge. What *was* he going to do with himself? Not just today, but tomorrow and the next day and the day after that? Before Iraq he hadn't been the type to be bored; he remembered being excited about free time for reading or listening to music or cutting out magazine clippings for his bulletin board. Clipping trees and shrubs in the backyard. And walking around on his hands. Coach Shelton had suggested handstands as a way of calming his nerves before a race, but Jefferson had come to think of being upside down as one of his favorite pastimes.

"Esco thinks I'm seeing that VA doctor again today," he said now, without explanation.

"Yeah?"

"Yep."

"So?"

"So what?"

"So . . ." This was one communication technique the cousins shared, conversation Ping-Pong. With nothing but grunts and sighs and one-syllable replies, there could be a lot of talk with little chance of any significant communication. Jefferson felt it was just what he needed.

Besides, his mind was still stuck on Josephina.

Toward the end of senior year, when things were getting serious and it was starting to sink in that Jefferson really had signed on the army's dotted line—he'd received a letter in the mail with an actual start date for basic training—he'd found he couldn't stop thinking about Josephina. He wanted to talk to her, to let her in on the secret he had yet to share with his grandmother or Nigel, to make up for all the times he'd hesitated, for all the times he'd watched her walk by on the other side of the street without saying more than "Hey, Josephina, how's it goin'?" He began to imagine normal conversations with her, and then he began to imagine that all those conversations in his head were real.

When that chance came and went, and Jefferson had gone for his basic training right after graduation and immediately after that for duty station training and had returned once again to Santa Fe with only ten days' break before shipping out to Iraq, he'd planned it all out. He was going to tell Josephina he cared for her, and he planned to use the word *love* and maybe even the word *deeply*. He would explain that he was being deployed to Iraq, that he didn't know exactly when or if he would return, and that he wanted her to know his true feelings before he left because, god forbid, she might run off with another rough guy if she didn't know how he really felt. Jefferson felt full of the possibility of changing the course of their two lives.

Saturday mornings Josephina almost always came into the store for a few things for her mom. So on that last Saturday before Jefferson left for Iraq, he waited, ready to call her by her full name. *Josephina Maria C de Baca*. But on that particular day, Joz had not come to the store. All day he waited, and at 5:05 p.m., after helping Esco turn off the lights and lock the front door, Jefferson walked the block and a half to her house on Brae Street and knocked. He knocked and knocked, but no one answered, and the next morning he left for war. Later, in that faraway desert, whenever Jefferson found himself missing home, he also found himself thinking about Josephina as a child who had grown up to be his friend.

"Look, Nigel," he said now. "Can we talk about you and your plans for once? I mean it, man. I'm sick of being in the spotlight with nothing to say. Literally sick of it. Can you please come up with your own story, something really interesting about what you're planning to do with yourself once the motorbike is fixed?"

But instead of talking, Nigel undertook the bold effort of standing up, an effort that required several deep breaths and a long red-faced pause once he was upright. He gave his sweatpants a tug, walked over to Jefferson, and handed him a piece he had torn from the newspaper. "Looka here. Last one in the far column. Read it."

Jefferson followed his cousin's pointed finger to an ad in the bottom corner:

Need a Pseudo-Doctor to talk to you about your problems? First session complimentary. 555-1212.

"Thanks, Nigel. Just what I need. A pseudo-doctor."

"You need sump'n, cousin."

Jefferson gave Nigel the look he'd always used when his cousin tried to jive-talk him, his palms up around his ears in an exaggerated *wuzzup?* pose and his lips all wrinkled. Nigel had taught him this pose years ago, and Jefferson loved giving it back to his cousin at opportune moments.

Nigel returned to whatever it was he was working on, and Jefferson stuck the slip of paper in his pocket and headed back out of the shed. It had been exactly one month. The Bee Gees followed him as he walked back through the scrubby yard, shrieking at him to use his walk to show he was a woman's man, shrieking at him to live. He thought he was out of range when Nigel's voice found him, his feet already on the curb.

"Hey, Jefferson, you listen here," Nigel said, his large frame again filling the shed's doorway, his eyes lost but intense nonetheless deep within his heavy face. "You best forget about you-know-who, you know what I mean? She's nothin' but trouble, I don't care how nice she used to be in second grade or whatever. And anyways, cousin, her boyfriend'll kill you."

But Jefferson was smiling, his mind back on GGM and all his descriptions of children who played together as kids and grew up to love one another as adults, and of the misery of men missing women they'd never truly held. It was more proof that the writer understood Jefferson's life. Jefferson had heard the syllables of Josephina's name in the call of Iraqi birds outside his window, and in the metallic grind of the gate as it had opened and closed to release him into the war-zone hinterlands. He'd begun to believe that there was something inevitable about her, and sometimes he imagined that the young woman of his dreams—the Josephina he had thought of as he entered the dark bedrooms of captured towns, who had materialized in the smell of bandages, in the metallic brutality of gunfire, in the sheer horror of human death screams—would somehow yet reveal herself in a new way, smiling at him in the middle of it all perhaps, a flower tucked behind her ear.

FROM THE PATH that ran along the railroad tracks, Jefferson could see nothing but the top of the stadium lights and the back of the cafeteria. He cut through the old parking lot—the one where the unlicensed drivers practiced parallel parking—left the bike against the chain-link fence, and walked down into the visitors' side of the old concrete stadium, sunken like an imperfect oasis within the desert. Way down, there was real grass, but up here a plastic grocery bag rode the gritty wind.

He'd waited until three to begin his ride so he could watch some of practice, which had always begun around 3:45. Should have been starting soon, so he waited as one runner grew to two and then a small group to over a dozen, stretching at the far corner of the track. And then there he was: Coach Shelton in his blue warm-ups, holding his clipboard as if it was 2005. His crisp voice was almost audible, directing the distance runners to set off toward the arroyo and then decreeing what the sprinters probably already knew, that today would be a day of 200-meter killers. Wednesdays had always been tough. It came back to him now.

It all looked so serious. High school track. He remembered his own intensity—much more consequential than anything having to do with academics—about the time he'd need to beat to secure a place in the 200 at the state meet. Now the number was gone from his mind, though he thought it had been less than 25 seconds.

The first group of four sprinters took off with the whistle, making good time halfway around the loop. The determination of their strides reached him at the top row of the stadium. A second whistle sounded, sending off a second group of four, and then a third and a fourth in quick succession. The runners rested a minute or so, hands on their hips and chests, heaving for oxygen. He could feel it. And before they were ready, the coach's whistle, forcing them on to another 200 meters, and another and another. By the sixth run, it had hurt worse than anything else he could imagine at that time.

Jefferson's last race had been just before graduation at the UNM stadium, an oval that, though regulation size, seemed made of an entirely different substance than any high school track he'd ever been around. He'd run a decent time, though not his best, and not good enough to place. At the time he'd thought the disappointment had killed something inside him. He'd skipped the end-of-year awards dinner, feeling that going would only make his failure to place at the state meet more noticeable. Before that last race he'd always finished ahead of Tommy Rutledge—god, he hadn't thought of that kid in five years—the other runner from Santa Fe High, who'd ended up first that day, and with a scholarship to Baylor to boot. Jefferson hadn't wanted to talk about it at the time, and he'd told anyone who asked that he didn't care and that he hadn't trained that hard anyway. But his stomach clenched now as he watched the young runners down below.

He'd always thought going back to the old places would be a comfort—he had thought of those places so many times when lying on his bunk in Iraq—but he was finding that to have been a false assumption. He didn't feel better or more himself sitting here at his old high school stadium, staring down at his old track coach. He didn't feel like walking down there and saying hello and meeting the young runners who'd taken his place. An emptiness louder than the previous emptiness was taking up all the space inside him, a brooding, malignant presence. It was an inarticulate sickness, and it would kill him if he didn't find a cure.

In a funk he left the high school and rode the trails that followed the big arroyo out to the south part of town, behind the Chavez Center with its indoor pool and basketball courts and ice skating rink—all that running and sweating and stroking of ice and water—behind the weathered, half-empty mall, out to where the houses had no trees in their small yards. It was another beautiful day in the high desert, and all around him life was abuzz, but Jefferson could think of nothing in the world he wanted to do as he gazed at the snow-tipped mountains way off in the distance.

EVENTUALLY THERE CAME the day—it was a Thursday—when Jefferson fished out the slip of newspaper from his pocket and called the pseudo-doctor and explained his situation.

Could he come over right now? She didn't have any appointments for the rest of the day.

Dr. Monika owned a compound on the East Side, infamous for the man who'd designed and built it, a political activist and painter from Santa Fe's roaring 1960s. Tucked back down an overgrown dirt lane, Jefferson guessed the place must have been under the care of a professional gardener. She met him at the door in an orange caftan and rubber flip-flops. "Welcome—Jefferson, is it?" she said, and led him through the thick-walled serenity.

He imagined her story—almost sixty, weekly massages, no real job ever, a lifetime of summers at the beach, at least one stint at an Indian ashram. Very beautiful, in fact so beautiful that it was weird for him to think how old she must be. The women he knew worked too hard to be this youthful at sixty. He felt bad momentarily for having had that thought— he meant no offense to all the beautiful hardworking women of the world—but it was true.

They passed through a long whitewashed hall hung with paintings and woodcuts he felt sure were important, ending up in a sunken sunroom, its many windows looking out onto a square of green lawn and a fountain. Who was this woman?

"Wowee," Dr. Monika said after he'd told her the whole story—at least, as much as he could dredge up in forty-five minutes. "So, let me get this right. You've made it home—you survived the war, but you witnessed unbelievable loss while you were over there—and everyone, your family and friends, are ecstatic to have you home, but you don't feel right, you don't feel yourself, you want to feel better. Is that it?"

"Well."

"I mean, that's what it seems to me," she said.

"I'm not sure."

"I know, I know, you hesitate to apply terms to yourself. You don't want to be a victim. You don't want it all to get the best of you, poor kid. You poor, poor kid."

"I'm not sure what I have has a label—I mean . . ." But he didn't know what else to say.

"Are you jumpy?"

"Jumpy?"

"Yeah. Jumpy. You know—*Ho!*" Dr. Monika yelled in his face, and he did in fact jump. Her breath needed a squirt of toothpaste.

This conversation was veering off into mucky marshland. It reminded him of what he imagined Louisiana bayou to be like.

"Could we talk a bit about Gabriel García Márquez?" Surely Dr. Monika, being the high-cultured sort of woman who had a fountain in her back courtyard and who wore a caftan at midday, would have something to say about GGM.

"Sure. So what about him? Great, great writer." Her eyes were seriously blue when she said this.

"Yeah. He's really my savior." He couldn't look at her when he said this—it was too serious an admission. He couldn't take it if she wasn't taking him seriously.

"Yes. Well. I can certainly relate to the power of great literature. I went through a Henry James phase when I was in grad school—read all of his novels one summer. Just beautiful." She seemed to be off in a neverland, probably the green lawn of some Ivy League college somewhere.

"I'm not really talking about beauty so much as—"

"Well, sure you are. You're just calling it something else."

"Maybe, but I don't think so. He saved my life, Dr. Monika."

"Who?" Her eyebrows strained toward one another.

"GGM."

"Who?"

He refused to answer this question. Maybe this hadn't been such a good idea.

"Oh, are you still talking about Gabriel García Márquez?"

Now he was sure it had been a stupid idea. This woman wasn't even a good listener. She had a lot of money, and she probably knew a lot about art and culture, maybe even books, but she had nothing to offer him.

But the woman was persistent, and luckily she didn't seem to be able to read Jefferson's mind, or he might have offended her. She just kept on talking and peering inquisitively into his eyes. "Look, Jefferson. Why don't you tell me a little more about what you're talking about—I'm curious."

He thought about his options, going back down to Albuquerque and trying again with the young doctor from the VA, or trying to find another psychoanalyst somewhere else, or just talking about it all with Nigel or with strangers down on the plaza. He thought about not talking about any of it ever again, and he wondered what sort of internal damage that might cause. And then he looked around him again— the beautiful older woman who claimed to be curious, sitting before him on a white couch.

"Have you read *One Hundred Years of Solitude*, Dr. Monika?"

"Oh, yes, of course. I think so. In college. That was a long time ago."

"Have you ever had a book you felt you had to carry with you everywhere, all the time, Dr. Monika? I mean, do you think it's normal to do that? To feel fragile and shaky at the very idea of losing that book?"

He paused to look at her. She was still listening.

"Because that's what I'm going through. That's my life. I feel sometimes things are stable all around me. I feel I'm home. I'm alive. There's no one asking me to get in a Humvee and go put myself in danger. I haven't touched a gun for over a month, and yet my hands shake. And when my hands stop shaking, I realize my brain's jittery. Jumping from one image, one phrase, one bit of memory to the next. It's never quiet in my head. I'm not myself, Dr. Monika. At least, I'm not the myself I used to be. The only thing that seems to make me feel okay is this one book."

"*One Hundred Years of Solitude*, you mean?"

"Yes."

"And isn't that a healthy response to all you've been through? I mean, it's not like you're doing drugs. It's not like you're racing a hundred and twenty miles per hour on the highway, trying to kill yourself. It seems to me that reading is the very sort of thing that might help you. I wouldn't worry about it at all."

The pseudo-doctor had such a nice voice, and Jefferson had no real criticism of the things she was saying to him, but nonetheless he suddenly felt he could not talk about any of this anymore. He felt he did not want to try so hard.

She went on. "I was just thinking it might be helpful for you to read a few more things—I was thinking what other novels I might suggest—who knows? You might find that with each novel you read, you feel better and a little bit more like yourself. You know . . . I know! I've got a great list of classics filed away somewhere. I'm just gonna go get it for you—I'll make a copy. I think this may be just what you need. And you know, it can be entirely free. The public library is a great resource. I'll be right back, okay? It'll only take a minute—"

And with that, Dr. Monika dashed back down the long hallway and disappeared around a corner. He heard a door open.

But it wasn't what he needed. He knew that. The idea of her eager fingers sorting through files, trying to find this list of classics, formed a heavy lump in his stomach. What was worse than suffering alone was witnessing complete strangers trying to heal you in a day with a piece of paper. Did she really think a list of novels could help him answer the question *Why?*

He clutched at *One Hundred Years* under his shirt and considered a new approach. What he needed was to show Dr. Monika that it was not the general habit of reading but rather the particular practice of reciting and chanting and singing García Márquez's words that he needed. He thought that by identifying just the right lines and sharing his practice with her, she would understand. She might stop trying to come up with another solution for him.

He struggled, trying to think of just the right line. If only Gabriel were there, he'd know which one would do the trick.

Jefferson's first idea was the line about people being so extreme, they would wage war over things they could not touch with their own hands. He thought what a great line it was and how, no matter what war you might think of, it was true. But it was so simple. Perhaps too simple for such a thick novel. So he stored it away in a mental bin and moved on. What was a line, perhaps a longer excerpt, that showed more of GGM's complex side? He thought about one of the many lines dealing with relationships between young boys and their much older aunties. There were some really interesting ones in that category, but the thought of Auntie Linda had always prevented him from fully appreciating them; they suggested ideas he found difficult to keep abstract. And so he moved on, back in the direction of Gabriel's ideas about war.

Dr. Monika was headed back down the hall toward him with the list of suggested reading. Ugh. She placed the multi-page packet on the coffee table in front of him. "You want some tea? Coffee? Bottled water? I'm going to get something for myself."

"No, thanks."

"You sure? I've got some really great Thai coconut iced teas."

It wasn't that he was against caffeine or sugar or chocolate or anything. He just found it all distracting. And what he needed in the moment was to settle on the perfect line. He was considering the one that always got him in the gut, the one that really cut a little too close for comfort, causing the face of his sergeant, RT, to take the form of a pulsing anagram eight inches from his nose. It might offend Dr. Monika for its specificity, and though it was longish, Jefferson felt fairly confident he had the gist of it in his mind. It began:

The sergeant ordered a house-to-house search, and this time the soldiers even took the people's tools. They grabbed a doctor and tied him to a bush and then they shot him.

Jefferson paused. The next bit was about the old priest. Terrible.

The old priest tried to show off by levitating, but the military authorities were not impressed and split his head open with the butt of a rifle.

There was one more bit about a woman who had been bitten by a mad dog who was then killed with a rifle butt as well. Jefferson shuddered as he thought of it. He couldn't repeat that part.

Dr. Monika had returned back down the hall, to the kitchen for her beverage, he guessed, and he felt a little shaky. Too shaky, in fact, to chant that line in its entirety to a well-meaning almost-stranger with crystal-blue eyes. It was bad enough to recall it in his own mind. He had to think of a different one.

Maybe he should go for simple. Two of his all-time favorites—lines that he'd recited and sung hundreds of times in the dining hall for all to hear—were very, very simple. It would be difficult to choose between them. God, he wished GGM were there to help him out.

The first was more hopeful than the second, but its rhythm wasn't quite as easy. The second rolled off his tongue; he had found he could almost fall asleep while chanting the second one. In both cases Jefferson had adapted the original lines so they would feel like his own. He thought of the two lines now, weighing the pros and cons.

War . . . it's such a waste! Why can't it just be a bad dream?
And:
I don't know why we are fighting.

But something was missing in each of these for this present circumstance with the pseudo-doctor. As great as each one was, Jefferson feared none was quite personal enough to capture her attention. He needed a line that showed more of what he'd been experiencing since he'd returned home. He needed a line to grip Dr. Monika with the precise flavor of sickness that had overtaken him. A riff on García Márquez's words that would simplify all the issues Jefferson was having a very hard time talking about. Jefferson thought of one now that came pretty close:

A deep chill has come over me.
It tortures me.
Even in the heat of the day
it will not let me sleep.
It stalks me.

Yes. If he had to start with one line, this would be the one. Jefferson knew there was no guarantee Dr. Monika would connect with the words—and he did not expect her to curl up on the floor and sob as he had the first time he'd chanted them—but he would share them with her anyway.

"Okay, I'm back." She held a glass of clear, bubbly beverage surrounding perfectly formed ice cubes. Just like in the movies. And again the question came to his mind: Who was this woman, and what was he doing in her house?

"Listen—I was thinking—why don't we pick a few books from the list and read them together? You know, like our own little book club?"

God, she was so well-meaning. Truly good.

"Whaddya think, Jefferson Long Soldier?" Beautiful too. A beautiful old rich white woman.

He didn't want to be rude. He didn't want to burn any bridges.

"Jefferson?"

It seemed best to leave the questions for a moment and just go ahead with the line he'd chosen, the most appropriate line he could think of in the moment to help her understand the current distractions of his mind, the dark places he'd traveled, the nightmares. Dr. Monika's very beautiful skin glistened all the more in that instant, compelling him onward in the direction he knew was best.

"Wait a sec," he managed, as he stood up from the white couch, adjusted his sweats, and considered his options. "Just a sec," he said, as he thought whether the pine coffee table strewn with magazines or the somewhat ancient-looking leather drum the size of a small kitchen table would be better for his purpose. It was important, he'd always thought, to add a little height to his presentation if at all possible. He was normally so shy. It helped to be taller.

She had taken her seat on the white couch, crossing her legs under her caftan and sipping her bubbly beverage, when Jefferson made his decision and stepped up onto the somewhat ancient-looking leather drum.

"Oh my god—what in the world?"

"Just a sec, Dr. Monika. I want you to hear something." And with that he launched into his take on Gabriel García Márquez's line about an inner coldness having shattered his bones, the one he'd just settled on moments earlier in his mind. He'd done this one so many times in Iraq that the words began to slip off his tongue into the crisp blue light of the room like an ancient fable. As was usually the case, he closed his eyes and opened his mouth and after having filled himself with air down to the bottom of his belly he bellowed,

I am so cold.

A deep chill has come over me.

A deep, deep chill.

He sang in his unique chant, the way he imagined all those old monks chanting in all those dark passageways. The way he imagined his great-grandfathers chanting from within the embrace of rocky enclaves and flat in the middle of the wide-open plains. He tilted his head back and sang,

It waits for me,

It tortures me.

He swayed on top of the drum with bent knees, singing on,

It waits for me and tortures me.

I say, it waits for me and tortures me.

It tortures me.

And so, even in the heat of the sun I cannot rest.

Even in the heat of the sun I cannot rest.

I tell you, I cannot rest.

He raised his hands above his head, and as he imagined old-time Baptist preachers from under the white tents of old-time revivals, Jefferson screamed out his hope for comprehension and connection.

I said, I cannot rest!

I said, I cannot rest!

I said,

I CANNOT REST!

Out of breath and seeing now through the slits of his eyes that Dr. Monika was gazing up at him with a strained expression, he finished the lines in what he thought of as a humble whisper.

For several months, even in the heat of the sun, I am so cold I cannot rest.
The chill stalks me,
It stalks me,
It stalks—me.

His performance of the lines, his articulation of the words and the precise way in which he'd drawn out and repeated certain syllables, was, if Jefferson had to say so himself, a perfect representation of his emotional state. He could not speak for all those other soldiers, but he had no choice about whether or not to speak for himself. And he was proud to have made it to the end without crying—sometimes that happened, and it was okay, but he was glad for this first time with Dr. Monika that he had kept it professional and sort of, if he thought about it, academic. This was the best way for her to experience the words—without his overwhelmed emotions getting in the way.

He stepped down from the drum, which fortunately had proved strong, and he looked at her, waiting. He had a lot of experience with this sort of thing and knew that he could not expect a positive response. Still, he always hoped.

There were tears in her eyes.

"Wow–wee," she said, clasping her hands together under her chin. It must have been the only word that came to her mind.

They reached a point not long afterward in which any more talking about any of it became awkward, and so Jefferson left, with plans to visit the pseudo-doctor again three days later. He didn't expect much, but then again, there was something to be said for having a stranger willing to listen. Though Dr. Wesleyan in Albuquerque had meant well, and though she had been a bona fide MD with framed certificates on her office wall, there was something altogether more helpful about this older lady who'd advertised on the back page of the weekly paper. He had no name for the feeling he was having as he rode back down her dirt drive and back through the tangle of eastside estates, but his hands did not shake as they steered the bike back home.

After that Jefferson kept going back to see her two or three times a week, and though he continued to bring the novel with him, after a month of the storytelling he removed it from the Ace bandage and began to carry it in a backpack.

What the skill was, precisely, and where she had learned it, Jefferson never determined, but Dr. Monika, who had no medical degree, who had nothing behind her but a lifetime of beautiful living, began to help him feel better. She was a good listener. "You just tell me whatever it is you need to get off your chest, Jefferson. Just start talking."

And talk Jefferson did. He began with generalities, as if slogging through a quagmire. *It was intense. I couldn't ever catch my breath. I knew it was gonna be bad, but I had no idea.* There were several weeks of this undefined muck spilling out of him, always ending with Jefferson in a ball on the white couch, weeping, Dr. Monika sitting next to him, patting his back. And then Jefferson felt he'd run through all that material and there was new stuff, specific stuff, an entire list of stories ready to be aired. It began when Dr. Monika asked the question, "So when exactly did you start chanting from *One Hundred Years of Solitude?*"

He paused to remember.

It had been the evening of his forty-seventh day, after Ramon from Las Cruces had been shot in the throat next to him. The line he'd chosen on that day had been a long one, one of Jefferson's abiding favorites because it ended with a hopeful notion. Jefferson believed that this notion—that there could exist a machine to help a person forget his nightmares—was reason enough to love Gabriel García Márquez. Even if the man had written no other noteworthy sentence, this one idea would have been enough. Ah . . . *A machine to take away one's bad memories.*

After that, using the list he'd kept of all those losses, he'd told her a story each time he visited. About the loss of a close companion or a guy he'd just met. And how, in each instance, he pulled his book out from under the Ace bandage and chanted the line from *One Hundred Years of Solitude* that seemed most appropriate.

The list was long. Jefferson did not plan to get through the whole thing when he started sharing stories with her, but in the end he told Dr. Monika everything he could remember about each of those losses he had witnessed at close range.

Without fail, after Jefferson had talked for thirty or forty five minutes, Dr. Monika would ask him what he planned for the rest of his day in a tone so neutral that it made it simple for him to admit just how simple his life really was. He was riding his bike home, or he was stopping at the store to help Esco unload an order, or he was going to think about checking in on Josephina C De Baca, finally going to do something about his feelings about that girl. Dr. Monika shared her plans as well— sometimes yoga in the backyard, sometimes a hike up Atalaya, sometimes early dinner plans with an old friend.

On his rides up to Dr. Monika's on the eastside and back home again, those several times a week for all those months, despite the changing seasons, despite his easing breath, despite his growing trust in the pseudo-doctor and the movement of the novel from the Ace bandage to his backpack, Jefferson did not stop loving Gabriel García Márquez. Most of his day-dreams were of the writer, and when he was not dreaming, he was speaking to the old man in his mind and occasionally, in great bursts of verbal enthusiasm, yelling out actual questions to which he awaited actual replies.

Oh my god, how did you know what it would be like to return home from war?

What should I do now?

Sometimes it was not a question.

God, I wish I could talk to you, Old Man.

Sometimes it was a plea.

I really need to see you, GGM. If I came to see you, would you open the door?

GARCÍA MÁRQUEZ'S DESCRIPTIONS of Úrsula Iguarán's husband—José Arcadio Buendía, the eccentric patriarch of the Buendía clan—his experiments and his unwitting neglect of his family, had immediately reminded Jefferson of what he knew of his late grandfather. Jefferson had never met the wild Lakota musician with whom Esco had fallen in love and raised a family, but he'd heard plenty of stories. The two men were similar beasts. Ursula's husband began as a family man and ended up a solitary lunatic after years of failed experimentation and ranting. He spent the last years of his life tied to the trunk of a chestnut tree in the courtyard, and he died a lonely death.

Likewise, Jefferson's grandfather had died alone, a musician chasing a dream. A banjo player with a lithe voice, he had traveled the Southwest with a little country band, forever hoping for a break. Nothing, not even his wife and their young daughters, filled his heart like writing songs and plucking the banjo's strings on stage. Jefferson figured that music had been for his grandfather what laboratory work had been for Arcadio Buendía, an addiction.

And then he had died in a boating accident outside Austin while touring the Lone Star State. Esco was forty-four years old, with a ten-year-old grandson, Nigel, and a second grandson,

Jefferson, just two weeks from being born. She had never told anyone (to whom would she have shown her soft side?), but her husband's death, coming like that out of nowhere, had turned her numb. They had gotten into a habit of talking on the phone about being grandparents again together, of helping their younger daughter raise her child, just as they'd helped Linda. They had reminisced about the days when their girls were little, of taking them to concerts at Paolo Soleri, of picnicking up in the mountains. He'd been nostalgic. I'll be home for the birth, he said. Get her to name him Jefferson Long Soldier, after me, he'd said.

And then he'd hit his head wrong on the rocklike surface of the lake as he tried to jump the wake with his water skis, a typically freakish accident. He'd died without ever regaining consciousness. "He was always doing stupid things," Esco said every time she told Jefferson the story. "He was full of life and scared of nothing. Just like your mother," she usually added, shaking her head.

Just like José Arcadio Buendía, Jefferson thought as he read the lines in the novel.

15

HE TOOK HIS time, allowing each story to pull at him as it would. When possible he shared a detail he'd known about the person who had died, something she'd said just before the explosion, the expression in his eyes when he made a truce with the pain, a smile that reminded Jefferson of a friend from elementary school or of a season of the year. Some stories tugged at internal body parts—his esophagus, his inner ear, the ocular nerve attaching his eye to his brain—and others threatened to annihilate his various extremities—the thumbnail of his left hand, the callus on his right heel, the tip of his nose. Because each loss played uniquely upon his mind, Jefferson housed each one in a different place. Although he had a list, some stories were still hard to find.

The boy who'd told him about his grandmother's pierogies made him cry for Esco's hands as she wrapped tamales. For the young woman whose left ear was blown off prior to her mortal bleeding, he cried for her first favorite song, for all the time she must have spent on her bed as a middle-schooler listening to songs via headphones, for her first iPod and earbuds that, he imagined, her mother had given her as a high school graduation present. For the older guy whose helicopter went down less than an hour after he handed Jefferson a fistful of good-luck bubble gum, Jefferson cried for his own good and fortunate life and for the man's sweet tongue and his teeth and his lips. Some of the stories were more difficult to tell than others—the old man with his goats, the family in their Toyota, the seventeen-year-old and the hound. He told each one, and he cried his unique set of tears to the alert one-person audience on the white couch before him.

In all, there were forty-one stories in twenty weeks.

HE WAS A high school dropout, approximately two hundred pounds overweight, a fact that caused his eyes to almost disappear into an expanse of perspiring skin. Almost exactly a decade older than Jefferson, he was an unlikely optimist who appreciated the hard questions brought on by life. Later, as Jefferson was accounting for all the small miracles that had helped him heal, he realized that it was his cousin's subdued hopefulness that had lifted him out of harm's way at a critical moment. Nigel's mindset—that life was made up of puzzles, not problems—was part of the life-saving recipe.

During Jefferson's first several weeks home, Nigel had laid low, telling his cousin to take it easy, to listen to music, to give it time. He listened to Jefferson complain about Esco's incessant gentle knocking on his bedroom door, her constant offer of fake chicken soup, as if it could heal him. Nigel told Jefferson that he understood that Jefferson's problem had nothing to do with soup or fake chicken, or, for that matter, any food item their grandmother might prepare.

This went on for weeks, all through that summer of 2009, and then the aspens turned yellow up in the mountains and the light took on that nostalgic low slant. Winter was coming, as it always did, and aside from his having told Dr. Monika a bunch of stories, Jefferson thought, nothing much seemed to have happened.

Then came the morning Jefferson finally decided to contact Ray Soto, his friend from Iraq who also loved García Márquez, to see if he wanted to get together now that they were both survivors back in Santa Fe, and discovered that Ray had hanged himself in his apartment off San Mateo, a whole year earlier.

Jefferson slouched in the metal chair, drinking his fourth Dr Pepper of the day, alternating mindless slurps with fistfuls of Cool Ranch Doritos, as his cousin changed the spark plugs on the Kawasaki. It was a breezeless, mosquito-less October evening, the kind of evening white people call Indian summer, whatever that means, and yet Jefferson could not erase the image of Ray hanging from his ceiling fan less than a mile from where Jefferson now sat. It was as loud as a mortar explosion in his head, as unexpected as hiccups and as difficult to forget. He felt he might be sick.

Nigel was smearing away the corrosion and grease from the bike's engine with a dirty rag, paying attention in an inattentive manner. Jefferson fully assumed that his cousin was not listening. This was okay. What Jefferson felt he most needed on that evening was to be solitary without being alone, to talk without his words having any consequences, and somehow miraculously to arrive at a decision about which fork in the road to take. There seemed to be two options: sign up for another tour of duty or get on with things as best he could back in Santa Fe. An explosion sounded in the near distance—a car backfiring on Cerrillos, or a handgun over on Hopewell Street—shaking Jefferson's skin against his bones. Could he do it? Go back out there again?

"Isn't there anything you'd like to do with yourself, dude?" Nigel asked.

The question interrupted Jefferson's consideration of the option Ray had chosen, to end his own life after making it home alive. It was unbelievable news—such a nice guy, a guy who'd loved Gabriel just as Jefferson loved him.

Jefferson remembered the night a shrill whirring had heralded the arrival of a mortar in their barracks—in truth it had hit the next building, not theirs, but who could tell the precise landing point of such fiery violence?—uprooting Jefferson and Ray Soto and all the other guys who were on the verge of sleep, slamming their bunks into each other and spilling the contents of their drawers into heaps of disarray, snatching their cell phones and laptops, smashing their skinny arms and legs and butts onto the cold, hard floor. There was a pause of intense silence, and then there was moaning and tears. Jefferson had been thrown against Ray, both alive, thank god, but Ray had cried into Jefferson's shoulder and clung to him like a child. No blood on either of them, but then again, blood wasn't the only sign of a wound.

He hadn't told that story to Dr. Monika. He'd forgotten that one.

Nigel was looking at him, waiting for something, it seemed.

"I got some bad news today," Jefferson finally said, unable to look his cousin in the eyes, staring instead down into the dirt.

"Yeah," said Nigel. "Sorry to hear, cousin." His large frame hovered, motionless.

"Yep," said Jefferson. "I found out a friend of mine died. Not too far from here," he said, pointing to the ground. He was preparing to go on, to tell Nigel about Ray, about how they'd shared a love for the great writer García Márquez, when he realized his throat had closed up and that he would not be able to speak anymore.

"I can't talk about it," he said finally, sobbing into his hands as he thought all the sad thoughts about why any of it had had to happen.

Nigel could not have been further from understanding his cousin's infatuation with the famous writer, but he knew

Jefferson was a dreamer who rarely acted. And he knew Jefferson, who had seemed extremely weird and disconnected when he'd first returned from war, had calmed down a little bit over the past months, but was still not at all well. Nigel had watched Jefferson jump and cower at the sound of a shopping cart rattling across the grocery store parking lot. He had seen Jefferson's finger-crochet projects hanging from the clothesline next to the van in Esco's backyard. From his spot in his sleeping bag on the floor, he had witnessed Jefferson's screams in the night and had documented daily the thickening glaze over his cousin's eyes. He appreciated, as only an obese man can, the large quantity of Doritos Jefferson consumed, along with the increasing bagginess of his clothes.

"Come on, cousin," Nigel said now. "It's gonna be okay."

An intuitive naturalist, Nigel believed in neither talk therapy nor antidepressants when it came to mental health. Perhaps nothing would help his cousin, he thought, but staying in Santa Fe was probably the worst thing he could do. Although he did not think Jefferson was suicidal, whenever he saw that faraway glaze across Jefferson's eyes, he imagined it had something to do with death fantasies. He had a smirk and a standby line: *Come on, man, eat some ice cream or somethin'. Go ride your bike down to the stadium.* It might not have been enough to help everyone, but for Jefferson—who loved Nigel and who, despite the murkiness of his solitude, despite the pain of his memories always found himself wanting to live—it was just enough to see him through a bad moment.

"Come on, man. Eat some ice cream or somethin'. Go ride your bike down to the stadium," Nigel said now.

So far it had worked every time, but now Nigel was sensing a deeper level of grayness in his cousin's blank face, a degree of absence he hadn't seen before. Something close to unreachable. He knew he had to keep his cousin engaged—conversant and awake, so to speak. All the brochures from the VA talked about how family members needed to pay attention to their loved ones once they returned home, not to ignore subtle changes in expression or skin tone or general energy level. And so, though he generally tried to avoid using his own large body to intimidate other people, Nigel decided to make an exception. He was out of options. So he heaved himself down onto the ground in front of his cousin, bent his knees under himself, grabbed Jefferson's bony wrists, and brought his meaty face right up close. Pressing firmly into Jefferson's hands and ignoring his attempts to pull away, Nigel told him to shut up and listen in the harshest tone he could muster.

"Now this is what you're gonna do, Jefferson, ya hear? You're taking the Kawasaki, and you're going to drive it far away, out of Santa Fe somewhere, do you understand me?"

Jefferson did not answer, just sat there with his chin against his chest, his eyes closed. It was difficult to tell whether he'd heard.

"You can go wherever you want—to Las Cruces or El Paso or Phoenix—I don't care where you go. But you gotta get out of town. You gotta find yourself, man. You gotta do what you gotta do. You hear me?"

Nigel was sweating, and his knees seemed to be buckling under the weight, so he took a deep breath and stared way off in the distance, out of the shed and toward where he knew the Jemez Mountains rested. He'd dreamed himself of riding the Kawasaki off and away somewhere, someday, perhaps a lady friend along to share the journey. It was a dream that could still happen. But for now Jefferson needed help, and at least one thing was clear: Jefferson needed to get out of town. And Nigel's bike could make this happen.

But Jefferson was thinking about Ray, and how it had all unfolded. How he'd been wanting to contact Ray for weeks, see what he thought about going off on a road trip to find

Gabriel García Márquez together. How he'd gone on Facebook that morning to send him a message. He knew it was probably a dumb idea, unrealistic at least, but maybe it would feel good to talk to Ray about it in theory.

But why was Nigel so close-up and in his face? What was he saying? Something, it seemed, about the Kawasaki. Something about getting out of Santa Fe.

All of it was almost too much for Jefferson to bear. He'd had this idea about finding the great writer, and he did believe it was a decent idea, and he'd thought about sharing it with his friend who he'd now discovered was no longer alive. What was he to make of it all? He looked straight into Nigel's big face, into his long, narrow eyes, and he tried to make sense of everything that had brought him to that moment. It was almost too much.

And then he found the words to say the thing he needed to say.

"You think it'd be insane for me to go find Gabriel García Márquez down in Mexico City?"

Nigel sat back down on his stool and wiped his brow with a rag. What was Jefferson talking about?

"I mean, he's had cancer for over a decade," Jefferson went on in a rush, "and he's super old anyway. If I could get myself down there, you think I could just knock on his door? You think he'd answer?"

"Who are you talking about?" Nigel said, but he liked the energy he was hearing in Jefferson's voice. It was a bit of the old spontaneous Jefferson.

"I told you. Gabriel García Márquez."

Jefferson was speaking faster with each new syllable in each new question. The glaze over his eyes had begun to dissipate, though, so Nigel stopped trying to make sense of what his cousin was saying and just stared at him with newfound hope.

"I mean, did you just say something about your bike, Nigel? I could borrow your bike? I'd take good care. I promise

OUT THERE

I'd be careful—do you really mean I could take it? Are you serious, I mean? Do you think it'd make it all the way to Mexico City? I mean, you wouldn't mind if I tried?" Though the excess sugar from the four Dr Peppers accounted for part of Jefferson's excitement, Nigel recognized the larger part as genuine hope. A trip on the Kawasaki. A chance to talk with some old dude who was obviously a big deal, maybe a musician he'd never heard of?

"Look," said Nigel, his slow, deliberate eyes finding their way out through his good thick skin. "I have no idea who this Gabriel Montez dude is—someone you met in Iraq who's in Mexico now?—but given how bad off you are, you really have no choice, man. Sounds like you need to go find this dude. Maybe it would help. You won't know unless you go."

"Gabriel García *Márquez*," Jefferson said. "His name is Gabriel García *Márquez*."

THE 47TH DAY. *Ramon, 20, from Las Cruces shot in the throat next to me.*
Adair, from Hollidaysburg, Pennsylvania. 22.
Dudzinski, 22, of Mangilao, Guam, who died in a Humvee crash. I was in the vehicle behind him. He called me "buddy boy."
Hazelton, 29, of Edinburgh, Indiana.
Teresa Blue, 23, of Rosedale, Maryland. I saw the explosions and later helped carry her body.
26 yrs old. His name was Alton. Bellevue, Nebraska. His vehicle was behind mine when an IED blew it off the road. I'd never spoken to him but he had a real nice smile.
Father and three young girls in old Toyota station wagon near Fallujah. Their young eyes were scared out the back window at me—I don't know why. I hope nothing ever happens to them. I watched until their car disappeared into the dusty landscape.
27-yr-old Barker of West Seneca, New York.
40-yr-old Benton of Winona, Minnesota.
Dan Logan from another little town in Pennsylvania. Watsontown.
Debree, 20, of Evansville, Indiana.
Tristan's hand. He's alive and has been sent home. 24.
Cheever, Jr., 31, of Charlotte, NC.
Daniel Waterford, 19, of Auburn, California. A real nice guy.

Hume, 21, of Appleton, Maine. Stupid IED. Sang in the evenings like Johnny Cash.

Thomas. Mount Vernon, Washington. Only 21. I was with him on his birthday.

Dvorak, 24, of East Brunswick, New Jersey.

Gomez, 20, of Irving, Texas, who died in the National Naval Medical Center in Bethesda, MD. I was there when he went down but heard later of his death.

A young guy from Pleasant Prairie, Wisconsin.

25-yr-old from Gilmanton, New Hampshire.

Dorn, 32, of Minnesota, his helicopter went down in the Tigris River. He was the first one to call me crazy to my face.

Harry Wisener, 26, Golden, CO.

Master Sgt. Pinga Pinau, 33, of Watertown, New York. Loved this guy. He was so funny and what a beautiful name.

Zach LeBlanc who was younger than I was. Damned IEDs. From Buffalo.

Lawrence from New York City. 26 years old.

A guy from Rochester Hills, Michigan. I think his name was Aron. Never got his last name. 23.

19-year-old Galen from Albuquerque. Went down after telling me about his grandparents surviving the Nazis.

Johnston, 46, of Sackets Harbor, New York. When an IED detonated nearby he was injured and died two weeks later at Walter Reed Army Medical Center in DC. I saw him the day they shipped him back home and he said he'd always loved the way I read from my book even if everyone else might have thought I was crazy.

Anderson. Something about the physical training in Baghdad. He was from Pittsfield, Massachusetts. 24 years old.

A guy name Jeff Kleiner from Stockbridge, Georgia, 25, who drowned in a lake on the palace compound in Al Fallujah.

Dwight from Cass Lake, Minnesota. Another 20-year-old. Could have been a stand-up comedian.

The old man and his goats, pleading in an unknown tongue.

Sgt. Schoener from Ohio. Also a sprinter in high school. 26 years old.

OUT THERE

Steiner, 29, of Chattanooga, Tennessee.
Thomas T. Stromberg, III. 18, of Lopez, Pennsylvania.
Johnson, 28, of Sarasota, Florida. His helicopter was attacked. I
saw him board the helicopter. He'd just given me a handful of gum
and said he really liked my sneakers.
Richard Seiders. Gettysburg, PA.
The 17-year-old and then the hound. They were both accidents.
A guy from Missouri named Lincoln flew through the air and died
on top of me. Also immediately: Baxter Flavius, 20, of Boise, Idaho;
Burkland, 26, of Rockville, Maryland; Ferre, 21, of Bakersfield,
California; Connor, 19, of Jamestown, New York; Sgt. Monday
from Newark, Delaware. And later, Howell, 32, of Philadelphia,
New York; Lamb, 23, from New Orleans; Charles Terrazas, 25, of
Clarksville, Tennessee; Nick Warren's leg, 24, of Fairview Heights,
Illinois; and Rich Rosales's feet, 21, Saint Louis, Michigan.
Ray Soto, 26. He loved Gabriel Garcia Marquez, he told me once.
Loved him. Why did this have to happen?

HE DECIDED TO present his decision in the kitchen to his grandmother and Nigel as if it were final, rather than appear to be asking them for advice. He figured they would say it wasn't the best idea, that there were so many reasons not to go, and besides, why? He'd just returned home.

"Aw, honey . . . ," was all Esco said at first. After a few minutes of settling, she said, "Tell me one good reason."

But then, before he could begin to explain, she was off and away, telling him how Mexico wasn't safe for Americans traveling alone, that there were regularly reported tales of drug traffickers killing whoever happened to cross their path, that anyways, Jefferson was still jumpy. "Every time someone walks up behind you, you freeze like a stunned jackrabbit," she said, and then went on to recount the incident at the post office when Jefferson had jumped to the ground and covered his head, screaming, after a man dropped his pile of junk mail. She said she was going to call his therapist ("Esco, I don't have a therapist") and ask if it was safe for a young veteran in his state to leave home again so soon. And besides, she was curious where he was going to get the money to pay for his international travel, and anyway, didn't he care about her and his cousin, who had been waiting all this time for him to get home safe so they could get on with their lives? When was he going to start reading again? As she talked, she shoved plates and glasses into the upper cabinet, jamming a few saucepans and skillets down below.

Nigel just leaned against the kitchen wall, his eyes closed, seemingly humming a silent tune.

Jefferson waited. Despite his grandmother's words whirling about him, he felt calm.

"Here's what I wanna know—," said Nigel, when Esco had slowed down a bit and begun to repeat her arguments.

She immediately took Nigel's words as support for her view, interrupting him. "See, Jefferson, your cousin has a problem with this coco-minnie idea too, see?"

"Cockamamie, Esco. Cock-a-MAMIE," said Jefferson.

Nigel seemed to be waiting for the talkers in his family to take another breath. When the pause had lasted a full ten seconds, he started up again, pushing back away from the wall and standing wide-legged between the kitchen counter and the dishwasher, using his hands like a football coach describing a play. "One question," he said, holding up the pointer finger of his right hand at Jefferson. "Are you taking the dog?"

But Esco continued on in her own line of thought. "You're not taking the Corolla," she said.

Jefferson had an answer to Nigel's question, but he turned to Esco first. He'd wanted to talk to Nigel once more privately about taking his motorbike, to seal the deal, but it looked like he wasn't going to have that chance. He wanted to tell her that he was planning to take the Kawasaki, but she interrupted, saying, "There's the camper van in the backyard, but I think it's been sitting out there too long. I doubt even Nigel could get that thing runnin' again." Then she put her hand on her forehead and sat down in the nearest kitchen chair, as if mention of the van or the suggestion of Jefferson's mom or both had been too much for her. "That van's been sitting out there over twenty years, boys."

"Not twenty years, Esco," Nigel said, but then he paused and seemed to calculate in the air. "Oh, well, yeah, I guess you're right. Hmm . . ." He was now looking at Jefferson with raised emphatic eyebrows, encouraging him to tell their grandmother what the two of them had already discussed.

Jefferson smirked, looked up at the ceiling and way off beyond that to a faraway place that seemed to be materializing before him.

"I was gonna ask Nigel to borrow his motorbike, Esco," Jefferson said finally. He had been mulling the idea over for two full days since their first conversation about it. "And I was planning to put a little carrier or basket thingie on the back for Remedios," he said, now turning to face his cousin. "—of course I'm takin' her."

Nigel wrinkled up the right side of his face.

"I just can't believe we're really talking about this," Esco said into the kitchen tablecloth, her fingers now squeezing the bridge of her nose. It seemed to her that once again the ground was moving under her feet, that the stability she'd yearned for after Jefferson's return from war had not come to be. Some part of her had known it was too much to expect. He'd been out there in a hostile world, doing things, seeing things, she could not imagine. And though she had done her best all along to raise him, to love him, she knew that Jefferson had suffered losses before he ever left for war. She had done her best, but Esco knew that this was sometimes not enough.

Nigel'd been reworking that bike since before Jefferson had graduated from Santa Fe High. When he'd bought the scrap parts from the owner's widow, he'd weighed under two hundred pounds and had been dating a girl named Marissa. He'd told her he was going to take her on rides down to the Rio Grande in Albuquerque, and to the balloon fiesta. There was a moment back then when Nigel'd thought he'd marry Marissa.

"I'm one hundred and ten percent for it," said Nigel, "but you need to practice riding before you head out, cousin."

"I know how to ride a bike," said Jefferson.

"I never seen you ride one."

The conversation went round and round—Esco with her head propped between her hands, mostly silent and Nigel with his swaying hulk hammering at the practicalities—until the sun's last glare angled through a broken slat in the front window blinds, hitting him in the eyes as he sat on the living room couch. It was all too much. "Let's get outside and watch the sunset," Jefferson said finally.

Out of weariness as well as the desire that came each day at this time to see something beautiful, the two followed Jefferson onto the back stoop. Esco plopped down in her metal chair, Nigel leaned against the house near the back door, and Jefferson perched on the stoop, his feet swinging above the scrag grass. The yard—a rectangular patch of scrub and dirt and empty plastic yogurt tubs and a tumbledown shed and Jefferson's mom's old camper van—provided the counterweight for the sky's display. It could not have been so beautiful without the contrast of the ugly yard. Jefferson had figured this out back in high school when he needed a reason to feel okay about the junk that surrounded them. Tonight, far off in the west, the orange fireball eased toward the horizon as the three of them watched.

He didn't have any answers for their concerns. It was true what Nigel had said: he didn't really know how to ride a motorbike. Each of his grandmother's amorphous fears was also probably valid. There were lots of things she hadn't considered, Jefferson guessed, that were valid concerns as well. Concerns more at the heart of the matter. What was the point? And what were the chances he'd get to see GGM, even after he'd traveled all that way, even if he could find where he lived, in the fifth or seventh or tenth largest city on the face of the planet? Assuming he did find the courage to knock on the heavy antique door Jefferson imagined, lifting the tarnished brass doorknocker he imagined, formed in the shape of a lion's head, what then? It was possible that García Márquez would stare at Jefferson through the peephole of his thick wood door and refuse to open it. It was also possible that he would let Jefferson in, and Jefferson would then find himself tongue-tied, with absolutely no words to express why he had searched García Márquez down over a thousand miles from home, on a borrowed motorbike, with his dog. So many potential failures awaited him.

He needed a good reason to do what he wanted to do.

What was it? What was the one good reason?

In the quiet of that evening, as the distant star became a semicircle and then a sliver and then nothing but a source of dim light and heat below the horizon, Jefferson told himself that this trip might be the most important thing he would ever do. That it could be the beginning of his personal revolution. That it would change the world as he knew it, and the way he knew himself in the world. He told himself he had to go find García Márquez to end the nightmares and the horrible daydreams and the feeling of empty solitude that followed him around. So that he might continue breathing in and out, so that he could taste his grandmother's *posole* when she set it down in a white bowl on the green place mat in front of him. He had to go to Mexico City so he could once again recognize the good heat of the sun on his skin, experience the ever-so-slight-but-real tingle of his birthday, November 18, a day unlike any other.

No one but Dr. Monika knew all forty-one stories. Jefferson hadn't wanted to burden his grandmother or Nigel. They both worried plenty already. Though she said she was happy to have him home, that he looked so well, Jefferson knew Esco still worried all the time. She still slept at the foot of his bed when he wasn't sleeping out in the van, and she was still afraid he'd hang himself from the ceiling fan if she left him alone for even twenty minutes. She'd admitted this after a few days of his return when he'd said he was okay, that she could go back to sleeping in her own room. She kept hearing stories about soldiers returning home and pretending to be okay, and she wasn't taking any chances, she told him. He'd have to push aside his poor old grandmother sleeping on a cot at the foot of his bed if he was going to try to kill himself.

"I'm not going to kill myself," he'd told her, again and again.

"That's exactly right, Jefferson—and that's why I'm sleeping in here with you."

The darkening dusk, his grandmother and his cousin sitting and standing quietly there with him, the everyday hum of cars along Cerrillos Road, these things grounded Jefferson. It all seemed so clear to him now.

"I love you guys," he said.

Esco patted his shoulder, and Nigel began to hum. The distinct smell of burning piñon—most likely a fire down at Manny's—buoyed him.

He told them what he could. "It's hard to explain, and I don't want to talk about any of it, but I experienced a lot of loss over there. I'm not the same as when I left."

Esco squeezed his shoulder, and Nigel came to kneel down behind them on the stoop. His large hands covered hers on the back of Jefferson's shoulder.

"I have to go find him. I have to try. I'm not sure I have a good reason, but I'm going anyway."

Still so much needed to be said, and yet the silence continued into the now dark night, eventually giving way to Nigel's sweet humming and the hooting of the turtledove who, along with his ancestors, had inhabited the large ponderosa pine at the back of the yard for as long as Jefferson could remember.

Later, as he lay in his bed listening to his grandmother's ragged breathing, Jefferson arrived at his One Good Reason for traveling to Mexico City to find García Márquez in that mysterious way that people everywhere, through all of history, have made decisions. His very life cried out to him. A miracle.

OUT THERE

Just like Colonel Aureliano Buendía, Jefferson had failed to die. His very life encompassed the idea of joy coming from sorrow, for what can be more joyful than surviving a tragedy and going on to live a full life afterward? And Gabriel García Márquez was the man who had covered bloody streets with rivers of yellow flowers. He was the one who had imagined a world in which incest and insanity reside alongside pots of geraniums and true romance. Jefferson had to find this man. This good man whose story had not only lightened his load but saved his life.

This one good reason was all he needed.

THAT FIRST NIGHT, Jefferson rode 250 miles on the Kawasaki, the black wind in his face and the bright stars overhead, cheering him across each new mile. When finally he crossed the border into Ciudad Juárez, he followed the road to the first bright grocery store and parked his bike under the streetlamp closest to the entrance. Sitting down, he propped himself against the lamp, Remedios curled at his feet, and slept the hard, relieved sleep of having begun a necessary journey. When he awoke, it was to the conversation of two old women bickering as they shuffled along. Across the parking lot two young children followed their parents, and the sun burned hot and true on his face.

After buying a baseball cap, two bananas, dog food, a cinnamon roll, and a coffee, he fed Remedios and studied his map in the shade of the building. He'd drawn a yellow highlighter line from Santa Fe to Mexico City, a straight shot south through Ciudad Juárez, Chihuahua, Torreón, Zacatecas, San Luis Potosí, and Querétaro. It was a long way down. Aside from Iraq, this was the only time he'd left the United States.

All around him, the world was awakening.

The day before, Nigel had taken him to the Santa Fe High parking lot for a quick lesson and taught him some basics, like the fact that a tank of gas would last a long time. Now, on the road, Jefferson had no choice but to fill in the gaps in his knowledge. This proved to be familiar territory for him, sort of like figuring out how to load an automatic grenade launcher when lying on his back in a deserted school under attack from snipers. He learned quickly that it was necessary to learn quickly or die. Before that trip Jefferson had ridden on the back of Nigel's bike a handful of times, but he'd never driven the thing himself. Jefferson was a walker by nature and preference. He'd thought about walking to Mexico City. It would not have been impossible. People had done it before him, and people would do it after him.

He coasted down the gradual incline of a high plain of low cacti, a landscape so much like La Bajada Hill between Santa Fe and Albuquerque that he questioned for a moment where he was, as if he'd woken from a dream, disoriented. Ah, yes. Somewhere between Ciudad Juárez and Chihuahua, on his way to find the old writer. The day after Thanksgiving. Hightops on his feet, and newly woven traveling headband across his forehead. The pup, Remedios, his solitary companion.

The Monday before, Jefferson had told Dr. Monika the story of the last time he chanted in Iraq. "And then I came home," he said. They were sitting on the facing white couches. Outside, the sunflowers bent wearily toward the dirt, their petals faded, most of their seeds stolen away by birds. Dr. Monika looked as if she was waiting for him to say something more, but he had nothing more to say. All the talk that had passed between them did not in this moment seem to offer any additional momentum. She would make herself available to him as long as he kept coming, he guessed. She would maintain an interest in his recovery, even if it took him the rest of his life. Her white couches would always sit in that crisp sunroom, looking out on the garden, going through the seasons as it did.

It was then that he had told her of his plan to borrow Nigel's motorbike and drive down to Mexico and find GGM.

The idea seemed to become real as he spoke it aloud. "I've gotta go find him, Dr. Monika," he'd said. "I won't know—I'll always wonder if I never go."

Part of him had not wanted to say the idea out loud. Saying it aloud made him vulnerable. It might have been better to keep the plan to himself, tell Dr. Monika about it all once he'd succeeded and had a complete story to share. He didn't want to face her criticism, not at the same moment in which he was trying to buoy himself into action.

But when Jefferson found the courage to look up at her, when he made the decision to look into her eyes, he saw that the muscles of Dr. Monika's face had relaxed. She was looking upon him as if he were her own son, smiling a smile of hope.

"Just don't say anything," he said anyway, not trusting what seemed to be her great faith in him. But she behaved as if she hadn't heard him. She turned and marched away down her long hall, returning a few minutes later with a wad of cash and a kiss on his cheek. She called him an inspiration for dreamers everywhere. "I love you, Jefferson," she said, and she wished him great success.

Everything within view struck him as patient and persistent, a landscape barren and untamed but somehow also forgiving. Though he was full of fears about all that could still go wrong, his heart beat a little lighter within his chest and his blood coursed a little more steadily—a little less noticeably—within his veins. He was in Mexico. There hadn't been any pickpockets in the parking lot in Juárez, the bike engine wasn't sputtering, and he hadn't seen a single sign of drugs or bandits. The only real worry was whether Gabriel would still be alive by the time Jefferson got to his house. How would he find his house? He thought of how Nigel would be asking him this question if he'd come along—he was always the practical planner—and he clicked his tongue and shook his head as he pushed the Kawasaki on, anticipating all the people he was going to meet along the way. All the adventuring. The chance, most likely, of miracles.

"I can't say good-bye again," Esco had told him. "You better be careful." And she had walked down the hall with her tall glass of ice water and closed the door of her bedroom behind her. She knew the basics, his rough itinerary, and she'd handed him a wad of cash stuffed in an envelope, with some of which he'd bought a used rear-mounted motorcycle dog carrier, so Remedios would be comfortable on the road.

So far, none of it had been as scary as he'd feared. He'd never been across the border—he'd never been south of Cruces before yesterday—but the people he'd seen and the land he'd traveled across so far didn't seem that different from the people and land of home. That Esco was half Mexican, which made him one-eighth, explained part of his comfort, the easy way he breathed. The sand and the chamisa and the scrub were familiar to his New Mexican eyes—familiar and forgiving, like family.

One thing Jefferson had not predicted was the drowsiness. Having never had a motorcycle, much less his own car, he'd not had the chance to drive on long, deserted highways before. He'd had his driver's license since the age of sixteen, and he used Esco's car to go to the store sometimes and once to Santa Fe High's homecoming, but Jefferson had never driven, say, all the way to Albuquerque. In Iraq he'd driven the Humvee only a handful of times, usually for short distances in some sort of emergency. That accident with the poor dog happened because he was not all that used to driving, and he thought he'd put it in drive, when actually it had been in reverse. And he'd never driven so far that he'd started to fall asleep. So when Jefferson started to feel drowsy as the high country of Mexico scrolled past, he knew he had to do something.

He started by reciting a line from *One Hundred Years* out loud for five or ten miles, over and over again, matching the words to whatever catchy tune happened to cross his mind until he reached the point at which the exercise no longer held his attention, and he began to feel drowsy again. On that second day, somewhere south of Juárez, he transitioned from popular hits to what he imagined as Old World monk-style chanting. The line was one he'd memorized first for Ms. Tolan and then had revised once he was a soldier.

I did not know why we were fighting.

He dragged out the word *fighting* into two long syllables—*figh . . . ting . . .*—just as always. And while he began by imagining monks in windowless cells, he transitioned into thinking about ancient people walking across the American plains. The syllables meshed with the deeply resonant melody, and Jefferson bellowed in the deepest of baritones.

I did not know why we were FIGH . . . TING . . .
I did not know why we were FIGH . . . TING . . .
I did not know why we were FIGH . . . TING . . .

But after about five miles his head began nodding again. He tried to fight against the drowsiness by holding his left foot up slightly off the pedal—his grandmother had taught him that trick—but even that didn't work. He'd seen those pictures in driver's ed of people who'd driven their cars off the side of the road or across the middle stripe, and he figured falling asleep on a motorbike would be worse. He thought of pulling off the road to try to slap himself awake, but he didn't want to interrupt his forward momentum. That was when the idea occurred to him, somewhere outside the little town of Café. He would write his own completely original lines. He would mimic the great writer. And that is how it began, Jefferson's traveling exercise to stay awake and improve his literary skills all at the same time.

His results were humble at best. If he were to be really honest, the lines he composed sort of stunk. But the writing he did in his head that day did keep him alert and alive on the highway, and moving in the direction of Mexico City, and that was what mattered.

The first line Jefferson created, and then chanted in what he thought of as Mexican style for the next ten miles, shaking his head in the wind and sending his voice in the direction of any animals he happened to see, was this:

I am coasting the desert of Chihuahua,
In search of the writer who saved me.
In search of the writer who sa-aaaaved me.
Who sa-aaaved me.

Jefferson became almost lost in these lines as he sang them, time sliding by, imagining himself to be an inspired writer, some traveling priest sailing free. Sometimes Remedios howled along with him, but mostly she remained silent, her nose to the wind. He followed that first line with many more, each based upon the reality of the highway and his growing attempt to see his life as he imagined García Márquez might see it. It was possible, he decided, to change one's reality by interpreting the nearby world through a more magical lens. Thus he began to compose a long series of lines, lines intended to mend those situations in life that Jefferson felt needed mending.

In the castle dwelled a magician,
whose job it was to free anyone who had been charged unjustly,
and to return the money to those who had ever been cheated because of greed.
Because of GRE—EEED.
GRE—EEED.

This one covered so many injustices, and Jefferson chanted the word *greed,* divided into two syllables and in his deepest baritone, in honor of the many good people who'd suffered because of that one word over the eons. As he chanted and sang, Jefferson thought of the opposite of greed, which he thought of as love, and at some point he began to chant that word instead. *Love. Love. Love.* He thought of all the heroes in the world, of people who ran into burning buildings to save other people, of people who took care of old people and sick people. He thought of teachers. He thought of all the pain in the world and of all the people who forgave the people who had hurt them. Love was such a big concept, and it covered so many people, that he felt the need to chant the word *love*, divided into two syllables and skipping around from the lowest part of his range up to the squeakiest whisper of a falsetto, for about forty-five minutes as the bike swooped along the ups and downs of the road.

LO—OOOVE.

He did not feel at all drowsy anymore.

Somewhere after the little town of La Parrita, Jefferson saw a figure at the edge of the road. As he rode closer, he realized it was a man teetering with his toes on the road, his heels on the rough ground. For as far as Jefferson could see, there were no houses or any other form of shelter that might suggest that this rough sandy patch could be a dwelling place, and yet here this man stood. He decided from a distance that he would not risk stopping. The man could be crazy or dangerous—a lone thief, or even some sort of alien-zombie—so as Jefferson came to within ten feet of the guy he edged the bike leftward, crossing over the median, in order not to hit him. As he passed, the man remained perfectly still, and Jefferson felt a wave of fear pass over him. Though he tried not to look, Jefferson had seen the man's face in that instant, noting the pocked skin on his cheekbones and his sad and motionless eyes. He urged the motorbike on, willing it to speed up and leave this solitary figure, and for many miles his mind was filled only with a desire for escape.

But as he put more and more distance between himself and that solitary man, the encounter began to haunt him. He tried to understand why the man had frightened him so much, and why he had not stopped to talk with him. After he'd traveled several more miles, Jefferson began to feel pity for the man on the side of the road, and he began to write the story of the man's childhood in his mind.

His face, with deep pockets on the cheeks left by a difficult adolescence, seemed to have been forgiven in its old age by a tub of peppermint water.

To the tune of a country-western song he'd always liked, Jefferson twanged the line to himself and to the pup and to any living creature that might be listening alongside the highway, hidden inside culverts or behind scraggly bushes. Jefferson had suffered from the cruelty of acne many long months and years, and he'd always felt he needed some kind of forgiveness. The idea of soaking in a tub of peppermint water to wash away your sins seemed now to be what he'd been looking for all those years.

Miles passed like so much good conversation among *simpáticos*, and the wide expanses of caliche and scraggly bushes began to be dotted by the occasional junk car and spare tire. A ramshackle barn on the left. Telephone poles and wires in the offing. A faint but indefatigable hint of fry grease, possibly French fries.

Finally, civilization began to form around him in small pockets, and Jefferson's heart quickened ever so slightly. The tingling in his fingers, previously a sign of fear, now had an undeniably optimistic flutter to it, tinged with something he might call hope. As he rode into the outskirts of Chihuahua, Jefferson felt some small sense of accomplishment, as if this trip had already changed something within him. Though he could not change the dark past, his relationship with that past was changing. He thought of the list, and realized he had not read it yet that day, a fact that made him slightly anxious—for he had made an informal promise to himself to read it every day—but also a little jubilant. The chanting of the list never failed to inspire him.

From where could he read the list on this day? He scanned the near horizon and identified a tree a hundred yards off in the scrub. There it was. His tribute place.

Off the road he directed the bike as far as he could and then left it in the sand and walked the rest of the way, Remedios at his heels, to what looked like a tangled thirsty oak. It was an inexplicable beauty in the middle of the desert and for this reason Jefferson knew it was the place for which he had been searching without knowing he had been searching for anything at all.

Leaving the pup to watch from below, he climbed the tree with the list, then, looking out over the land to see that the moment was right, he gathered his breath to read out the names and the ages and the other details he had written on the page.

This made sense to him. This was what he was meant to do as he made his way through the dry mountains of Mexico. Even if he was unable to find the great writer, even if the great writer turned out to be inhospitable or aloof or uncooperative or—God bless Our Lady of Guadalupe—dead, Jefferson would have this moment in the oak tree, reading and chanting and singing the list that was becoming both more a part of him and less a nightmare with each passing mile. Inexplicable though it was, Jefferson began to feel a nostalgia for all that it documented. The memories were what helped now as he breathed, as he searched the sky for patches of understanding clouds, as he began to sing quietly, letting his voice grow in volume, making his mind traverse through the many losses he had witnessed.

On the forty-seventh day, Ramon, twenty, from Las Cruces was shot in the throat next to me.

He perched high in the tree like an eagle, and he made his way through the list, vocalizing a line now and then as a particular memory called out to be sung or chanted or shrieked or whispered.

Father and three young girls in Toyota near Fallujah.
Oh my god, what can I do?

All this struck him as the only thing to do in that moment. It was heavy work, the interstices of which he filled with weeping and pleas to God for help. What was he to do? In other pauses he called out to Gabriel García Márquez, who was a deity closer and more tangible than God, and all this he did like a young man learning to be human.

Hume, twenty-one, of Appleton, Maine. Stupid IED.
Sang in the evenings like Johnny Cash.

The rough bark of the tree cut into his thighs and elbows as the position that had begun as secure and comfortable started to feel pinched.

A guy name Jeff Kleiner from Stockbridge, Georgia, twenty-five,
who drowned in a lake on the palace compound in Al Fallujah.

He was less than halfway through the list and not willing to stop, so he readjusted his weight, told himself he'd practice a handstand on the ground for a while afterward to level himself out, and kept on going.

Sergeant Schoener from Ohio.

It must have taken almost an hour for him to get to the end of the list that first day in the oak tree, for by the time he was singing about Ray Soto, his friend from Iraq who also loved Gabriel, Jefferson's feet were numb, and the sun's globe was resting upon the distant hills.

Finally, his task complete, he scrambled to the lowest branch and leaped to the ground, tumbling as he hit the hard earth only to receive the wet kisses of his pup. It was late, and he had miles to go and decisions to make about what to do for dinner and where to spend the night, and so he folded the paper carefully back into the book and stuffed both back into the bandage on his chest, for this had again become the right place for the book, he believed. He breathed in deeply once more, identified a patch of level ground in front of him, threw his hands upon it, and kicked his heels behind him and up in the air above his body, securing himself in the inverted pose that had come to be so important to him. Being upside down never failed to bring a rush of activity to his head and, usually, a welcome change in perspective. Remedios seemed versed in the behavior required of her, so she sat near him, quiet, as he stared out at the open plain then—the earth above, the sky below—and as he laughed at the joy of having the full weight of gravity, for the moment, off his feet.

OUT THERE

As he drove on into Chihuahua, Esco's wariness and Nigel's encouragement and Dr. Monika's faith—all of it love, it seemed to him now—joined the wind in his ears, the straight road south, its occasional hill, its rocks, its lizards and roadside crows, all of it arriving in fact and fantasy without the clenching of his jaw, without the holding of his breath, without even a hint of nerves. And not since he'd decided to do this thing had the shaking of his hands overwhelmed him. It could have been because gripping of the handlebars at fifty-five miles per hour required great concentration, but Jefferson was beginning to think that his hands might have stopped shaking for a different reason altogether.

THAT NIGHT IN Chihuahua Jefferson spent $15 for a single room in a small motel, a place with a shower down the hall. Once he had eaten a sandwich and gotten Remedios settled next to him in a nest of towels on the bed, he studied the black-and-white photo of García Márquez on the back cover of the novel, the photo in which the old guy's eyebrows looked as if they could strangle you from behind, and he thought of the start of it all.

As is true of so many great love affairs, Jefferson had not loved the writer right away. No. It had been a slow painful process. Having been assigned to read what he thought of as the old guy's thick novel, full of names that all sounded alike and sentences that rambled across two and three pages, Jefferson initially found Gabriel García Márquez irritating, some smart-ass writer from some intellectual family in South America who had no idea what a pain in the ass he'd made every high school senior's life.

In truth, Jefferson hadn't read much of the novel at Santa Fe High; he'd spent more of his energy debating with the same counselor who would later try to help him with college applications. When Jefferson might have been reading, he was skipping class to sit in her office and listen to her explain once more why she thought so much about young kids sitting inside at stiff desks discussing big ideas. He didn't care so much for being indoors, sitting at a desk next to the honor roll students at Santa Fe High, discussing big ideas, he told her. Wouldn't it be better if he could just go outside? Wouldn't it be better for young people to go out into the world and climb trees and decide for themselves? Who was she to decide what was best for him? he asked, in the most polite way he knew how.

"Get back to class, Jefferson," she'd said. "Just get your rear end back to English class."

"Gabriel García Márquez. Have you heard of him?" Ms. Tolan asked the Honors English class the second week of second semester of senior year, and some valedictory *chica* on the second row raised her hand and recited something she must have looked up online the previous night. Jefferson stopped listening after the bit about the writer being a Communist from Colombia.

It was just nine months after this classroom discussion the fall after he had graduated from Santa Fe High—that Jefferson Long Soldier packed his copy of the novel into his duffel, Ms. Tolan having told him to keep it at the end of the semester. No one else had given him a going-away present, unless you counted the two packs each of clean white socks and underwear Esco got him at Walmart.

Jefferson knew that many things in life did not make sense. He had experienced the confusion and hyperventilation, the standing on his head and the holding of his breath, the still not comprehending why things were the way they were. The fact that he packed his copy of *One Hundred Years of Solitude* into his duffel and took it with him across the ocean to Iraq despite his antagonism toward the book, despite his resentment of superintellectual men—this was one of those confounding things that did not make sense. It did not make sense, and yet it happened.

One possible and partial explanation was that Jefferson
liked Ms. Tolan. She called him "dear," but she wasn't over-
the-top—she was also the kind of lady who sometimes dyed
her hair pink, and never pretended to know all the answers.
It is possible that because Jefferson liked her so much, he
wanted to indulge her. He imagined that Ms. Tolan would
love it if he took a piece of literature with him. The García
Márquez novel was the last one they'd spent any real time on
that spring; after spring break, the teachers knew not to expect
much from the seniors. Jefferson couldn't say for sure, but he
guessed they'd read some short stories and poetry in April and
May. But he hadn't forgotten *One Hundred Years of Solitude*, the
novel that had beached itself in the dry sands of New Mexico
that spring and threatened him from his desk day after day.
What a pain that novel had been to him then. And on top of
it all, Ms. Tolan *loved* it. She wasn't a bit Hispanic, but she'd
pulled out her Spanish accent as she'd discussed the Buendía
family—José Aureliano and José Arcadio and Fernanda and
Remedios—from the front of the classroom, making them
construct collages using magazine photos that reminded them
of their favorite character. Jefferson knew Ms. Tolan would not
have known if he'd left the book under his bed at home, but
the most honorable part of him wanted to show his teacher
some respect. While she was older than all the students, she
wasn't all that much older, and besides all that, she was the
only white woman he'd ever really talked to, so he took her
advice and packed the book, even though he had no plans to
ever touch the thing again.

Ms. Tolan believed Jefferson had connected with some of
the characters and understood why they behaved the way they
behaved. It was surprising how many kids didn't even try to
give this impression. And because of his effort, Ms. Tolan must
have thought the story was meaningful to Jefferson—that it was
something that would remind him of home when Jefferson was
off and away being a soldier. She was sick to her stomach when

Jefferson told her he'd signed up for the army. She told him so. "Why are you doing this?" she'd said, shaking her head. "You don't have to do this. Please don't do this, Jefferson."

It wasn't her fault, but Ms. Tolan probably didn't realize how hard life could be, living in Santa Fe with a dirt yard and nothing but a broken-down camper van back by the trash cans to remind him that he'd ever had anyone but a grandmother. She tried to be a good English teacher. She always wore nice clothes, and she seemed to know what she was talking about. She wrote lots of comments on his papers. She was no slacker. But still, when she told Jefferson that day that he should take an important book with him—if he was really going to go through with his crazy plan to be in the army, he should at least pack an important piece of literature!—Jefferson might have laughed in her face. He might have said, "Ms. Tolan, you haven't got a friggin' clue." He might have said "Adiós," and "Hasta luego."

The fact that he didn't say anything at all, that he held his tongue that day, is also one of those inexplicable facts of life. Not even Jefferson could explain why he left the room and walked down the hall, musing silently about his teacher's mind. Take the novel? Why? Because it would make him less scared? Because the book would be his friend? Is that what college had taught her?

He hadn't cracked the cover of *One Hundred Years*, didn't even remember the thing, until about five weeks in, when things started getting rough. He'd met guys from all over the country. Chattanooga, Irving, Little Rock, Memphis. And also a few from New Mexico. Hobbs, Española, Farmington, Las Cruces. His platoon leader was a guy who went by the initials RT, though Jefferson never learned what they stood for. One thing it didn't take Jefferson long to learn: either RT was not the kind of leader the US Army should have trusted in the first place, or he had been at war too long.

It was then, five weeks in, when Jefferson's brain started spinning. What had he done, getting himself caught up in that war? All he'd have had to do was say no to that recruiter, and yes to the Santa Fe High counselor, who just wanted him to meet after school a few afternoons so she could help him with college applications. Beginning in September of his senior year, she'd said he could go almost anywhere he wanted—all kinds of places he'd never heard of—given his combination of good grades, unexpectedly sweet test scores, and the fact that he was three-quarters Native with no real money. One grandma's love was nice, the counselor said, but it couldn't pay for college. Even after he'd missed a lot of the deadlines, the counselor didn't give up. "It's not too late, Jefferson," she said—until it was.

But he was eighteen and full of ideas about digging in the dirt and trimming the trees and all the other things he'd always wanted to do in the backyard. That and climbing the highest peaks in New Mexico and Colorado, even. All those places he wanted to go. The idea of filling out all those applications and moving into a dorm room just so he could study a lot sounded like something a white boy in the movies would go for. What was it going to do for his life? How could reading a bunch more books help?

Jefferson's default idea was to get a job outside the store and start helping Esco with the bills. If he got a job and spent more time outside of the house, maybe Josephina would start paying him some attention or maybe he'd meet another nice girl. Maybe he'd have a little extra cash to take a nice girl to the movies. The idea of a nice girl sounded distant, like Hollywood as well, but Jefferson thought that a job and some cash might boost his chances more than a stack of books, and he also thought that a nice girl was probably less distant, if he was really being honest about it, than any chance he had with Josephina, her long dark eyelashes, her sweet round face, and the supple dark skin on her bones. This, too, figured into his decision to join the army. It must have.

Certainly none of it had seemed very serious, not really dangerous. Jefferson had lived his first sixteen years in peacetime. He'd just started his freshman year at Santa Fe High, fifteen years old, when the planes crashed into those buildings in New York. He could tell it was a big deal by the way all the adults reacted, by the fact that school was closed for a couple of days, by all the crying and candles down on the plaza. And it was pretty unreal to watch the clips over and over again on TV. Like a scene out of a video game.

Lots of older guys at school began talking to recruiters, signing up at the Mall, going away to defend the country, and Jefferson watched and tried to understand how he actually felt about it all. He didn't really like the idea of war, but maybe this one, with all its high-tech weaponry and computerized bombs and stuff, wasn't really like those wars they'd studied in American history, those terrible wars in England and Germany and Japan and Korea and Vietnam. Plus, maybe he wouldn't really have to fight. Everybody always seemed to think that being in the army was about guns and artillery and killing, but what about all those support jobs, all those jobs far away from the front? He didn't have a girlfriend to talk to, and he knew what Esco and Nigel would say. His whole family seemed to think he was headed for college and some better life beyond that, but no one talked about the details, because, he guessed, no one in his family really knew how to go to college or beyond, a fact that, frankly, scared him a whole lot more than the idea of wearing a uniform and learning to handle a gun.

So Jefferson thought a lot about it, in the solitude of his own room, staring out at the Jemez Mountains, off and on during ninth and tenth and eleventh grades. When all the college talk began in earnest, senior year, he'd started weighing the pros and cons in a more methodical fashion—a list of pluses and minuses on the back inside cover of his English spiral—and then, over the course of a long weekend in the spring of senior year, his eighteen-year-old brain spit out the answer. *Why not? I'll join the army.*

And he had felt pretty good about the decision. Forward movement out into the world. This was the sort of education that made sense to him. This was the opposite of sitting in a classroom, discussing big ideas with other smart kids in Santa Fe. Besides, he had no real plans to compete with this possibility. There was a chance, he thought, he could make some small difference for his country—maybe save a life or two—and that this would help him be a better person once he was out, back home, setting out on the rest of life's journey. He assumed he would not be hurt or scarred or changed in any substantial way. It had seemed like it would be nice to have a little money in the bank.

Looking back down now at the black-and-white photo, Jefferson guessed that after a decade of cancer and amber liquor and cigarettes, GGM would be even scarier-looking now. The photo must have been one of the writer's better ones, seeing as he had agreed to have it printed on thousands of copies of his book. And it had been taken sometime before 1998—a long time ago. Jefferson's mind rotated on its axis: not only was the guy more than ten years older and possibly scarier looking by now, he could die at any moment.

Again, he tried to doze, but there was no reasoning with his anxiety. He envisioned meetings with García Márquez in his book-filled house in which the writer smiled vacantly, then just turned his back on Jefferson and walked away. He imagined García Márquez's heavy door slamming in his face, like when Dorothy was refused entry to Oz. The motel ceiling had, he discovered, an intriguing swirling pattern. He wanted to sleep but could not fend off his fears, the back-and-forth inside his head. *You are so anxious, Jefferson. Why are you so anxious, Jefferson? I'm not anxious.*

Finally, he turned to the method he'd relied upon for so long. Turning on the lamp, Jefferson retrieved the book from his backpack, opened it up to a slip of paper on which he'd written FEAR, and held it in his lap, remembering Gabriel's lines, the lines that had helped him so many previous nights. Now he thought of Gabriel as he sang, with his own words and in his own voice:

I do not need many words to explain

because one is enough: FEAR.

He repeated the sentence slowly, many times, until the words were engraved upon his mind. He did not think about the technical definition of the words. Rather he reflected upon how the words felt on his tongue and the ways in which the spirit of them filled his belly.

I do not need many words to explain
because one is enough: FEAR.
I do not need many words to explain
because one is enough: FEAR.

With eyes closed, Jefferson wrapped the end of one line around until it tangled with the beginning of the next line, and his tongue became encircled by the sounds, and the softened sentiment began to hold him in its silky cocoon.

Jefferson did not make peace with his fear that night, but he did face some of the bleakness, and in so doing he made peace with that bleakness and saw the chance to move beyond it. It was possible that Gabriel of the tangled eyebrows, whose words had saved him from war's bleakest realities, would be dead by the time Jefferson arrived at his doorstep. That he might have traveled all this way, only to be disappointed.

So on that hard bed on the second night of his journey to find García Márquez, Jefferson proclaimed the truth as he knew it. He sang in a new cadence to the imagined strut of a snare drum, attempting to prove to himself and to anyone who happened to be eavesdropping that he was not delusional.

Gabriel García Márquez may be DEAD . . .
Gabriel García Márquez may be DEAD . . .
Gabriel García Márquez may be DEAD . . .
Deaay—uuuud . . .
Deaay—uuuud . . .
Deaay—uuuud . . .
DEAD.

And finally he curled up with the pup, and slept.

IN THE MORNING Jefferson drove on toward a town named Jiménez, a place he knew nothing about beyond the fact that it marked the road he needed to travel, the road that was taking him farther away from his life as a soldier, the road that was helping him to remember what it felt like to just be himself, Jefferson Long Soldier. He did not know if it was possible, but he would try to live an entire day without thinking about Iraq. Or, if that proved impossible, at least an entire day without crying about it. Jefferson had always been taught that crying was a healthy response to intense emotions—Esco said she had learned this from her husband—but Jefferson felt he had reached the point of diminishing returns. Enough crying already. A day without sad tears was a day worth journeying for. So as he cruised his way past the isolated homesteads that became villages in the miles outside Jiménez, he found a new goal: a day without sad tears. *A day without sad tears*, Jefferson chanted aloud to himself and the wind, *is a good reason for journeying!*

As was often the case, this outburst was followed by many miles of contemplation, which was followed by a memory. The memory of why he'd reached for the book in Iraq.

He had been lying on his bunk, thinking about the Jemez Mountains, that oceanic blue-gray presence that for most of his life had beckoned out his bedroom window. He had been closing his eyes and imagining the hard, flat dirt surrounding his barracks to be that hard, flat homeland of New Mexico, the distant rises in that Iraqi landscape to be familiar. Because at one time a pulsing, rocking mass of water had connected this to that, because whales and fishes had once swum unfettered from Timbuktu to Albuquerque, because the wind still knew no bounds, Jefferson thought that none of this was impossible to imagine.

The daydream had led in its way to his sweet grandmother, driving to Walmart to buy him those socks and underwear, the Jemez Mountains pulsing steady before her as she drove her Corolla down Cerrillos Road. Nothing, not even two miles of 1980s auto repair shops and fast food and bargain stores, could be ugly with the Jemez Mountains as a backdrop, she had always said. He saw Esco in his mind's eye then, sitting among scrabbly chamisa and sage in her folding chair in the backyard, watching the sunset. He imagined her telling him to come outside with her, to come see the fire in the sky. *Look at those orange flames, Jefferson! Look at those magenta cactus flowers!* The hot palette of the New Mexico sky at dusk twisted and turned in his mind. Boys just like him from Kansas and New Jersey and Pennsylvania and, yes, New Mexico, sleeping and eating and waking and doing what they had to do.

He'd curled himself up into a ball on his bed, his chest heaving, wet tears making a mess of his face, wishing that his grandmother were there to sit on the edge of his bed and tell him she was sorry and that it would all be okay. He'd cried for a while, and then he'd thought of the book. He'd gotten down off his bed, retrieved the novel from his T-shirt drawer, and begun to flip through the pages, reading scattered passages. He did not know why.

God, was this land in Mexico beautiful. And all these simple people, natives most of them, living along this simple road. Jefferson was certain that if he could stay long enough in this sparse landscape, along a simple road such as this, if he could eliminate from his view any shopping malls and gigantic parking lots and television shows about people killing people, that he would get better. It was important to realize that it wasn't just the shooting and the exploding in the war zone that made things so difficult. It was that when you came home, your kind grandmother was still making a decent tofu breakfast burrito, and that she was now sleeping at the foot of your bed.

On the outskirts of towns, stray dogs and roosters ran alongside the motorbike, but the pup kept her nose to the sky, letting out only an occasional bay. And Jefferson began again to chant, once again imagining the monks. Simple, tonal syllables to begin with, and then word upon word until the combination of sounds became a line he'd written in his mind at some point, a line based on so much he'd learned from Gabriel.

He became lost in fecund memories . . . in a sensuality he did not know he had experienced . . . in abundant rivers of forgiveness and hope . . .

. . . of forgiveness and hope

. . . of forgiveness and HO-ope.

It seemed to him a reorienting sort of line, a line meant to turn him from discouragement. The idea of it, and then the chanting of it, led him to picture himself with Gabriel under that willow tree next to the Rio Grande, one of his favorite imagined moments. The writer was explaining in precise terms how it was that water could bring forgiveness and hope.

"In little rivulets," he told Jefferson, pointing a finger. "In the hop-skip-and-jump of a flat stone across the surface. See."

Jefferson and García Márquez skipped stones together in the vision after that, each searching along the shore for just the right stone among the multitudes.

In abundant rivers of forgiveness and hope . . .

Jefferson lost himself on the final word, chanting it in two long deep syllables many times as he drove on down the road.

Ho . . . ope . . .

Ho . . . ope . . .

Ho . . . ope . . .

SOMETIMES THE READER'S love of a story is immediate and bright, jumping like a belly flop into his lap on page 1, basking until the beautiful end. Other times the love builds slowly and surely, like nostalgia. It hovers on the edge of recognition for many chapters, a suggestion waiting to be spoken, until that innocuous detail announces itself as a sort of secret communiqué to the reader, this particular reader, telling him that this story was written for him. Telling him that the writer, as unlikely as it might seem, has known the same people, has worried over the same small anxieties, has suffered the same meager disappointments, has been humiliated by precisely the same set of slights and calluses. Telling him that the writer's hopes and dreams and celebrations have followed the same course as the reader's. None of this makes logical sense, of course. The writer is much older than the reader, and he has lived his life on a different continent, in an earlier era, and yet the feeling is undeniable. The reader, jubilant with this discovery, runs to the edge of a great chasm and jumps. He can fly! He smiles and lets out an enormous sigh, a full mile of air below him and nothing but blue above. He approaches the other edge of the abyss. He stretches out his fingertips, reaches, grabs.

129

That one small detail, the handhold on the other side, might not seem worthy of mention. It might not bear the weight of the literary world. It is ancillary to the theme. It might be read past by hundreds of other readers. And yet there it is, this one small something that offers this reader a grip, this one thing that moves this reader's heart. Here it is! The detail that means he will love the story forever.

For Jefferson it was the scorpions. From that first time Jefferson came upon a line about a scorpion in *One Hundred Years*—in this case the scorpion that stung Rebecca on her wedding night—he knew García Márquez was on his side. Almost every time he browsed the novel after that first sighting, there was another one! As if GGM had placed another of the little beasts there to keep him awake. To remind him of his family, to offer perspective. Jefferson was in a war zone, yes, but at least his cousin Nigel was not chasing him around the house with a scorpion on the end of a stick, like when they'd been kids. Yes, Jefferson was fighting in a war he didn't understand, but at least he wasn't being stung on the toe by one of the stealthy suckers in his sheets as he slept. At least his enemies were big enough to see. At least the Iraqi insurgency had not taken the form of giant bugs with pincers.

More than stories about loss in war, about unexpected love, about perverted family dynamics, about the rich enslaving the poor, Gabriel García Márquez's scorpions told Jefferson—in a secret communiqué—that the writer was real and alive, a human being walking the earth. He was living and breathing and loving, fearing the day he'd be stung, just like everyone else.

SOMEWHERE AFTER JIMÉNEZ, Jefferson, plenty tired and hot, not to mention hoarse from his own chanting of memorized lines and newly created poetry, ran the motorbike onto the wide sandy shoulder and parked. The sky was big here, not unlike the sky in New Mexico or Iraq, and in the sudden quiet he felt the presence of Nigel, of each person who had helped him. A few cars passed by, a raven cawed from high up in a thirsty tree, Remedios sniffed around beneath a nearby clump of brush. He was not alone. And in the presence of those few drivers and that one bird and his dog, as well as the many unseen spirits who he imagined to be traveling along with him, taking it upon themselves to help, Jefferson dropped down on his knees and kissed the sandy earth. He closed his eyes, saying a prayer of thanksgiving for his good cousin Nigel, so generous and patient and funny, and then filled his lungs with the brilliant Mexican air and bellowed in a southerly direction, "Here I come, Gabriel! Here I come!"

How far Jefferson had come, to now be calling the famous writer by his first name as he stood on this sandy shoulder of Autopista 49, on his way to see the great man. It was a journey that had begun so unexpectedly, so unconsciously, in that distant-seeming classroom, Honors English 4. Jefferson thought now of those tears in Ms. Tolan's eyes that first day she'd spoken of GGM. He'd not forgotten those tears, shed for García Márquez as well as a handful of other writers she referred to as literary geniuses. The tears had been a mystery to him. He had no doubt that they were stirred by something real, and yet intangible. What had his teacher found in the words of these particular writers?

The mistiness in her eyes and the crackle in her voice usually came when she spoke about a particular writer's journey toward creating what she called "a great work of literature." She had told the story of GGM's struggle to find just the right way to tell the story we now know as *One Hundred Years of Solitude*. Just the right voice. How he had struggled for many years with the ghosts of the story inhabiting the catacombs of his skull, trying to coax it out, and that he had not given up until he had heard his own grandmother narrating the story inside his head. Ms. Tolan had spoken with the same crackle in her voice about a woman writer, a woman from England, Jefferson thought, but he could not remember her name. She'd been depressed, had drowned herself. He would never forget that, because they had watched a film in class—fictional, of course—about the woman's walk down to the river, the way she tied rocks into her skirt. Jefferson would never forget the sad beauty of that writer as she breathed her last breaths among the rocks and the fishes, looking up to the blue sky. Ms. Tolan had most definitely had red eyes when she told that woman's story—how brilliant her writing, how troubled her mind. There had been a few others who had summoned his teacher's tears but he could not remember any names.

The reading in that last year of English had been hard, and most of the time he'd gotten too drowsy to finish his assignments, staying up late, drinking coffee, but his curiosity had been enough to keep him working and wondering. What was it that kept a woman like Ms. Tolan—and English teachers everywhere—reading books and talking to students about stories and making them write papers about those stories? Something deep within him did not want to disappoint his teacher. She truly seemed to believe that a book could make a difference in her students' lives. And something deeper still told him there must be magic hidden within the text.

So he had compensated. Every day at lunch, just before fourth-period English, Jefferson got out his copy of whatever novel they were reading at the time and flipped through the pages that had been assigned that day, back and forth randomly, using his thumbs. He'd close his eyes and stop when he felt like stopping, and he'd point randomly to a sentence on the open page. He'd read the sentence, and maybe another one that followed if the first one was short, and then he'd begin to see the sentence floating in his mind, like a translucent jellyfish, its tentacles swaying to the sound of a beautiful lullaby. In this way the sentences began to live in his mind, and he walked into class, eager to share what was now a part of him. Every day Ms. Tolan asked some version of, "So, what did you guys think about the reading last night?" and every day Jefferson popped his hand in the air and recited.

The results were several: Ms. Tolan came to love Jefferson, and would often stop him after class and tell him what a pleasure it was to have a student like him contributing so much to class discussions, and a few times she suggested that he think about studying literature in college. At the end of the year, she told him to keep his copy of *One Hundred Years*, because, she said, he would probably want to have it at some point in the future. In the end, Jefferson made an A in her class both fall and spring semesters without ever having really read one of those novels Ms. Tolan loved so much.

In Iraq he turned to the novel as a comfort, a distinct memory from home, not because he expected any real help from the book. But it proved to be a good distraction from reality and, in all honesty, he had never forgotten the mystery of Ms. Tolan's tears. Within a week he had slipped back into the routine of the flipping back and forth of pages, and the rote memorization of a line or two. He did this every night after dinner, as he pulled his mind away from Ramon and Adams and Dudzinski. As he pulled his mind away from the three little girls' scared eyes asking him for help out the back of their father's Toyota. Not in an attempt to bury anything, but rather as a way to help him breathe as he remembered. He'd had an infected plantar wart on his heel as a middle-schooler, a festering sore that prevented him from running in the district track meet his eighth-grade year, so he knew the dangers of ignoring and pretending something bad would disappear.

Each evening he sat on his bed, back against the wall, and reviewed as many details of the day as he could. He never lingered too long on any single memory, and eventually he made it to the end of the day, to dinner in the dining hall, an event that became a natural segue to thinking about dinner at home with Esco, wondering what she had eaten that evening. Jefferson often thought about how it must have been simpler for her, a sort of bonus for having him gone, that she could eat what she wanted without worrying about his vegetarianism. Had she eaten carne asada with fresh tortillas? A hamburger with green chile?

After he thought about green chile for a while, Jefferson closed his eyes and held the novel in his lap. He pretended he was sitting on his bed at home, or at one of the outdoor lunch tables at Santa Fe High. He crossed his ankles because that was a natural position for him, and Jefferson believed the point was to be as relaxed as possible. He breathed slowly in and out for a few minutes, trying to remember who he was: a nineteen-year-old from Santa Fe, three-quarters Lakota, one-eighth Mexican, one-sixteenth German, and one-sixteenth Scots-Irish, who had a whole body with a jittery heart and a bleeding soul. Though sometimes the sound of heavy trucks and an occasional explosion encroached upon him, in those moments Iraq seemed for the most part to be a dream.

He flipped through the pages, back and forth with his thumbs, just like in high school, and the pages fell open naturally, and a particular spot on the page called to him, and he would read.

Jefferson would remember forever the feeling the sentence his finger had found that very first night gave him. It was the sentence about new gypsies and oily skins and parrots painted many colors and a hen laying a hundred golden eggs. It was the sentence about a monkey who could read minds and a device that could both sew on buttons and reduce fevers. It was the line that mentioned the machine that could take away one's bad memories. How could anyone ever forget the feeling brought on by a sentence like that? When Jefferson had read the last bit, the muscles of his face had formed into a smile, and a feeling of measured joy had entered his heart. He had imagined on that night what Gabriel García Márquez might have meant by an "uproarious joy," and how the writer had envisioned a machine that could eliminate bad memories. What an idea. Jefferson needed that machine, he thought as he sat on his bunk that night, and he began to imagine all the other soldiers who needed it as well.

He kept his eyes closed a bit longer, picturing the great writer in the barracks with him, that unforgettable face from the back cover. This was Gabriel, the angelic writer who had brought tears to Ms. Tolan's eyes, a man who seemed both human and otherworldly and who, in that moment, was right there in Jefferson's head with him, laughing. It was if the old man had known Jefferson and the entirety of his life long before any of it had begun. And for the moment, on that first of many nights, the writer reached out and grabbed Jefferson, telling him it would all be okay.

Jefferson knew that the novel had not literally been written for him. He was not stupid. He remembered enough from English class to know that *One Hundred Years of Solitude* did not take place in Iraq, and that it was not about a young soldier from Santa Fe. It was a South American story. It was about several generations of a large family—two brothers with similar names, and all their descendants, one of them, a soldier, though not a soldier like Jefferson. More like a commanding officer, a general.

Still, Jefferson had slept that night with a little less nervousness in his stomach, just knowing the writer was out there somewhere, living and breathing, and most likely aware of the war in Iraq. In that intangible but very real way, Jefferson felt Gabriel was with him, and that he was a little less alone. Jefferson began to call him GGM on that night, and sometimes simply Gabriel, because the whole thing—Gabriel García Márquez—took too much energy. Besides, that was what everyone else in the world called him. Gabriel García Márquez—yes, that was his name. But to Jefferson he became GGM, his very own Gabriel.

The next night Jefferson did it again. He flipped through the novel with his thumbs until a group of words caught his eye. He memorized the words. He adapted the words. He made them his own. And he repeated the practice the following night. Again and again, night after night, until it became his religion. And like any true faith, it began to help. In the restless hours between midnight and dawn, Gabriel's words resurrected Jefferson's hope.

Not too long after that, Jefferson began reciting aloud. If you had asked him, he would have given an upbeat explanation, would have cast himself as a morale builder among the troops. Would have said that he memorized and recited not just for himself, but for anyone with ears to hear. That these words, these beautifully insightful words, by the great writer from across the ocean, were life buoys cast out to save soldiers adrift on the raw ocean of war. He would not have used the term *chaplain* or *healer*, yet he arrived promptly on the scene of any crisis, providing aid and comfort. He had a quote for any circumstance, for any man or woman who cried out in pain, for any miracle or tragedy. Often he spoke of Colonel Aureliano Buendía as if he was a figure from pop culture: "Well, you know what Colonel Aureliano Buendía would say about this, don't you?" And for this, the men and women of the Tenth Mountain Division as well as many others based on Anaconda came both to love and pity Jefferson. Most had no idea what the dark young soldier from Santa Fe was talking about, so they just nodded and let him share his lovely, incomprehensible chants.

JEFFERSON WAS ALWAYS bemused by people who thought they could protect themselves from trouble, people who told themselves they were living safe lives out of harm's way. Bottled water in the basement. Travel insurance. A book on surviving bird flu. Jefferson understood that about tragedy: that at any time it can find you, enter your life through a door you didn't know was there. There was no denying it when it came for you.

But could you identify a miracle? Were you in tune with the possibility of something very good coming out of something very bad? Of grace in tragedy? Of life kicking death into the stratosphere? This, Jefferson felt, was far more important—or in any case, it was how his brain worked. He tended to see light rather than dark.

Jefferson was thinking about miracles on that second day of riding through Mexico when he heard what he thought was a distant helicopter. The sky had turned a mesmerizing shade of turquoise, white voile wisps strewn across it. He was on his way to Torreón, a good bit past Chihuahua, where he'd begun that morning, but still at an unknown point between the two, somewhere in the middle of the high Sonoran Desert. And there were rocks—giant boulders, really—flanking the highway as he rode.

Sarah Stark

He was chanting an upbeat *Torreón! Torreón! Olé! Torreón! Olé!*—a chant he thought might be appropriate for the upcoming city, even though, in truth, Jefferson didn't know a single thing about Torreón. The sound of the name reminded him of bullfighting, a tradition he guessed existed in Mexico, though he knew it was really a Spanish thing. He knew the difference between Mexico and Spain, but still. Part of the reason for the upbeat chant was his need to flush out all negative thoughts from his mind. Though he was trying to focus on the possibility of miracles—as he usually did—he had sensed in the last ten miles a change in the landscape. It felt as if the light on the rocks, the light of the beautiful sky, had suddenly turned stark, dissonant. Despite his efforts to resist them, stories of Mexican violence—a series of beheadings he'd heard about near San Miguel, clippings Auntie had passed along about child abductions—began to crowd into his mind.

But god, those beautiful rocks, lining the road for miles— so immense he found himself shaking his head at their size. They seemed like guardians of life, anchored so deeply to the earth that they made small human worries seem trivial. He rode on long enough to think about the people who tried to capture such beauty, all those artists, and to remember the name of that really old woman—Georgia O'Keeffe—and her paintings of bones. An English teacher he'd had in ninth grade—Jefferson couldn't remember his name—had been crazy about Georgia O'Keeffe and the fact that she could spend so much time and energy perfecting the painting of a single bone or a single flower. The teacher related it to being a careful writer. *Be like O'Keeffe!* he'd shout from the front of the classroom. *Don't do a goddamn-nother thing until you've written the best freakin' sentence you can possibly write!* Jefferson was thinking that the teacher might have been a little more right than he'd thought at the time, and he still trying to remember his name as he sailed along, when suddenly he saw that the sky had unmistakably darkened all around him.

140

Still, he pushed the implications of this darkening away. It was better to think of the history of these great rocks. What sort of events had formed them, exactly? He thought of the lava and the water and the ice that he knew must each have covered this place at some time in history, and of the whole generations of rocks that lay below these noble boulders, and below his own feet, the sand and the pebbles and the common stones, when the thundering became so loud above him that Jefferson had to look up. Remedios was barking and baring her teeth.

But oh, what a beautiful surprise awaited him up there. A giant swarm of swallows and crows and ravens filled the sky, swooping in great loops, following what seemed to him an orchestrated pattern, arabesques and curlicues and leaps and dives, all of it at high speed and close together, so that he had to wonder when they had learned the choreography, how they had practiced. Their songs rose above the whir of his Kawasaki, above what he had initially thought might have been a helicopter, in a dense symphony, filling him with wonder and delight—sopranos and mezzo-sopranos, altos and tenors and basses. Jefferson pulled over to the roadside, shut off the engine, and stood looking up at the show. All around him birds descended, making gentle contact with the earth, touching down like skirted acrobats from parachutes, like jellyfish floating in the air.

And then there was a voice—a distinctly human, female voice, speaking, possibly yelling, in harsh tones. It sounded very close, but because he'd been looking up at the birds, the sun had blinded him, and he could see nothing more than blurred dark shapes hovering above him. The birds seemed to have vanished, though, as had the beautiful songs they had been singing. Remedios was still snarling, and Jefferson looked back at her to check that she was okay before he returned his gaze to the dark forms surrounding him. Suddenly they resolved themselves into solid objects, large men with angry faces.

And then they seemed to be rushing toward him from all sides and angles, in such a surge of manpower and sports utility vehicles and horses that though Jefferson was scared, he could also see that this ambush possessed an undeniable beauty of orchestration—worthy of the big screen, larger than life. In his almost four years at war, nothing he'd seen approached this restrained and, yes, truly beautiful violence.

When you find yourself on a motorbike near Torreón, surrounded by fifteen angry men, he thought, there's no room for doubt. There was no need to wonder about the identity or occupation of men like these, in their leather jackets and somber T-shirts and sturdy jeans, their lips and eyelids a purplish ochre despite the heat of the day. He did not for an instant think they were cattle ranchers protecting their livestock.

They flung dust in his eyes; their breath stank of stale coffee and nicotine. A guy pointed a handgun at Jefferson's right temple, his face inches from Jefferson's own, while the rest wielded their rifles like skateboards. A woman was shouting at him, rattling her words off so rapidly that her Spanish could as easily have been Chinese. Reflexively Jefferson raised his hands up to his face and shouted back, "Don't shoot! Don't shoot!"

Suddenly he thought of the old Iraqi man and his goats. It had happened near the sad trees, the trees that had reminded him of the tired piñons along the dry bed of the Santa Fe River. Jefferson saw those sad trees, leafless and forlorn, saw the old man on his knees, begging RT not to slaughter his goats, saw the old man's good eyes in the face of very bad luck.

The images pressed in on Jefferson, even as he tried to focus on the very real situation that was developing around him. Three of the bikers were on top of him now, patting him down to make sure that he was unarmed, speaking now in a broken but comprehensible English. He took the switch to English as a good sign, a sign that they might be persuaded toward pity. His experience told him that nothing he did or did not do, nothing he said or did not say, would make a difference. These men and this woman were on a mission more complicated than Jefferson could comprehend, a mission that had nothing to do with him.

"What you doing? CIA? DEA?" This one held the tip of what looked like an M9 at his cheekbone. Jefferson shook his head, only saying, "No . . . no!" There was no point in rhetoric. Rhetoric had not helped the poor old Iraqi man. Even the old man's prayerful pose had not been enough to convince RT that he was a real and harmless goat farmer.

Even Jefferson knew that the story of how he came to be on the highway to Torreón would be difficult for anyone else to believe. That he was on a borrowed motorbike on his way to find Gabriel García Márquez; that he, a graduate of Santa Fe High, a veteran of Iraq, believed that the famous writer had reached across the ocean and desert to save him; that *One Hundred Years* had been written for that purpose—it was the truth, but Jefferson did not want to tell it to these complete strangers, who would most likely kill him anyway. The story was worth more than that to him.

His cheek was pressed against the hard-packed earth; he could feel the barrel of a gun at the back of his head, a heel under his left shoulder blade. An ant trail came into focus at the far right of his field of vision, winding up and down and around the contours of the pebbles and rocks. *The ants go marching one by one, hurrah, hurrah.* If he lived, he'd become a painter, he'd paint ants and their lovely little trails. Someone was pulling his thin wallet out of his pocket. He hoped Remedios was okay.

"Jefferson Long Soldier," a voice said, reading. "Santa Fe, New Mexico. Six-seventy-five in cash."

After a short pause Jefferson detected a measured approach from somewhere in the middle of the group. Someone was nearby, bending into his space. Warm breath on his left earlobe. "Why are you here?" A coarse whisper. The woman. English as quick and clear as anyone from north of the border.

Jefferson kept his eyes trained on the ants, lifting his chin just enough so that he could speak. "I'm a soldier returned from war, and I'm on my way to Mexico City to see a writer." He stopped, feeling that this was as much time as he was allowed.

The men had long since stopped yelling. In what seemed to be a well-rehearsed ritual, the woman became the director of the scene. She held Jefferson's small head in a tight grip and waited a moment before whispering, "You're a fool if you think I believe that story." Malicious sniggering broke out from several among the group, the sound of encroaching death.

A weighted pause. The pause, as Jefferson had experienced it, before the rifle cracks the skull. Before the automatic gunfire guts the spinal column. Before the two or three quick shots slice the throat. It was the pause in which the killer grits his teeth and reminds himself that he has bigger problems than the dumbass who's foolishly crossed his path. Jefferson had no interest in considering the details of how they would do it, so he prayed that they would kill him quickly and give his mind a rest. He prayed that they would spare the dog. He'd seen so much death, he'd been so close so many times, that he knew there was not all that much to dying. He feared the few intense moments of pain—he'd certainly seen that—but the dying never lasted long, and it always ended. That much was certain. The worst part, Jefferson believed, was the anxiety that came right beforehand. In war, with mortars coming unannounced from all directions, there was often no time for this anxiety. He wouldn't claim that he'd change places with any of the soldiers he'd watched die, but now, as his own fear was building, he was thinking that most of those soldiers had not had to endure a prolonged period of anxiety preceding death.

On the dirt, below the guns, the pause continued. Too long.

His mind, instead of doing what he wanted it to do, what he had hoped it would do—surfing peaceably through lovely memories—became anxious. And in that sharpest of all anxieties in the face of death, it clenched down on the memory of the old man and his goats.

RT, the platoon leader, had decided too soon that the old guy was an insurgent. So many things had been wrong about the decision, and Jefferson guessed that it had more to do with RT being at war too long, and less to do with the old man who they'd happened upon that dusty afternoon in the washed-out town near the sad trees. RT must have had a lot more go wrong in his life, Jefferson guessed, than a mother and father deserting him at birth. But the blessing was that when RT had decided to act, he was fast. The time when the old man knew beyond any doubt that he would be shot was very short, probably less than two minutes. That's the only real credit Jefferson could give RT: he didn't torture his captives by making them wait.

But now Jefferson was waiting, considering what possible coincidence might intervene to spare him yet one more time. Might the woman have detected a familiar scent on the back of his neck as she straddled him? Could his tattered backpack remind her of her life as a student? Did the very straightness of his hair sweep up nostalgia for her mother? Was it possible that his long-lost father could be among those in the group? Might he have recognized Jefferson?

Anything was possible.

Though he had come so close so often, as a mortar man with the Tenth Mountain Division in Iraq, he had escaped death every time. He had not been killed in the first day and a half of driving a motorbike in Mexico. So now, once again facing the prospect of death, Jefferson set his mind on the possibility of life. He thought of his desire to live. He thought of the fact that he was on his way to GGM's very house. The fact that he was still so young, and that he wanted to live. The fact that he had a long list of things he still wanted to do.

Finally the woman seemed to prepare to whisper in his ear, even as he imagined her directing the assassins with her eyes. She smelled faintly of bergamot, and because Esco had a thing for Earl Grey tea—it cleared the mind and prevented headaches, she said; it was the scent of knowledge—Jefferson took this as a hopeful sign. If only she knew the reason for his journey, he told himself, the bergamot woman might spare him, and he clung to this possibility even as he began to calculate the shuffling steps of five or six men in the circle. It sounded as if they were lining up about ten feet from where he knelt, in perfect firing-squad formation.

There must have been a lot of nonverbal communication going on; no one had said a word, yet suddenly the group shifted into action. Jefferson was forced to his knees by one man as another tied his hands behind his back and yet another began the process of blindfolding. Before completing his task, this last one must have been distracted, leaving the kerchief down around his neck like a collar. This interested Jefferson; he had actually thought a lot about the blindfold theory. If old photographs and some seemingly realistic historical films were anything to go by, blindfolds seemed to be part of the dresscode for firing squads. Still, he failed to understand their purpose. Was it so the man being shot would not witness the bullet's approach? Was it so the murderers did not have to look into the victim's eyes? RT had not made members of his platoon use blindfolds.

This could be the beginning of the end, kneeling on the hard ground, hands bound tight, able to see death coming. Jefferson began to reckon with the idea, forcing himself to think that he might never meet Gabriel. What if all the things undone were to be left undone?

The men found their places and shuffled their feet. Jefferson knew, but he didn't know. Was it wrong to assume that their preparations mirrored his own nauseated participation in several makeshift firing squads? He wanted to believe that at least one of those guys did not want to shoot. Though RT had insisted upon a certain brisk efficiency in killing, it had never been quick enough for Jefferson to avoid the sinking feeling.

Once he'd realized that RT would spare no one, that the circumstances did not matter, Jefferson's preference would have been for quick shots to the back of the head, like in old movies about the Nazis or the Khmer Rouge or American gangsters. But despite his insistence on speed, RT never gave up the formality of the firing squad. Old man down on his knees, his goats huddled nearby. Five young men—three or four years older than Jefferson at the time—down on their knees. Always the hands tied at the wrists. Always the uncovered eyes.

"Can't we get on with it?" he said finally to the woman, who still stood close to him. "I'm impatient for death." And with this most honest assertion he felt a slight breeze across his face. "If you insist on killing me, an innocent lover of books, then you should be kind enough to do it quickly. Otherwise, let me be on my way." He paused and considered the truth of his statement. It was entirely true. He was innocent, and as much as it would have surprised Ms. Tolan, he had become quite a bit more than a guy who got A's on his in-class essays. He had, in fact, become a lover of *One Hundred Years of Solitude* by GGM. And though Jefferson's passion was concentrated in that one book by that one writer at the moment, the adrenaline in his veins encouraged him to exaggerate. He had become, in these few desperate moments, a young man destined to be a great lover of books. If he survived, he would live to read. Not knowing whether these would be the words that saved his life, or the words that annoyed the woman into moving ahead with a quick slice of his throat, Jefferson spoke again. "There are few things worse than the anxiety preceding death, don't you agree?"

"Who are you?" the woman asked him again. "And stop trying to play mind games. You're a dead man."

And because Jefferson believed her, he turned philosophical even as his blood turned cold. He did not want to die.

"I'd like to quote a man I love from a book that is very important to me." He didn't want to sound uppity and use the words *writer* or *novel.* "If these are to be my last words, I'd like them to be important ones. I would also like you to call my grandmother after you shoot me, and tell her what happened." And then he proceeded to ask for a piece of paper to write down Esco's name and number. "It's the humane thing to do," he said, staring straight into those bergamot eyes. And then, because it felt final, he prepared to recite his favorite excerpt from *One Hundred Years of Solitude,* the bit about Colonel Aureliano Buendía and his miraculous failure to die.

But his mind was a jumble. What was the line? Why couldn't he remember it?

So many inexplicable things happened in a life.

All those good people who helped when you were having a rough time. All those near misses. All those misunderstandings and explanations and worries and apologies. All that hurt and healing. All that anger and scowling. All those smiles.

"Are you going to say these last words, or aren't you? Get on with it," the woman said, though she too seemed distracted.

He searched through the lists of quotes he held in his mind, so many lines he'd chanted and sung so many times, but the one about Colonel Aureliano Buendía was hidden in the scrubland of his memory. Instead, he found his mind lighting on that last day before he'd returned to the recruitment office and signed the papers. He'd taken a really tough geography class, and he knew that Iraq was part of the Middle East and of course he knew about Saddam Hussein and Osama bin Laden, but he didn't comprehend the seriousness of it all. Vietnam was a jungle in war movies from many lifetimes ago. And none of these had anything to do with his real life. He knew that terrorists had hijacked planes and flown them into the Twin Towers and the Pentagon when he was a ninth-grader, but that seemed so long ago.

In that midmorning moment outside Torreón, as Jefferson knelt on the hard earth, he still could not remember that favorite line, that mantra from his metal bunk, but he could see clearly that recruiter's office, the yellowed walls, the guy's broad smile across the desk.

Had the words abandoned him in this final moment?

The men made the gun-clicking, foot-shuffling noises he knew so well, the sounds that meant they were both anxious and prepared. Jefferson had a picture of RT in his head the moment before he commanded the shooting of the old man and each of his bleating goats, clenching his jaw as the old man kept trying to explain his life situation in his garbled yet intelligible Arabic-English gobbledygook.

The bergamot woman's boot pinched Jefferson's left calf as it rested on the gritty ground, and she told him to say his last prayers to whichever god he called his own, and go ahead with the quote, already, if he must, because he was out of time.

Jefferson thought of Esco, her keen intuition sensing something wrong. And of Nigel, weeping for the loss of both his cousin and his motorbike. This was to be the last scene in his rather short life. It seemed almost too perfect, though, like an absurd portion of GGM's own brain that hadn't made the final cut of his novel. Ex-Soldier Traveling to Meet Hero Writer Killed by Angry Men. Wouldn't this have made a great scene? In that moment, he vowed to the gods of literature that if his life was somehow spared, he would do his best to write a story capturing the absurdity of it all. Or, better yet, to pass the material on to his hero so he could write it. He'd know how to do the story justice.

"On your marks!" shouted the bergamot woman against the nervous whimperings of Remedios the Pup, and Jefferson was thinking how this piece of dialogue would fit nicely into a GGM-style story when the line, the one that had alluded him moments previously, returned to him. Each perfect word of what he thought of as a perfect scene. The one in which Colonel Aureliano Buendía skirts death. And then, the entire quote in all its simple perfection flashed in his mind. A miracle.

Jefferson saw the slow-motion bullet, the one intended by

Colonel Buendía to end his own life, as it entered his chest on its miraculously unscathing journey through his body, and exited out his back, failing to kill him. Because time was short, he began reciting his version of Gabriel's mind without permission from his captors.

Buendía was out of danger!

The bullet did not hurt him!

It went straight through his body and out the other side without touching any vital organs!

A miracle.

Straight through his body and out the other side without touching any vital organs!

Jefferson completed the recitation just as the rifles marked him. There were no goats to worry about in this scene, but he was aware that someone had forgotten after all to pull the blindfold up over his eyes, and so Jefferson stared into the eyes of his killers. They did not want to proceed. He understood their conundrum.

There was a pause, and perhaps because they were trying to make sense of his odd chanting, and because Jefferson was in no mood to wait silently, he repeated the recitation, his eyes closed this time in tribute to his hero, the great writer, the man who really was more to him than he imagined even an angel could have been if she had flown down from the clouds at that moment and rescued him. Jefferson raised his hands over his head and looked to the then cerulean sky and sang.

I said, the bullet did not hurt him!

A miracle.

Straight through his body and out the other side without touching any vital organs!

The caliber of his chanting in that moment, his voice somehow rounder and more committed than usual, surprised him.

But nothing happened with the guns and their bullets. He didn't know why. If he had been the old man with the goats, he'd have bled dry by this time, all pain erased. He had lost track of the bergamot woman, but it was clear that her boot was no longer digging into his left calf. He imagined she was smart enough to have moved out of harm's way.

But then his mind shifted and he began to believe, again, that life was possible.

Buendía was out of danger! Out of danger. A miracle.

He kept his eyes shut tight, and tried to eliminate from his mind all thoughts of impending execution. The chanting, he now felt, had brought him into ethereal contact with GGM and all he had ever intended in his novel. It was as if Jefferson had become part of the fictional Buendía household, sitting there in the kitchen as Colonel Aureliano Buendía, returning from many years of war, shared a meal with his mother, Úrsula Iguarán. As he sat at their table, Jefferson observed the tired profile of that former soldier, the one who was said to be taller than when he had left, paler and bonier, and who, according to his mother, showed the first symptoms of resistance to nostalgia. The colonel turned to Jefferson and tipped his heavy head ever so slightly in what Jefferson took as an acknowledgment of all his pain and loss and sin. It was only a moment, and nothing but a daydream, but it was also real, requiring him to gasp at the sharp air around him.

But now the bergamot woman was yelling—HALT! HALT! HALT! NO SHOT! NO SHOT!—and running between Jefferson and the rifles. In a simplified Spanish he now understood, she told the men to put down their weapons, move back and give her some space, put down their goddamn weapons! She sent them away to sit under the shade of a large rock, explaining that she needed time to think. And then she came up beside Jefferson and asked in a gruff whisper if he was serious. Was he shitting her? Was he really on his way to meet Gabriel García Márquez? Gabo?

"Of course," said Jefferson. "Why would I lie about something like that?"

"You'd be surprised," she said, but the lilt in her voice told him he had made a connection with her. The shift was baromet-ric; like a summer thunderstorm that's blown over, the murder-ous energy was now gone. As surely as he had understood that they would execute him, Jefferson now knew that his life would be spared, that this was one more in the long string of near misses from which he had emerged unharmed. He squeezed his hands together and acknowledged the gift with a broad smile and a kick of his sneaker against the hard earth.

The bergamot woman shook as she untied his wrists and sat down on the ground next to Jefferson, a sudden peer. Even though he could feel the closeness of her body, her spirit was nostalgic and faraway. All breezes ceased in that moment, and from somewhere nearby Remedios loped up to him, whining and licking his hands.

"I'd forgotten about that part," she said finally. "What a hero, that Colonel Aureliano Buendía, no? What a man!" And she shook her head even as a tear formed in the corner of her eye, a tear that looked quite like those Jefferson remembered Ms. Tolan shedding on a number of occasions in the classroom at Santa Fe High. And then, as if from a deep reservoir, she looked off toward one of those giant stones, the ones that had mesmerized him in the first place, and began speaking in a singsong fashion not unlike Jefferson's own chanting.

"*The air was so full of wetness, the fishes danced around in the courtyard and in and out the window* Can you imagine it?" she continued to him, but also to no one in particular. Jefferson couldn't say he remembered that line though he loved the idea of it, and wondered if she too had taken liberties with the famous words. "If only... The air could be so full of wetness that... *fish could dance in the courtyard*! Wouldn't that be lovely. Oh, if only it would rain," she said, looking to the sky as if the drought was to blame for all her present ills.

The rest of her group had dissipated, wandering back in the directions from which they had appeared. He thought he could hear the rustle of birds' wings again, off in some nearby trees. One of the men approached the bergamot woman, exchanged a few words with her, and then motioned for the others to go on with their business. It seemed this sudden turn of events, as unlikely as it felt to Jefferson, was not giving any of the others pause.

The woman continued in her slumped position, reminding Jefferson of himself now, her eyes glazed and the words, begun like an assignment, having turned into a rhythmic incantation. She began to repeat the few phrases, as song, and he felt the ease of participating in a known ritual. As she recited, he began to feel he had known her since childhood.

The air was so full of wetness, the fishes could have danced in the courtyard. In the courtyard. Could have danced in the court—yard!

She stood then, a tall vision between him and the place in the hard earth where the line of men with semiautomatic weapons had stood moments earlier, and waved her arms southward.

"You've got a long way to go," she said.

She looked so hard at him that her gaze traveled straight through. "And it's important, what you're doing. Brave. Imagine—on your way to meet the great García Márquez . . ." The woman's voice trailed off as she said this, looking now above and beyond him, her eyes lost way out in the sky. She laughed softly, something occurring to her as funny or odd, and Jefferson got back on the Kawasaki and called for the pup to follow. The bergamot woman was waving and saying "Godspeed, *muchacho*" as he turned the bike toward Torreón, and he felt once again that it could all have been a movie, this woman behaving exactly as he imagined a character from *One Hundred Years of Solitude* might, saying just what would be expected to a young man whose life she has inexplicably spared.

IN THE BRILLIANT moments just prior to sunset, it began as nothing, and then the nothing took form and became a shimmer far off in the distance, a reflective concentration of energy. Minutes passed, and a dark form materialized within the mirage, a form both nebulous and certain. It was human—a large human—moving toward Jefferson up the highway, and he thought momentarily of hiding. But Jefferson's need for human conversation, for someone who might listen to the story of the bergamot woman, outweighed his fear. Look into the eyes of the one who hunts you, Esco had always said, and so he stood still and watched as the dark form approached. It was at least half a mile off and moving laboriously, so there was plenty of time to change his mind.

It was late in the day and many miles down the highway after his brush with death, and he had stationed himself at the base of a grandmother oak several hundred feet off the road, the tree's serpentine roots both pillow to his whirling frightened head and ottoman to his throbbing frightened feet, Remedios asleep with her head on his chest. The motorbike lay in the tall grass nearby, now that it had done its job, helping him to hightail it down the highway. His hands had been shaking much more violently than he would have expected, given all the times he'd skirted death before. In the war, he had known it was war, and that death might come at any moment, but now he realized that death lurked in this new non-war-zone life as well, like the undertow hidden beneath the gentle swells of the ocean on a calm, sunny day.

Jefferson had tried to distract himself from these thoughts by working on the collage, this idea he'd been developing over the past few days as he rode, something new he could create out of some of his favorite lines from Gabriel's novel. Ideas had flown into his mind—a viscous bitter substance, someone dead under the ground, a scorpion in the sheets—but though he copied and recopied them onto a piece of paper he'd tucked between the book's pages, they hadn't led him anywhere. He still could not tear his mind away from the bergamot wom-an's life. And so he'd just sat there under the tree and thought about luck and fear and being thankful. Someone had once told him that how we feel about things is a choice, and that he could choose to feel grateful for whatever came his way, that this was the best way to live a good life. That was when he'd first decided to watch the shimmer approach, not run away from it. But try as he might, Jefferson could not stop shaking.

The grandmother oak stood steady and firm. Far above him it lifted its branches to the sky, holding up all those hundreds of small, bright leaves, rustling their applause like an uproari-ous crowd at a concert. All else was quiet as the shimmer wore off, and the single form became two. With his eyes Jefferson traced a periphery around two distinct objects. Husband and wife? Grandfather and grandson? Cousins? He could not tell. He detected the bend and swing of two sets of knees and legs moving in a forward direction, carrying heavy loads, coming closer. Both heads seemed to be wrapped turban-style, or possi-bly in bandannas, which made sense, given the sun's intensity. The grandmother oak above offered Jefferson its cool, friendly shade, and he closed his eyes in gratitude and breathed despite the knowledge that strangers were headed his way.

OUT THERE

When less than fifty feet separated him from the figures, Jefferson confirmed that they were women, tilted forward against some weight on their backs, steady as snares—step, step, step, step—though he could determine very little else about them. The heavy loads implied an important mission, but their pace was unhurried. Had they noticed his orange T-shirt against the tree? He did a long handstand, watching them all the while, and tried to think of what García Márquez might say, but really, this didn't seem to be like anything out of the novel.

The distance became grenade-throwing range, slightly more than the distance he used to span in the triple jump in high school, and approximately double the four paces between his old bed and the bathroom. If someone had been with him, if he had felt the need to communicate, it would not have been safe to whisper.

The women were covered in heavy canvas clothing, multiple skirts and overtops, identical except for the fact that the one on the far side had chosen mostly greens and turquoise, and the one nearer to Jefferson wore light reds and oranges. On their backs they carried matching messes of rope and twine, wrapped in a tangle around a few short wooden posts. And now that they were so close, he realized exactly who they would have been if they had been in the story: these were the gypsies.

At a distance of ten feet he saw their beauty, a beauty that proved what good works God and the angels could do when they worked together. They were identical twins, their bronze skin glistening under the heat of the sun and their chocolate eyes bespeaking a frank calm. The women were by now nearly close enough to touch, but looked as if they might walk right past without seeing Jefferson. He knew that they might be unsightly on the inside, but the outer loveliness of these two women was enough to make him forgive all possible insufficiencies, abandon his defensive position among the tree roots, and rise eagerly to meet them.

"Hello there, ladies," he said, waggling the fingers on his right hand in what he had always thought to be a reflection of his good humor and kindness. "I do believe you are the first humans I have seen on this road in half a day. How do you do?"

The women stopped to look at him from under their velvety camel's eyelashes. Dark wisps of close-cropped, wavy black hair escaped their headscarves, and beads of sweat sparkled at their temples and behind their ears and at the napes of their long necks. Though the mirage-like shimmer around them had long disappeared, the richness of their lovely brown skin glistened all the more at close range. They were of medium height, and though they appeared to be identical in the genetic sense, Jefferson quickly began to notice differences between them. The one in greens and turquoise, who had been walking half a pace ahead, was slightly more wiry and athletic, with a taut quickness in her gestures and a sharper face, with keen, expressive features and a thinner nose.

The woman dressed in light reds and oranges was more rounded, with grace in her slower, more methodical movements. Her mouth quirked to one side in a near-query. She struck Jefferson as having a better sense of humor than her sister, though he knew that he might be projecting his personal history onto her; the quick, skinny girls he'd observed in high school had never appealed to him, while the one girl he thought he'd ever love, Josephina, was round. Jefferson, a skin-and-bones guy who'd always had to work at keeping the weight on, thought it was basic algebra. You had to keep the two sides of the equation equal, like balancing a seesaw: skinny guys and round girls on one side, big guys and skinny girls on the other.

He had a theory about the difference between round girls and skinny girls that he now applied to these two. The rounded one in reds and oranges would run late for her appointments. Rounded women were like that—they enjoyed themselves too much to be prompt. He loved that. Skinny girls, on the other hand, were skinny in large part because they rushed everywhere they went, their whole lives through. Skinny girls were always worried about being late or getting into trouble. He did not want to be judgmental, and he was sure that some skinny girl out there existed to prove him wrong, but so far in his life, Jefferson had found that skinny girls made him nervous and round girls made him breathe deeply and smile.

He broke off this train of thought, noticing that they were still striding forward, and soon would have passed him.

He smiled and waved again. Remedios had woken up now, and she yipped in their direction too. "Hey, don't you two wanna rest a bit?"

They exchanged glances of near comprehension, followed by a few quick Spanish responses, too fast for his brain, before stepping from the road toward him. They swung their bundles down from their backs, whispering and giggling as they approached. The rounded one asked a question, but Jefferson didn't understand her, and shrugged. "No sé, no sé."

He had begun to feel a sense of ownership over the space under the oak, as if it were his living room. As the women made their way toward him, he shifted his arms off his hips and into an outspread and beckoning posture, like the host at a party, coming to the door. *Come in, come in, you must be tired,* he said in his mind.

The tangled bundles of rope and wood on their backs, he could now see, were hammocks, and the women laid them on the ground only long enough to scope out good hanging spots in the branches. They greeted him with preliminary smiles, but hurried right to work, as if it were understood that the visiting, the getting to know each other, would come after the hammocks were in place.

"Can I help you?" Jefferson asked from behind. "Would you like some water?"

Both turned and smiled knowing smiles at him and then at each other, and then resumed their hoisting of ropes and their

159

tying of knots. Jefferson did not understand why they might be putting up their hammocks but he didn't think it could be dangerous. He'd recovered from his shock at his near-execution, and now was feeling somewhat entertained. He'd even begun thinking how he might relay this story to Nigel and Esco. Both of these, he felt, were good indications that he was not afraid.

By then it was clear that the twins spoke no English. As they worked, Jefferson performed a panicked review of Spanish III from senior year—he had learned much more about writing Spanish than he had about speaking it, and even that was three years stale.

"So . . . cómo está?" he blurted out, wanting to continue his impression that he was a harmless young guy who knew *un poquito de español.* "Muy bien?" he prompted, after almost a minute had passed with no response. "Sí, muy bien!" he said again, another thirty seconds later, laughing a bit to himself. Ever since he had left Santa Fe, with the brief exception of those few minutes on the ground with the bergamot woman and her bandits, his hands had been shaking less, and something told him that he would continue to fail to die, and that this plan to visit GGM had been, in fact, a good one.

He was not afraid. He was certain of that now.

The hammocks hung securely, the twins turned to look at him, standing still for the first time at close range. They were not as old as he'd first thought, probably in their late twenties, and their bodies reminded him of those of high school dancers. He saw skin for the first time as the one in greens and turquoise sat on the ground and began disrobing. She unwrapped what looked to be a long scarf from around her neck and shoulders—several complete circumnavigations of herself—and continued with what appeared to be a practiced shirring off of three layers of blouse and four layers of skirt until finally all that remained was a cotton lace camisole and loose cotton pants, both wild-egg blue. Her sister stripped down to her underlayers as well and began digging in a large duffel bag until she'd found a stainless steel cookset and several plastic bags of vegetables and grains.

They smelled of cinnamon and almond extract, a scent Jefferson could taste many years later if he concentrated, and it caused him to question their existence Could they be angels? The one in greens and turquoise, the quick one, took a snake of gauzy fabric from yet another bag— ten or fifteen yards, it must have been—and began creating a breezy tent around her hammock. The action recalled in him a distant memory of a woman he could not remember, possibly a dream, and he found himself groping for a reference point for how to behave. A sexual beast was stirring in him, though he was shy about making this assumption. These were beautiful women. They were twins! And so he told himself he was mistaken about what that quick woman in greens and turquoise was preparing for in the hammock under the gauzy tent beneath the giant oak's branches. Still, he felt a distinct tightening in his chest that he'd come to know as his heart, telling him, *You are still alive.* And so he smiled and reminded himself that he was not afraid.

I am alive.

The rounded twin was cooking what seemed to be a mole stew—lamb and chocolate and potatoes and cinnamon and chile. She paused to serve him a cool mint drink that began, almost immediately, to free him of his worries. Her loose cotton pants brushed his toes as she moved from the low fire to her bag of supplies, and a few times she paused in her work, knelt, and touched the top of his head.

He was alive.

Jefferson became caught up in the whirlpool of miracles once again as he took swig after swig of his cool mint drink. He had survived near-death at the hands of the bergamot woman and her boys less than four hours previously. Before that, he had survived Iraq. (Though he had in truth survived many near-death experiences while in Iraq, Jefferson thought of it at this moment as one big near-death experience.) Before that, he'd survived childhood in Santa Fe, with his loving grandmother doing the best she could. By definition this meant he had survived, first of all, abandonment by his mother as a baby. He had known no father—that went without saying.

He was alive! Jefferson closed his eyes and marveled at the miracle of miracles and smiled at the beauty of the mingling scents of cinnamon and chile and chocolate.

Jefferson didn't know when the pile of quilts had materialized below him, or how his shoes had been removed, but he was lying shoeless on a pile of lilac and coral-colored quilts, the sunlight filtered through the gauze dissolving any sense of time in its hazy radiance. The wild-blue-egg twin had taken a bottle of oil and, kneeling by his feet, begun to rub it into his parched ankles and cracked heels and tired toes.

Jefferson had not realized his skin's thirst until the oil touched his feet. He was aware of his muscles turning soft. His memory of the scene amongst the gigantic boulders, his face down and his knees in the hard-packed earth, floated before him, now miraculously tucked into a soft cloth basket of past-tense near-misses. He was in the process of living to tell that story.

There was little talking between the twins, just a flow of singsong and humming and nostalgic clicking of tongues and soft laughter. Jefferson was not afraid. Jefferson was alive.

He began to be aware of a loosening in his chest as his breath flowed into cavities within his chest that had been long closed. His breathing eased. In . . . and out. In . . . and out. There was nothing else he needed to do. The sky pulsed blue—an exceedingly blue blue—and nothing about any of this was frightening. He was fully awake. He was near to life. In fact, he was so near to life that he was, in fact, alive.

The wild-blue-egg twin, after finishing with Jefferson's feet, had moved up to his ankles and calves, and now she was working on his left knee. There was no doubt that she believed in the criticality of kneecaps. She kneaded in and out of the grooves for fifteen minutes before moving on to the right side, as if releasing toxin. Her sister refilled Jefferson's cup, gave the pot a stir, and sat down next to him, motioning for him to lift his head and place it in her lap. She glared maternally when he hesitated, and so he obeyed. Faceup, his head resting in the junction of her two crossed legs, Jefferson caught speckled sunlight as it found its way through the oak's leaves and branches, through the cotton of her camisole and the wisps of her hair.

"Relax, my friend," she said in near-perfect English, and began moving her fingertips in circular patterns in his scalp, along his hairline at first and then fully into the depth and breadth of his tired head, whispering as she rubbed, cooing like an evening bobwhite, reminding Jefferson of the way Esco had helped him overcome his fear of night as a child—tickling his shoulders and arms and back with her stubby-nailed fingertips, singing old lullabies.

The fire smoldered.

Jefferson's mind wanted both to race and to rest.

"Rest," said the woman holding his head. And though it seemed a miracle that Jefferson could understand them, that somehow their words sounded like English to him, he relaxed his mind and thought of the story in the Bible in which this had happened. He did not need to understand everything.

They wrapped him in heavy cotton blankets and left him hanging in the hammock, surrounded in gauze. A stone soup bowl steamed next to him on a stump.

"Eat," said the rounded one. She sat nearby on the ground, eating, feeding Remedios out of her hand. Jefferson had many questions, but he was overtaken by a sudden appetite, and so he propped himself up and he ate.

He had lost his appetite for entire days since he'd returned, finding the sound of Esco's earnest knife against cucumbers to be nauseating. He imagined that it was the sound of her trying to compensate for every deficiency, for all of him now missing, left behind across the ocean somewhere.

Jefferson spooned more stew into his mouth, identifying the distinct flavors on his tongue. Beyond goodness and warmth, it embodied a creamy dark trustworthiness mixed with the pep of tomatoes and the anonymity of a woman who knew nothing about him. Not his name or that he was a soldier or that his mother had been sixteen when she left.

After the first bowl he asked for more, and only into his second bowl did Jefferson's stomach proclaim just how empty it had been all those months, its solitary yearnings all those neglected years. That much was now clear as Jefferson ate almost three full bowls before pausing. And then, as if he had removed the tiniest of pins in a very large dam, the words began to trickle out. The twins sat on either side of him on the ground next to the fire. They huddled under the blankets as the high desert chill fell upon the night.

He was alive. He was warm. His pup was content.

"I was almost executed this morning," he told them, hoping the Pentecostal effect of the afternoon had lingered.

The women looked at him with wide eyes. "Tell us the story," said the rounded one.

"Bandits of some sort," Jefferson said. "They came out of the hills. They surrounded me." His voice began to shake, but he continued.

"You were scared, but you survived!" said the angular one.

"You were brave," said her twin.

"I was lucky," Jefferson said.

He felt the need to go on. It seemed they were willing, and his gut told him this was what he needed, to tell his story. It was of course a miracle that they understood each other. Thinking back on it, Jefferson could not say whether he was speaking their Spanish or they, his English, or whether instead all three of them were speaking some third and unknown hybrid.

"Why did the woman—that bergamot woman—why did she spare your life?" the one on his left asked finally, locking his eyes into the grip of hers as if she had reached the end of her expansiveness and now wanted to know, simply and truthfully, the answer.

Jefferson shook his head. He closed his eyes and shook his head. His index finger and thumb pinched the bridge of his nose, a ragged breath escaped his mouth, and suddenly he was crying, his upper lip bloated, his shoulders quaking, his chest heaving.

He could not explain what had happened.

He knew what he thought the answer was, but it made no sense.

The twins beheld his tearful silence. They did not touch him or invade the space around him. They began a soft cooing, a wordless chant of nostalgia.

"The woman didn't kill me because I am meant to go on living. My life is not over because there are things I still need to do." These last words settled around him, as close to the truth as Jefferson could imagine.

Excluding the several times his young mother had tried to breast-feed him, the once or twice his grandmother had held back his longish hair when he'd been sick in the toilet, and the time in sixth grade when Josephina had grabbed his hand on the walk home from school, Jefferson's physical experience of the opposite sex was confined to a handful of events inside a storage container with a woman he hardly knew and would never see again. Esco had told him many times, always, it seemed, as a sort of apology, that his mom had attempted to feed him with her tiny breasts. He remembered his grandmother holding him while he vomited. He remembered the thrill of Josephina's warm hand in his, even all those years later. He remembered those hurried encounters between stacks of canned tomatoes and processed cheeses. These formed his small collection. Memories of female touch.

Jefferson had not realized it at the time, but when he began reading *One Hundred Years* he'd been hungry for the aura of sex. What was it to be with a woman? He'd never realized the degree to which a classic piece of literature—a book not even available at the grocery store—could be doused in sex. In *One Hundred Years*, sex was everywhere, slathered across the pages like so many adjectives describing the weather. It was straightforward, it was unapologetic, and though none of it was pretty, all of it was inspirational. A prostitute teaching her own son the secrets of the flesh. A wrinkled auntie who caressed her virgin nephew in the bath. Men and women making love in cisterns and hammocks and sheds. It did not match any of Jefferson's preconceived notions of love, and yet he found it all strangely comforting; when he read these scenes he felt less like a lonely soldier lost in the Middle Eastern landscape, and more like a man journeying to find his real home.

Naturally, the novel became his sexual primer. He liked the idea of having gotten his ideas from literature rather than from anything he'd seen on TV or the Internet, but more importantly he thought the famous writer's ideas made sense. Nothing about sex had ever seemed sweet or sentimental to Jefferson; rather, it seemed like an animalistic urge to drive away loneliness. This honesty, Jefferson could live with.

And here was the best part. In García Márquez's novel, no man or woman was excluded. GGM didn't mention anything about good looks or money as prerequisites to sex. In fact, it seemed the only ones who didn't get love quite right in the novel were the truly beautiful women. Men who had left their families for world adventure, fat men covered in tattoos, men who fixed pianos, who could be mislead by gypsy tricks, who were chained to trees, who worked all day in their laboratories, who murdered other men for no good reason—even the least of these found sexual comfort in GGM's story. Even the lowest of the low found a lover to hold him. For Jefferson this was a secret message of good tidings: Jefferson Long Soldier, despite being left by his mother, despite never having known his father or either of his grandfathers, despite being poor, despite having seen what he had seen out there, would one day feel the comfort of a real woman's embrace.

And this good news made it impossible for him not to love Gabriel García Márquez. Though Jefferson had nothing more than phantom memories of having lain in the arms of a woman, he believed his day would come. And what was more, Jefferson believed that if asked, GGM would say Jefferson's day would come as well.

He fell asleep that night with this hope, and dreamed of the rounded reds-and-orange twin climbing into the hammock with him, a feat he'd have guessed would be awkward and uncomfortable but which was in reality full of pleasure. He smelled almond cookies and smoke and the oil of unnamed fruits from unknown kingdoms long ago. She was near him and with him and above him and below him and behind him and before him all at once and at the same time.

"Mmmm . . . ," she whispered in his ear. "Gzhoooozzz . . . hauuuum . . ." Her hands rubbed his ears and his shoulders, his satisfied stomach and throbbing thighs. And then, as if she'd become leechlike, the dense sediment of grief within Jefferson began to soften and break apart and leave him. Specific days and times, specific losses.

Galen from Albuquerque.

Tristan's hand.

The old man with his goats.

Adams from Hollidaysburg.

Jeff Kleiner.

The father and the three young girls in the Toyota.

Ramon from Las Cruces.

Sergeant Schoener.

Hume, twenty-one, of Appleton, Maine.

That sweet hound.

The seventeen-year-old.

Dudzinski from Guam.
Hazelton from Edinburgh, Indiana.
Ray Soto.

The next morning Jefferson awoke on that roadside in Mexico, curled up in a soft place among the roots of the grandmother oak, not another soul in sight and no hammocks or blankets or pots or pans. He was not sure what had happened or why. Had they simply left without saying good-bye? He stood up and surveyed the branches, looking for something the women might have left behind. A rope that had secured the hammock? A cotton head wrapping? A necklace? But there was no trace of them. His belly was full and his body warm, but even the rocks of the campfire sat cold and silent.

As he dusted off and prepared to get back on the motorbike, the lingering apparitions of the twins taunted him. Shy and inexperienced as he was, Jefferson had dreamed that this might have been his day. He had imagined that the time had come for his first salutory lovemaking, and that it would be exactly what he needed. He believed the fortuitous arrival of the twins had been part of a divine plan to heal his wounds. He imagined that the heavenly sisters would reciprocate his quiet eagerness, and that this episode would become a story of mythic proportions, a story he would remember for the rest of his days. But the morning was upon him, and he was no longer certain that the twins had been real.

Gabriel would understand. As much as he seemed to believe in a woman's ability to comfort, the writer seemed equally aware of a woman's power to drive a man to insanity. The great writer loved and believed in and was driven insane by women. It was one of the things Jefferson hoped to talk about face-to-face with the old man in Mexico City. He was hoping the great writer would share some of his real-life experiences. Was it his experience, for example, that a woman could be truly uninhibited sexually and that, absent familial boundaries, she would share herself with any man to whom she felt connected? Did he, like Jefferson, prefer round women to skinny ones? And what about the old grandmothers and aunties? Did the famous writer believe in a world in which wrinkled old women pleasured themselves with the young and old alike? And how much of this had GGM experienced first-hand? Had he fathered seventeen sons with seventeen different women, like Colonel Aureliano Buendía? Jefferson knew it was not any of his business, but he hoped Gabriel García Márquez would be willing to share the details.

He pushed the bike back toward the road, his backpack loaded, Remedios secure in the carrier, and his mind full of the day's itinerary. Yes, he was traveling hundreds of miles south through Mexico to find Gabriel García Márquez, but where was he going *today*, and what portion of the healing process might be on the agenda? Jefferson had begun to think of the process as piecemeal, each episode relieving its own distinct burden and forming a link in the chain of events he needed to heal. Leaving Santa Fe had been a link. Trusting himself to learn to ride the Kawasaki had been another link. Facing the bergamot woman with honesty and fear, yet another. And inviting the twins —apparitions or not—to share his oak tree for the evening was yet one more step in the process of reclaiming himself after war.

26

EVENTUALLY JEFFERSON REMEMBERED her, as if it had all been a very real dream. There had been the real flesh of a real woman in the real Iraqi desert in the very real war, and it had begun with a package of gum.

Her name was Tajia. She was a hairdresser from the Philippines who'd left her kids and spent all her life savings for the chance to cut soldiers' hair in Iraq for $300 a month. She lived with eight other hairdressers in a metal storage container in a barbed-wired compound within the larger Camp Anaconda. Though twice the age of Josephina C de Baca, Tajia seemed young and buoyant compared to Jefferson's grandmother and Auntie Linda. And there was no doubt of her passion.

He'd been chanting the various passages about one or the other of the various Aurelianos or José Arcadios being driven mad by the scent of imagined lovers. Frankly, the idea was so mesmerizing to him that he wondered why it had taken a novel to bring the idea to his mind. He'd experienced the crazed phenomenon of scent with Josephina, so he knew it was real, that his own nose was capable of this obsession.

What he realized on that Wednesday afternoon in March was that he desired a real woman to smell. Imagined scents

171

might work for some men—he couldn't say much about those Buendías in the novel, he hadn't known them personally—but he needed more. Josephina had not been near enough to smell in almost a decade.

Tajia the Filipina, on the other hand, was less than two feet away from him at least once a day, right next to the little shop where he bought his gum and candy bars and magazines. Those were real drops of perspiration he could see along her hairline. That was her breath on his face when she stared at him and sighed. He could smell her. Cumin and baby powder.

When she looked at him while buzzing the back of another soldier's neck, he shivered. Yes, Jefferson was in the middle of what García Márquez had called "the dung heap of war," but here with him, just across from the convenience shop counter, was a sweaty woman, a real one in the flesh, and he began to believe that his fears just might be turned into pleasure. Afterward he did not remember anything of Tajia's face except her deep amber eyes, flecked with blood spots of exertion. She was about his height and much heavier, making Jefferson chuckle at what the two of them would have looked like as a couple if they'd ever left the storage container together. There was no doubt that her bottom was fat, but it was also, in its own way, much more delightful than his own. In fairness, he was nothing but a skin-and-bones kid at that time, not too far into his first tour.

On the day they met, Jefferson had helped carry Teresa Blue's body from the site of that horrible series of explosions. Though hers was not the first death, she was the first woman he'd seen die. He had touched Blue's still-warm skin, and he had helped load her still-warm body on the humvee, and he had sat with her slowly cooling hand in his own as they'd driven back to Anaconda. He could not remember how it had begun, precisely, or what the middle part had been, or why they had been wherever they had been in the first place. A terrible lonely waste of a day.

He knew it might seem unfeeling of him to associate his passionate affair with the story of another young woman's death, but war had turned every one of Jefferson's beliefs inside out. Inside out and screwy. Several minutes before the fatal blast, Teresa had walked past Jefferson, close enough for him to smell her distinctly female scent, something vaguely musky and sweet. The scent in that moment had made him remember the calm of having been held at his mother's breast long ago, and at the same time race forward in his mind toward the full-blooded possibility of touching a woman with whom he was enraptured. He'd thought to himself in that moment that despite the horror of war, at least there remained human touch, skin to skin. And then the world had been rocked, and the woman named Blue had become a casualty of a series of improvised explosive devices, a sight Jefferson knew he would replay many times in his mind, over and over again, for the rest of his life.

Several hours later Jefferson was buying grape bubble gum at the convenience shop, thinking that if he stuffed three pieces into his mouth, it might buffer him against the terrible memory.

Tajia was sitting on a step stool, watching Jefferson buy his gum. That was all. But as he paid the man for his gum across the counter, Jefferson was aware of that cumin scent drifting into his space and making him shiver. Tajia watched him, put her scissors in her mouth, and bit down, laughing. There was no doubt she was laughing at Jefferson. He shuddered again, got his change, and left the shop. That night he could not escape the tormenting scent. In the sheets of his bed, in the hand towel as he dried his face, escaping his bathroom bag as he dug for his toothpaste, it lingered: cumin on fresh waves of baby powder.

The next day, after he'd paid for his gum, Jefferson walked the several paces to the hairdresser's booth and sat down in her chair. He could have waited another week or so for a haircut, but he could no longer ignore the anxiety in his blood, not now that the memory of Blue's death haunted him. Shy as always, he said nothing and hoped she'd be able to read his mind.

"Why gum?" she asked finally in a heavy Filipina accent as she combed through his coarse black hair. "I see you all the time, every day. You buy gum, so much gum. Why?"

"My nerves," he told her. "It helps."

"You need something more than gum," she said as she shaved the errant hairs away from the sides of his jaw and the back of his neck. When she was finished, Tajia gave Jefferson directions for finding her that evening. In less than two minutes in her strained English and on the back of his very small receipt she wrote directions to the storage container located deep within the barbed-wire compound. At the bottom of the note she wrote AFTER NINE with a happy face.

That night Jefferson followed the scent of cumin and powder all the way to the storage container, which, as Tajia had promised, was unlocked. He had guessed it would be the sleeping container she shared with her hairdresser friends, but it was nothing more than a room filled with shelves of nonperishable food. The fumes were too much in the container housing beauty supply and cleaning products, Tajia explained, and she was lucky enough to be friendly with the woman who kept all the keys. "She understands some of us need some privacy around here," Tajia told him.

What followed was an unexpected consequence of war, the animalistic passion of two lonely people far from home. Tajia taught him what she could, and Jefferson discovered the rest. He was quick to learn his way around her very large body, exploring her crevasses and inlets and hills and valleys. He let instinct take the place of thinking, his skinny body becoming lost in her luxurious wet folds. They spoke hardly at all as they converted their solitary fears into bites on the neck and clawings across the shoulders and consensual invasions. Unlike love, it was detached and violent and selfish, and in that way he left each night feeling sated and alive.

OUT THERE

The affair lasted almost three weeks among the bags of pancake mix and vats of canola oil, until without notice Tajia was nowhere to be found.

Later Jefferson learned she had been sent, along with four other Filipinas, by armored vehicle to a base 125 miles to the south to replace hairdressers killed by an explosion there. Though he never saw her again, her scent of cumin held on to his T-shirts and socks until he returned to New Mexico, and for a long time he dreamed of sweating happily between her thighs.

His eyes had been opened. No matter how he tried to minimize the experience later, no matter how he justified it as part of the craziness of war, Jefferson now believed in unbridled sex with the wrong woman in the wrong place. He believed sex would never be quite as good in bed as it was elsewhere. He believed it would never be quite as good if the woman was beautiful and kind and gentle. He imagined all the wrong places in which it might feel right. Washaterias and the stairwells in large public buildings and T.J. Maxx fitting rooms and unprotected benches within litter-strewn parks. He imagined all the wrong women. The therapist from the VA. His sixth-grade teacher from Kaune Elementary. Esco's old friend, MaryLou. Ms. Tolan. He even tried one afternoon to imagine making love to his own mother, but because he could not imagine her face or her body, he had to stop. Sometimes his mind wandered to Josephina Maria C de Baca, but because he believed she was beautiful and kind and gentle, and also because he still hoped that one day the two of them would truly love one another, he tried not to linger on her. He began to think that life was not about love. He began to think that life was just a series of attempts to do the best you could not to be lonely or afraid.

I CANNOT UNDERSTAND *why people go to war over things they cannot touch with their own hands.*

This idea, thought by Colonel Aureliano Buendía, the great revolutionary of Macondo, conceived by GGM, and later revised in his own words by Jefferson Long Soldier, member of the Army's Tenth Mountain Division, originally from Santa Fe, New Mexico.

Who, thought Jefferson, could understand?

That must have been why the reading helped him. It was as if he had his own personal conversation several times a day with a wise man, a man who was reminding him of a larger perspective. Of the possibility of hope. Some people read *One Hundred Years* and saw nothing but blood and family dysfunction and gratuitous incestuous sex and the trampling of the poor by the rich. Jefferson read those same passages, and instead of feeling trampled, he felt a beacon of the writer's love, as if his own great-grandfather was telling him family lore, all the good and all the bad of it, to buffet Jefferson against the rigors of life. It was as if the writer was saying, "You think you've got it bad? Well, let me tell you about this character named Colonel Aureliano Buendía, who fought and lost thirty-two wars and never experienced true love."

When nineteen-year-old Galen from Albuquerque went down several weeks later, so close to Jefferson that blood from the boy's head wound stained Jefferson's shoes, the timing was in fact lucky. Jefferson had entered an illuminated state by then, making him more equipped than ever before to handle close encounters with death. He wore the novel, now taped and tattered, strapped next to his chest with an Ace bandage he'd bought from the convenience stall. He'd seen the villain in so many movies wrap his chest around and around with gauze to stanch bleeding from a gunshot wound, so in the same way he wrapped his own chest, slipping the novel in tight next to his skin. The book was a comfort. At night, he kept it wrapped against him in case he had trouble sleeping, and needed to recite by the light of the moon. There was also the added protection—a 458-page shield—it would provide, were a stray bullet to find its way through the barracks and into his bed at just the right angle at just the right speed.

On that deadly day, Jefferson had squatted down next to Galen and held his still-warm hands. Just moments before, Galen had told the story of how his Polish grandparents lived through World War II. "The Nazis took over my grandmother's farm," he'd said. "They stole and butchered their cow. Can you imagine it? The Nazis, man! My grandfather was eight years old and starving to death."

The conversation had turned to why each of them had signed up for the army, and after Jefferson had said he didn't really know, Galen had returned to the topic of his grandparents. "I signed up right after nine/eleven," he told Jefferson. "They were still in New York at the time, and the whole thing freaked them out, like the sky was literally falling, you know? Like it was Hitler returning from the grave."

Jefferson held Galen's hands until they grew cold, and then he slipped the novel out from the bandage and out from under his shirt and began flipping through the pages, searching for words. He needed just the right ones, something to help make sense of this one death. The blood had pooled around Jefferson's feet by then and was trickling down a step where the two had been sitting. From his lap a few moments later the words *trickle of blood* caught his eyes. This was it, the perfect string of words for the circumstance, the sentence that might connect him to a larger world. With his finger he followed the passage backward to its beginning and then began to recite slowly the very long sentence about José Arcadio being shot and his blood trickling out under the door and down the street and around corners and over curbs, all the way to his mother's house, around the dining room table and into her kitchen, where she was cracking thirty-six eggs for bread, so that she might learn of his death.

As Galen's face lost its pink, as his blood turned from red to black, Jefferson chanted the words as he imagined the boy's mother and how she might discover the news. He did not know Galen's mother, but he imagined a woman getting ready to crack eggs for pierogi dough, and how a mother's intuition might tell her that her son, this Galen, had lost all his blood out of the backside of his skull.

How had García Márquez done it again? Sitting at his typewriter all those years before, writing about the blood pouring from poor Galen's head and down the steps and across the Middle Eastern sands all the way across Africa and then spilling into the wide blue Atlantic, a current of foreboding, until it hit American soil and found its way to the threshold of the home in Albuquerque, where it would proclaim to the boy's mother that her son was dead.

Jefferson recited the passage in slow melodic murmurs until help arrived. He had no memory of who drove him back to Anaconda that day, or what they did with Galen's body. What remained for him was the memory of that dark river as it trickled off and away, down the steps and across the sand.

Later, on other afternoons when the floors and walls around him became stained with different blood—from Americans and Sunnis and Shiites and Brits and Sri Lankans and Kurds, young kids of every color, each flag and faith contributing to the bloody irrigation of Iraqi sands—Jefferson perceived it as sad, yes, but also as an opportunity to recite the beautiful lines about José Arcadio's blood running under the door and down the street and into his mother's kitchen as she prepared to crack thirty-six eggs. It was a chance to pause within the chaos, and to thank God once again for the great writer, the man who had saved Jefferson's life once more with his words.

THE *HORCHATA* **STRUCK** Jefferson's tongue as oddly alive and tart, but the Zacatecas plaza—lime trees, small children eating lollipops with their aunties, dogs, an early-December bustle—was reminding him of blood. The birds from outside Torreón had followed him, and roosted now in the trees and bushes nearby, clucking and croaking and cooing. Jefferson could now see that it was a mixed flock: grackles and sparrows and ravens and terns. Peacocks and martins and owls. Chickens. The pup had bounded off to roll in a patch of grass, and Jefferson was content to sip his drink and watch as a late-season mosquito helped herself to a long snack on his forearm. He hoped the heaviness would pass. The unreality of all these birds swarming around might help.

He did not know exactly how he had arrived at this spot in central Mexico, though it must have been by riding Nigel's motorbike, which was parked a few feet away. He did not know what had happened to the beautiful twins with their hammocks. What he needed to decide was whether to spend the night here or push on another few hours to somewhere farther—San Luis Potosí possibly, but he'd heard that town might not be a good one in which to spend the night.

When the mosquito finished and flew away, one large drop of blood remained on his skin, a succulent leftover, and Jefferson stared at it, that virulent wet drop—what a deep, rich red it was—watching as it rested, with no desire to travel. He raised his hand in the air in front of him and watched as the drop fought gravity for a moment before dripping down in a neat line a few inches toward his elbow. Then he put his tongue to it, closed his eyes, and licked.

The taste of being alive.

It was late on the third day, and his body ached from gripping the handlebars and pressing against the wind. And though he felt a degree of relief over having passed the first several days of his trip, of being now that much closer to his destination, he was also beginning to experience moments of anxiety. What if he got all the way to Mexico City, and Gabriel could not help him answer the question *Why?*

The taste of the blood proved a healthy distraction. On his skin a diluted streak remained, and he watched it begin to dry, exposing the cracks of his skin below. Beautiful, the patterns of those cracks in his skin showing up in light brown relief below the red, like a network of electrical circuits. Like contemporary art on his own body. Life, so near he could touch it.

Up in the trees, the grackles and ravens were strangely quiet, as if waiting and witnessing. Chickens scratched nearby in the bushes. He sat and breathed with them now, holding their winged images in his mind as they shifted on the branches and scratched intently in the hard-packed earth, as they stretched their wings and breathed. It was an extraordinary combination of fowl, and as he sat and meditated on them, Jefferson began to feel some recognition. There were the three chicks hopping on the walkway, so clearly those little girls from the Toyota. There was the peacock who had so obviously grown up in New Orleans. The three ravens who were so obviously from New York City and Chattanooga and Hollidaysburg. There was the great horned owl, its feathers just visible from its perch way up high in the pine tree; that owl was from Albuquerque, Jefferson just knew it. He saw each face and remembered each hometown, although the names escaped him. It made perfect and beautiful sense that each of these had transformed and was now traveling the earth as a bird, and Jefferson found them a comfort as he sat in the plaza. For he was not alone, not in his current thoughts, not in his memories of loss, not in his recognition of the harsh beauty of life all around him.

As his gaze blurred in one direction on the sight of the dried blood, out of the other periphery he watched the approach of an old man under a tired straw hat, sweeping the stone walkway of the plaza.

The old man was intent on his job, he could tell; he might not see Jefferson sitting there on the ground under the lime tree. It seemed un-Mexican, this sitting on the bare ground, something in addition to his poor Spanish that announced his foreignness. But Jefferson stayed there in his spot and let the old man sweep. The sun was warm on his face, and the day, though reminding him of blood, seemed uncomplicated. He felt taxed by nothing, neither nausea nor regret, and he gave thanks for the mosquito and the birds and his pup, and he breathed.

When the old man reached the tips of Jefferson's shoes with his broom, he looked into Jefferson's face and smiled and spoke. "Buenos tardes, señor. Cómo está?"

Jefferson smiled and replied, "Hola," looking into the man's eyes.

The old man spoke again—"Bueno. Gracias, señor"—in a high-pitched singsong that transported Jefferson's mind back to that open space by the sad trees, that old man and his goats, his high-pitched repetitive pleas, which RT had not heeded.

There was a moment's pause, and then everything around Jefferson shifted. A streak of light struck his eyes, transforming the plaza into a sunbaked desert, and suddenly the old man's voice had crossed boundaries of time and space. Jefferson peered back into the old man's eyes, trying to decide if this miracle could really be true.

"You're alive!" Jefferson said, his mind leaping toward the marvelous possibility before he realized the absurdity of his wish that it be so. He looked back up through the dancing sunlight and smiled the biggest smile he could manage at the old man. He smiled so hard it hurt.

"Sí, sí bueno," the old man was saying, and then, as if to prove it, he propped his broom against a bush and bent low to show Jefferson a sore on the top of his left hand, possibly a burn, beginning to scab. The scab was a marvelous shade of deep purple, with flecks of rust scattered on the edges, where it was beginning to crust. Radiating out from it was an array of sunspots and veins, a complex pattern of purples and rusts and plum reds on top of his rich brown wrinkled skin.

"Horrible," the old man said, shaking his head and then beginning to speak quickly, telling Jefferson what seemed to be the story of how his hand had been injured.

A small group of sparrows was hopping around his feet, and up in the trees the ravens were beginning to croak to each other. As the old man talked on, Jefferson's eyes were open and his mind began to make connections and he realized it was all possible, and that he was not the only one being given a new chance to live in the highlands of central Mexico.

"I can't believe you're alive!" he said again to the old man, shaking his head before going on to touch the man's scab and to compliment him on the beauty of his hands and the great good fortune that he was healing so well. "You are a strong man," he said in English before spending the next several minutes trying to explain in mixed Spanish and English what he meant, using the words *las manos* and *guapo* and *muy* and *artístico* while he motioned back and forth between the man's hands and the stone walkway, the broom, the lime trees and the bushes, and then, with a much wider arc of his arms, to the sandy hard-packed country beyond the great sea where he believed the two of them had last crossed paths, trying so hard to explain. But the old guy just stared blankly at Jefferson and then down at his own hands. It seemed that the old man, if indeed he had grasped any of Jefferson's words, thought that he was merely complimenting his skin or the structure of his bones. It was possible that he had not recognized Jefferson—that was understandable, given how scared he must have been that day. And besides, Jefferson knew he himself had not been a hero to be remembered that day by the sad trees.

The old man moved back to his broom, and Jefferson's mind searched for the right line, a line he could recite to honor this moment with the old man under the lime trees, the birds looking on. It did not take him long to think of the perfect line, one he'd sung many times over a period of several long weeks in Iraq, one he would never forget. Jefferson kneeled down on the gravel walkway and began reciting and then singsonging in the old man's direction, hoping that he would somehow understand how sorry Jefferson was, how happy Jefferson was to see his wound healing. With his hand on top of his backpack where he could feel the outline of the book, Jefferson sang in what he thought of as a blues voice, raspy and slow and full of soul.

Oh, I do not understand.

No, I do not understand.

How I could go to war over something I could not touch with my hands?

Something I could not touch with my hands.

My hands.

Las manos.

Las manos.

He stayed in that spot until the late-afternoon light became dappled on the walkway, the *suuvwp, suuvwp, suuvwp* of the old man's broom only a memory as the cooler air of the evening rushed in. The man had not slowed his work or even turned around when Jefferson began chanting, but later, before leaving the plaza, he'd doubled back to the place where Jefferson sat and once again swept the section of walkway near his feet. Then he had stopped sweeping for a moment and, looking hard at Jefferson, as if acknowledging an extraordinary communication, smiled and nodded. He began to point at various places around the plaza, speaking dramatically, as if telling Jefferson about the plaza and various things that had happened there. As if he had not told a story for many years. As if something had inspired him, like Jefferson, to overcome his shyness. He pointed toward the large climbing rosebush, one whose dried blooms looked as if they'd once been yellow. Perhaps the old man's grandfather had planted that rose, Jefferson thought, or perhaps forty years ago the old man now before him had asked his sweetheart to marry him under its falling petals. Perhaps the old man was explaining what a lovely woman she had been to him, all these many years. Eventually the old man had finished his story. "Hasta luego," he said, and Jefferson remembered the expression from ninth-grade Spanish. *Until we meet again.* It was a good thing to say to another human being. Jefferson was going to remember that saying, in both Spanish and in English, and he was going to add it to his list of things to begin saying to other human beings when the time was right. *Hasta luego. Until we meet again.*

Eventually the old man packed up his broom and his dustpan and left the plaza, walking eastward. Jefferson watched him until the shadows of the coming dusk and the bend in the road made it impossible to see him anymore.

29

THE PLAZA WAS swimming with dogs and the hour was late and Jefferson needed a shower. Everyone, it seemed, had gone to bed except for the unseen people enjoying music and drinks in the bar at the end of the street, where Christmas lights shone out into the night. But now a pack of hounds and labs and sweet scruffy mutts had begun to congregate around Jefferson's bench, as if they'd all gotten some message. The pack seemed at first interested in Remedios, who, thankfully, was a social beast and so leaped to the ground and began a good-natured rough-and-tumble with some of the dogs. But after a few minutes of this most of them returned to Jefferson, clearly in search of food. He counted seven dogs in addition to his own.

He'd gone on to San Luis Potosí in the dark of night, his misgivings eventually overcome by his need to move on. It was late by the time he left, since he'd had a bit of trouble finding Remedios and getting her in the cart. Once he'd cornered her on a far end of the plaza under a café table, he'd spoken to her as if she were his child, a beautiful being for whom he was responsible, and who because of her young age did not always know what was best for her. It would be fun to drive on to San Luis Potosí, he'd reasoned; there would be more playmates there for her; she would enjoy new adventures.

187

And here they were, these seven dogs proving him true, politely taking the few scraps of a sandwich he had to give them, sharing these as he'd never before seen dogs do, and then running laps around the plaza with Remedios, jumping from benches and rolling on the hard-packed earth and barking greetings and playful taunts.

"Shhh," Jefferson said to them, "not so loud." He didn't want to wake the town.

As the dogs played on, Jefferson thought of his warm bed, the pink-tiled bathroom with its warm water, and for a moment he wished for home. It was cold, and he didn't want to spend the night outside again.

Just then, he saw a dog—a new dog, the eighth—up the street, approaching the plaza from the direction of the bar in an off-kilter hop. As the dog approached, Jefferson could see that it was a hound—mostly basset, he guessed, going by its long, loppy ears—and that it had only three legs. On its way toward Jefferson, the dog stopped momentarily to sniff a patch of dirt and then to watch at a distance the play of the other dogs, diversionary techniques that did not fool Jefferson. Knowing that the dog was a hound, knowing that it was maimed, knowing how the magic of the universe worked when his eyes were open, Jefferson had no doubt that the dog was headed his way, that it had spotted him and smelled him and known him from afar. He knew that the dog was pacing himself on an inevitable trajectory that must end at Jefferson's feet.

Though Jefferson had guessed that Remedios contained a trace of hound in her blood, at the shelter he'd purposefully avoided any of the dogs that seemed predominantly hound. He had too many traumatic memories when it came to that breed. Like scorpions and the sight of his peers staring off into the distance with scared, sad eyes, the sight of a hound awoke in him an instant melancholy. And that was nothing compared to the feeling that washed over Jefferson when he heard a distant baying carried on the wind at night. "Why, oh why?"

he muttered aloud to himself as he watched the hound's sure approach—it was now just fifteen feet away, and closing in—couldn't war just be a bad dream? Why couldn't it be real, the apparatus to make a man forget his bad memories?

It had happened the day he backed over the hound dog in the Humvee. It had been fresh in his mind when he'd heard the poor dog scream. At the time Jefferson's heart was so heavy that he could hardly register any additional losses, but nonetheless he had put his head against the steering wheel and sobbed when he realized what had happened to the dog.

Jefferson must have erased some of the details from his mind; he could not remember why he'd been walking on that deserted Iraqi village street on that particular day. It was a Thursday afternoon, late in 2008. If he tried to think about it, he knew he must have been scared. Lost, maybe? He thought it had happened in a town far from Anaconda, though he had no idea why he'd been there. And why had he been alone? He was never supposed to be alone—he knew that. He was certain his heart had been racing, his hands shaking. He could see now the hard lines of sunlight slicing through the narrow gaps between buildings, buildings two and three and four stories tall. It was a city, then, somewhere in that vast hard-packed desert, a place he'd never been before. He didn't know why he'd been there at all, why he'd been alone.

He remembered a sudden screeching of tires and car metal, a sudden confluence of screaming and radio signals, breaking into his feeling of being all alone in a distant land. Up ahead his way was blocked by cars, several rough-looking men standing next to them, talking into cell phones, so he'd turned down a side street, hoping for help. He began to run.

His hands shook with the sudden realization that he had a pistol in his belt, that he was prepared if it came to that. The street was narrow, too narrow for the sun to reach it now, and he was alone and scared and running. Behind him, he thought he heard cars closing in, trapping him in that narrow passage, and his heart pounded. He hoped it was all a dream, that he would soon wake, but the men were running after him and he was sure he had been left in this walled city and then he turned up yet another narrow alley, one final attempt to get away, and there was the guy three feet in front of him, screaming at him—he had a gun, he would shoot. But Jefferson was ready, his hands shaking in their preparations, waiting to do the thing he did not want to do. And the guy was screaming and Jefferson was alone and scared, and so he pulled the trigger. A quick movement that changed his life.

Not much later Jefferson had learned that the guy, only a kid, just seventeen years old, had been on his way home with groceries for his mother. Jefferson had fallen in a heap on top of the boy's body, next to the boy's shrieking mother, and he had not heard anything the other members of his unit were telling him about where they'd been and why he'd found himself all alone and scared and running. Instead he had lain with the boy and his mother, singing words he knew to be true of himself, words that had been inspired by Gabriel and had made him wonder *why* more than ever.

War has made me a killer of good people.
A killer of good people.
Worse than the worst.
Worse than the worst.

The boy had died immediately, though the hound had not. Its death was a slow march to an end that was inevitable as soon the heavy tires and steel rolled over its bony body. It chose as a final resting place a spot somewhere within earshot of Jefferson's bed, and so he had no choice but to listen to each of its solitary yelps toward death.

After that, Jefferson hadn't been able to face the idea of traveling home, even though he'd been due a visit, though he'd e-mailed Esco that he'd be taking leave soon. The killing of the boy and the killing of the hound all in one day had killed too much within him. Going home would not be possible.

Seeing this Mexican hound had brought all that loss back, but now, even as he registered the pain, Jefferson also glimpsed some degree of hope. For this inspired creature, with its glistening sable coat and its ears that nearly swept the ground, was using its three good legs in a perfectly synchronized motion—a triumphant motion it seemed to Jefferson— as he approached. This hound had prevailed over its fate, and for that, Jefferson was thankful. Maybe, he thought, what he needed was not an apparatus to make him forget his bad memories, precisely, but rather one that could shift the past's dark horrors into memories of perseverance and light. This was the fiction he needed to be real.

Jefferson sat for he knew not how long, rubbing the hound's ears and reciting lines to it and to the other dogs on the plaza. Finally, a woman came out into the street from a house down the way, wearing a robe and calling out for the hound. When she saw Jefferson and asked what he was doing outside so late, and discovered that he planned to sleep on the bench, she insisted that he and the pup come home and sleep on her couch, and in the morning he could have a warm shower and breakfast.

WHAT HAPPENED THAT day in the forest between Dolores Hidalgo and San Miguel de Allende? Like a dream, it began and ended on a road he never traveled again, with people who never again crossed his path. He was almost one hundred percent sure it had been real.

The incident began with a slim young girl whose magnetic eyes made it impossible for Jefferson to say no. He had to follow her.

He had stopped alongside the two-lane highway. A stretch of broad hills sloped away easily, clothed with shin-high grass punctuated here and there by the most interesting trees. He'd watched the trees pass by in his periphery for several miles before deciding to stop and take a closer look. Later he'd looked them up—Mexican piñons, a species related to the piñons in northern New Mexico, slow-growing conifers with sap-heavy bark, each with a distinct and forlorn asymmetry of twisted arms and knotted stubs. They looked out of place on the Mexican hillside, and he imagined them as exiles from the Holy Land. He'd never been to Palestine, but he'd been close enough, and these trees breathed a Middle Eastern breath to him.

On that day one particular piñon twenty feet off the road inspired him to stop and park. He walked the short distance uphill and pressed his palms against its gnarled trunk, breathing in the resinous scent which reminded him of jasmine tea. Raising his chin, he studied the branches—a few of them seemed to beg for pruning, but he resisted their call—and their geometric dissections of the sky. And then he decided to climb. His hands grasping the lowest branches, he'd placed his left foot in a natural foothold, gripped, and had pulled himself up when he felt a sharp tug on the back of his shirt and a small but imperious voice.

"Ayúdeme!"

Help me. Jefferson's mind traveled back to Spanish class, to a word he'd had no need to remember until that moment. He turned to find a slight girl standing just below him. She wore a thin cotton shift that fell loosely over her shoulders to her knobby knees. On her feet, a pair of rubber clogs, much too large.

"Por favor, mister. Ayúdeme!"

She motioned frantically, her breath short and shallow. "Pronto! Pronto!" she gasped and then turned, running up the hillside through the tall grass toward denser forest. Jefferson watched her run, the pup alongside her, unsure what to do. Should he follow? He felt the tug of the child's innocence. Could he leave the motorbike on the side of the road?

At the end of twenty yards she stopped and turned to see Jefferson still standing beside the tree. Even at that distance the child's brown eyes commanded him. What was he waiting for? She flapped her arms and jumped up and down, yelling, "Pronto! Pronto! Pronto!" And as she did so, Remedios yipped a similar injunction. *Hurry! Hurry! Hurry!*

After pulling the motorbike behind a bush, where he left it with a silent prayer that it would be there when he returned, Jefferson sprinted up the hill after the child and the pup, who by that time were far ahead, across the open hillside and running into the denser, flatter pine forest. In less than five minutes they'd come to a clearing, low grasses surrounded by mixed pines and cedars. The place had the feeling of a hollow, though it was not clear if the land was actually lower there or if the taller trees made it seem as if it were.

A hundred yards before they arrived at their destination Jefferson could hear low groans of pain, and dread grew within him. He had heard the sound of pain so many times in the war zone, he didn't know if he could face that sound—and the suffering person who inevitably came with it—again. A constable of ravens sat overhead in the tallest of the surrounding pines, and these gave him some comfort. Esco had always told him that people who feared ravens simply did not understand the species.

All he knew to expect was the damage done by gunfire or explosion, but what he came upon instead was the girl's mother in the midst of childbirth.

The woman lay on a quilt atop a bed of pine needles. Draped on low branches hung a few articles of clothing—a few small dresses that must have been the child's and a few larger ones, obviously the woman's. Two mugs, a saucepan, and two spoons perched on a circle of rocks around the charred remains of a campfire. So this was their home. Scattered around the base of the tree were a vinyl suitcase, a plastic doll dressed in denim, some blankets, and one large chopping knife on a wooden block.

The child took her place next to her mother, bent down, and whispered something into her ear. Then she stared with scared eyes at Jefferson. The woman had paused between two waves of pain, and Jefferson leaned down to try to talk to her.

"Are you okay? Do you need help?" he said, feeling a little stupid; it was plain that the child would not have come running if all was well. He also imagined that the woman spoke no English.

"Por favor," the child said, the only thing she knew to say as she held her mother's hand.

"I don't know what to do," Jefferson said, feeling his breath fall away. "I'm not a doctor—I have no idea what to do."

The woman arched backward with a terrifying scream that sent the girl into a fit of panicky babbling and tears. Once her pain had eased, Jefferson knelt down beside the two. He touched the mother's arm and then that of the girl. "I don't know what to do," he repeated, shaking his head, but then, seeing the fear in the woman's eyes, he changed his tone. "It's gonna be okay, okay? It's okay—I'll do my best, okay?"

He knew that though the woman's cries came from her mouth, and though her bulging belly was the location of her baby, neither of these were where the action was about to take place. He knew that if he was going to help this woman deliver this baby, he was going to have to kneel between her legs. His eyes were going to have to be wide open, his hands ready to touch and calm and cajole and hold. There was no time to ponder as the young girl begged him with her eyes and the woman clutched his wrists and the unseen baby made its inevitable way nearer to them all in the quiet hollow of that solitary wood.

He spoke to them to calm himself, to organize his thoughts in a time of stress, even though he knew they could not understand his words.

"I'm just going to move down here and see what I can see," he said, sliding between the woman's legs and lifting the blanket that covered her. At first he saw all the expected sights: knees, feet, skin. But when he forced his eyes down to below the woman's belly, he was momentarily confused.

"Wow. Okay. I think I can see the baby's head," he said. "That must be what that is—WOW," he said again, trying to appear calm, trying to mask his bewilderment. It was too much to ask of a young man with very little experience with women, to help deliver a baby. For an odd moment Jefferson tried to think if ever in his wildest dreams he had imagined this contortion of hips and vagina and vulva and anus. And there was definitely a small, wet head jammed in, like a cork, between all those lips and folds and wrinkles. He thought again that really, he was not the man for this job.

The young girl was at his side now, kneeling down with him and grasping her mother's ankles. The mother spoke a few quick words to her daughter and then looked at Jefferson again with pleading eyes, as if to remind him that this life is for the living. It did not matter what he had done or not done prior to this moment. This right here, this now, was all that mattered. A scattered line came to him in the moment, one that he could not place, and he began to chant it now as the woman set her jaw and attempted to gain purchase in the task at hand.

The best moments of life, she thirsted for those.
The best moments of life, she thirsted for those.
The best moments of life, she thirsted for those.

He chanted the line over and over as he rubbed the woman's stomach and patted the young girl on the head. He chanted because he did not know what else to do, because life had caught him unprepared. His need to make it to Mexico City, his memory of all those killed nearby in combat, all those lost limbs and all that blood, coagulated with the longtime sorrow of all he'd never had, and still, the baby made its way toward the light and air and the touch of its own mother's skin.

He tried to pray, but he could not. It had been so long since he had spoken directly to God. He tried to remember scenes from TV shows and movies dealing with childbirth, but nothing he could recall was helpful. The woman screamed and thrashed her knees from side to side, and there seemed nothing to do but hold her. He closed his eyes.

The child screamed something he interpreted as "Baby's coming!" and he nodded, believing it must be true. He repeated the words—*Baby's coming!*—to the woman, and she nodded between screams and took a series of deep breaths, as if preparing for something really big. The child squeezed his wrists, and the woman closed her eyes and groaned in a new deep tone, a sound Jefferson would have guessed meant death rather than life. He did his best to separate himself from the dark pain of her voice and her eyes, and he focused instead on that little wet head emerging. It popped out a bit more—he could see a forehead and the beginnings of ears—and then popped back inside. Then there was a pause as the woman caught her breath. It seemed the bursts of pain were separated by about twenty seconds. The next screams brought the baby's head completely out, half its purple neck too, and the child placed her small hands under the baby's head and screamed in delight to her agonized mother. The next scream and push brought the first shoulder and Jefferson reached in and held the baby, waiting for what seemed like the certain end. With a final whoosh the second shoulder and all the rest of him— because he was a boy!—poured forth from the woman and into Jefferson's arms.

Almost as soon as the heavenly light had begun to soften, the young girl stood at Jefferson's side with the big kitchen knife, gesturing to indicate that she would hold the baby and the cord if he would cut it, and so he did. Blood and wetness glistened upon every surface, on his fingers and hands and wrists and forearms and in his hair. There was a swath of blood across the thigh of his blue jeans—he noticed this later—but in the moment he was aware of a warm quiet and of a licorice scent and of the young girl's humming. He swaddled the baby in a towel, and handed him to his mother, whose face had been transformed, after the savage screaming of moments earlier, into that of a dewy damsel. She could not have been more than twenty-three.

The infant suckled, and the young girl arranged dandelions on her mother's bedsheets, and the woman smiled and then dozed, smiled and then dozed. All seemed well and good. Motes of light sifted through the leaves of the surrounding trees, abiding spirits to christen the moment. For indeed there was a tangible holiness in that clearing beneath the pines, and he recognized it, a feeling he had sometimes had among the newly dead. Whether it was the presence of God or of some other heavenly being, he could not say; he did not know how or what to call it, but the presence was unmistakable, and it was good.

By some mystery of nature or perhaps fate, mother and child and babe were healthy and whole. The infant's skin glowed a vibrant red, and when he was not cooing like a baby rabbit at his mother's breast, his lungs spewed the loud fury of hot, lively life.

Jefferson sat with his back against a tall sturdy pine, his mind brimming. He fought with his brain, and tried to stop all the thinking. He could not explain the reason for his deep, steady breath, but he guessed it was good for him, this steadiness. He had not known it would be like this, helping to deliver a baby. Was that what he'd done? Had he helped deliver a baby? The process had had a natural momentum and seemed not to have required his help, but nonetheless, he had followed the call of the young girl into the woods, he had knelt between the legs of the shrieking woman, and with his own two hands Jefferson had welcomed the baby into the world. A host of heavenly beasts flew in abundant loops in the sky overhead, and the quiet was full of the music of the ages, while from the tops of the trees the ravens kept watch and waited and chanted silent blessings and prayers of thanksgiving. An easy breeze accompanied the night as it came upon them, full of the twinklings of distant galaxies and the mother moon.

The three passed the night easily, and in the morning Jefferson prepared to leave.

"Will you be okay?" he said to the woman, hoping his tone would convey some of his meaning. He touched her shoulder—he was close enough to see the perspiration above her lip—and then took several steps back to survey the scene. The young girl—yesterday's sentinel—slept in the crook of her mother's arm, and the babe suckled, and the woman smiled a weightless smile.

"I'm leaving, okay?" he said. "Adiós?"

She nodded.

To turn and walk out of the hollow tore at Jefferson's heart, but he did it anyway, never looking back as he walked down the hill, the pup at this side, past the large piñon he'd been about to climb when the child had first found him. He pulled the motorbike up from the hard ground and walked it back down to the two-lane highway. Remedios leaped into her basket, and he pulled out onto the road, heading southeast for the outskirts of San Miguel, and beyond, toward Querétaro.

THE BIKE RACED along under Jefferson, carrying him onward
as his mind replayed the birthing in the hollow. Those forty
minutes had been intense, but something else was haunting
him now. He felt he'd experienced that same intensity before;
it was as if he'd seen those deafening rays of light and heard
those blinding screams in another lifetime. Jefferson had never
thought about it before, and even now, as he did so for the first
time, he told himself it was impossible.

Throughout his twenty-three years, similar flashes of
memory had occasionally lit up Jefferson's mind with wonder,
but he had never been able to identify their source. When
he was very young, they might have been set off by bright
sunlight shining directly into his eyes, or by too much sugar,
as his grandmother maintained. Later, after he'd been intro-
duced to the concept, Jefferson thought it might be the Holy
Spirit spreading comfort and insight. But now that he'd helped
a woman give birth, Jefferson wondered if this flash of memory might have originated in his very own birth. Could anyone
possibly remember his own birth?

Esco had told him a few stories, enough to prove that he'd
been born into the world just like every other baby. Much of
her banter about his mom he'd tried to ignore, however. Once

he reached fourth or fifth grade, when he emerged out of the haze of early childhood and had to face the fact that he did not have a mother's hand in which to place field-trip permission forms, Jefferson decided that the less he knew about her, the better. And his birth? He'd never actually thought about his birth.

Now he tried to remember enough of Esco's stories to begin to piece them all together. His mother had been sixteen years old, a sophomore at Santa Fe High. Her name was Faith. She'd stayed in school until her stomach gave her away, and then she'd dropped out, saying she was done with books anyway and that she refused to be part of what she called the Preggers Club, the ten or so other Santa Fe High student moms who that particular year had waddled around the high school, and eventually brought their new babies to the on-site day care. His grandmother hadn't known much about the boyfriend, Jefferson's dad. Only that he was Lakota, like Esco's husband, and that Faith had been crazy about him.

Once, when Jefferson had begun to think about his mother's choices, about the fact that she had chosen a life without him, he'd felt himself getting angry. Although he knew it wasn't Esco's fault, that Esco had not been the one to leave, he yelled at her anyway. "How could you have let her do that to me?" he yelled. "She left me! I was a tiny baby!"

"She was so young, Jefferson. Not a bad person." Then Esco gave him her I'm-serious look. "She couldn't face what she had done, but I tell myself she's out there somewhere, living a good life. And your father too. He must have been a good kid." Her voice trailed off then, and she looked away for several minutes, way out the window toward the Jemez. When she faced Jefferson again, she was composed. "Each of us comes into this world with challenges," she said, as if she were a trained therapist. "You should thank god she was smart enough to leave you behind with me as early as she did. Do you have any idea how lucky you are?"

OUT THERE

That was the first and last time Jefferson had raised the topic of his mother's personal merits. His perspective and that of his grandmother were too far apart, separated by too many circumstances. But he continued to think of his mother—Faith—just as anyone might. He wondered where she lived, whether she was in fact still alive at all, and which of her traits had *whooshed* with him through the birth canal and stuck to his very being. Was he a good reader because she had been a good reader? Was the 200 meters his best race because she had been a sprinter? Did she reject meat too? He thought about Esco long ago insisting that his mom had been a good person, and he wondered what specific examples she would give if asked.

Low hills pulsed alive around him as he rode on. On that day his mind spun with the fact—an irrefutable fact—that his own mother had been pregnant with him for nine whole months, carrying him around in her young little belly until it was time to push him out between her legs and into the big, bright world. He'd traveled through the *whoosh* just as that tiny baby boy in the hollow had, the nearness of life delighting his own vivid face, his wide-open eyes, his strong, firm fists. And just like the woman in the hollow, Jefferson's own mother had experienced the flash as he had nestled into her arms and suckled at her breast that very first time. He just knew it. It had been late in the night on November 18, 1986, and there must have been peace and love and thanksgiving, if only for a little while.

SHE'D GIVEN HIM a lot of money, and she'd hugged him, and he guessed all that meant she was probably thinking about him, sending him good vibes. He wished he could tell her about the twins and the bergamot woman—surviving that close call with those bandits. Boy, she'd have loved those stories, but he didn't have a phone, so he'd have to wait until he got back home. Jefferson didn't think he was going to tell Dr. Monika, or anyone else for that matter, about the baby being born in the hollow, though. Helping that little boy come into the world, fill his lungs up that first time—that was his own little miracle.

33

IN QUERÉTARO, AS Jefferson read the words LA BIBLIOTECA PÚBLICA GÓMEZ MORIN on the large contemporary building on Avenida Constituyentes, a wry smile spread across his face. Here he was, standing exactly where he needed to be.

The building pulsed in front of him on that sixth afternoon like an answer. He'd had no plan to end up there, no map, and in truth he could not remember the last time he'd stepped inside a public library, though it must have been sometime in sixth grade. He did not count the library at Santa Fe High, which he had been permitted to visit only once, his junior year, to complete a research report on Toni Morrison, but where students were not allowed to loiter during lunchtime or after school. As a child he had walked to the La Farge branch of the Santa Fe Public Library most Saturday mornings with Esco, but that had ended after elementary school, he thought. His grandmother still checked out a pile of books every week. Jefferson couldn't say why he had stopped going.

Jefferson leashed Remedios to the motorbike, crossed the street, climbed the several steps, and pulled on the heavy brass door handle.

Inside, he stood on the ground floor, looking up and around at the librarians ahead, at all the stacks of all the books. Stacks disappearing around corners. Stairwells suggesting more, both upstairs and down.

What was the question the library was answering?

Five steps nearer to the circulation desk, he gave what he thought was a clever nod to one of the librarians, who seemed to be watching him suspiciously. Looking her way, Jefferson gave his sweatpants a tug, resisted the celebratory good-luck handstand he really wanted to do, and tried to read the map of the place. Everything was in Spanish.

The librarian was beautiful, a librarian created by a heavenly casting director, he thought. She wore it all so well: her half-glasses askew at the tip of her nose, her dry smirk, her muted short-sleeved cardigan. She was a perfect part of the whole that was making him feel something really good in that moment.

Jefferson smiled a true smile at her—a smile meant to be read as *Don't worry, I love libraries*—and went on through the foyer and to the left, into a large reading room.

Old dust and old paper and old wooden armchairs creaking under the weight of generations of readers, all of it inside four contemporary concrete walls. He couldn't believe how lucky he was to have found this place.

Later—he didn't know how much time had passed—Jefferson found himself on the second floor, roaming between two long floor-to-ceiling stacks. The air was both crisp and calm as he let down his traveling guard and began running his fingertips across the spines. So many words. So many ideas. Such good work. Such hope.

Who were all these good people who had written all these good books?

He told himself the feeling he was feeling was not nostalgia, that the scratchy sensation at the back of his throat was not emotion. He told himself that the sense of homecoming could not be real, because this was a place he'd never been before. And yet.

OUT THERE

From what Jefferson remembered, and what he'd been told, and the little research he'd conducted on the subject, reading had come easily to him in first grade at Kaune Elementary. He'd been encouraged by the fact that Esco had learned alongside him.

He remembered it being like a code game, deciphering those twenty-six symbols into sounds, those combinations of sounds into meanings. He'd thought for so long—in pre-kindergarten and kindergarten—that that thing adults did with papers and books, holding them out twelve inches from their noses and shifting their eyes from left to right and back again, was just an adult joke, like Santa Claus. But then he'd deciphered his first code—S A T, "sat." C A T, "cat." B A T, "bat."

Shazam. It was real. Not a joke at all. Jefferson remembered this as a singular moment of piercing light behind his eyes, a moment in which the great bird within him took flight, his wings pushing the heavy air down below him, his heart lifting to the sun.

He remembered none of the details after that, only the magic of stories and the way some of them lit a candle inside him. But according to the elementary-school report cards Esco kept under her bed in the Rubbermaid box, Jefferson had mastered all the codes and puzzles presented to him. He had progressed, so that by eighth grade he was given the Language Arts Award by his nice teacher Ms. Johnson, whose face he remembered as pink and glowing. At the time he had dreaded walking in front of the entire DeVargas Middle School student body at the end-of-year awards assembly to accept the certificate, and Esco had been too shy to ask if picture taking was allowed, so she stood off to the side of the bleachers, her Instamatic 300 tucked in her purse. So only the off-white certificate in the Rubbermaid box remained to prove that he'd been something special.

Later, among the more than two thousand other students at Santa Fe High, Jefferson had reveled in anonymity. How he'd loved watching all the swarms of young people, the soccer players and cheerleaders and football players, the gangs, the pregnant young mothers, the artsy ones carrying portfolios, the actors. Jefferson continued to learn, and he always did his assignments, but he tried to avoid any bright lights. Many years later, as an adult, Jefferson was sometimes asked by his friends how he'd ever managed in such a huge high school, with so many dropouts and drama. The question always surprised him. He had enjoyed Santa Fe High. He'd never been to the circus, but he knew lots of people paid money to go see the show, and he imagined that was something similar to his experience, merely showing up at his high school.

A few days after his nineteenth birthday, his duffel packed and waiting by the front door, his high school diploma stashed in the Rubbermaid box under Esco's bed, Jefferson had made a flash decision that might have been predicted if his entire history of reading were to be studied. He told Esco to wait just a second, that he had to go get one more thing, and he turned around in the hall, ran back to his bedroom, and grabbed his copy of *One Hundred Years of Solitude* from under his bed.

Wouldn't he need it?

Now, lost in a far corner of Spanish Literature, a rectangle of heavy oak tables with low lamps off to the right, Jefferson followed signs to the M's. *M* for *Márquez*. When he did not find it under *M*, he found his way to the G's. *G* for *García Márquez*. And there it was.

Cien años de soledad.

Four copies. All in Spanish.

He pulled one out from the shelf, sat down on the hard, cold floor with it, opened to the first page, and began reading—first mouthing the words silently, then in a whisper, and finally out loud for anyone nearby to witness.

Muchos años después, frente al pelotón de fusilamiento, el coronel Aureliano Buendía había de recordar aquella tarde remota en que su padre lo llevó a conocer el hielo.

OUT THERE

It was one of his favorite lines, and though his Spanish was terrible and he stumbled along as he read, Jefferson spoke the line many times as he slumped against the stacks that day.

Muchos años después . . .

Muchos años después . . . su padre lo llevó a conocer el hielo.

Finally he stopped, unzipped his backpack, retrieved his own copy of the novel, and opened to its first page. He read the English words he'd come to know so well, the ones that for some reason on that particular day in the comfort of the Querétaro public library made him feel like a genuine lover of books rather than just one kid with an odd obsession for one famous writer. Jefferson imagined Gabriel García Márquez sitting at his desk, coming up with the words, probably having already written much of the novel that was to follow, and knowing that these words were the right ones, the perfect ones, with which to begin his story.

Many years later, as he faced the firing squad, Colonel Aureliano Buendía was to remember that distant afternoon when his father took him to discover ice.

ESCO HAD ALWAYS loved bookstores, even though she'd only occasionally had the extra money to make a purchase. That was the beauty of the public library. Those memories . . . Walking to the library with Jefferson when he was in elementary school. The click-clack of his metal wagon over the hackberries. He'd gone through a period after middle school of reading less and playing more basketball at the park, but she'd kept on walking to the library alone, trying her best to be a role model and, more importantly, doing what she had come to love. Maybe some day when he was older he'd remember how much reading had meant to his old grandmother, and that knowledge would make a difference.

That was why she'd never bought a TV. That and the fact that she couldn't stand the idea of all that sitting around while the earth rotated on its axis. Good German Scots-Irish Mexican Americans did not sit around waiting for life to be revealed on a screen.

The summer after his junior year in high school, when Esco was certain Jefferson was out drinking beer with friends, but when he'd actually just been lying on the couch at Nigel's, watching reruns, he had not read a single book. Even after she'd checked out copies of *The Howling* and *Kujo* for him and placed them on his bed with a note that read STEPHEN KING WILL ROCK YOUR WORLD!! That was also the year that he stopped going out with her anywhere. When he was home, he was in his room with the door closed, even taking his plate of food in there, muttering under his breath whenever she asked him to help unload the groceries or water the tomato plants in the back. He'd continued with the pruning, however. He'd always loved making the bushes into pretty shapes, sort of like their own botanical garden.

While Jefferson was away at war, Esco had sometimes visited one or the other of the two remaining local bookstores in town, just to feel closer to him; there were young people in those places, people who seemed to be home from college or doing their best to find healthy entertainment in the small town. Esco alternated between the cozy bookstore on the edge of the ritzy neighborhood and the larger downtown one, housed in an old brick mercantile with wood floors and large windows. Sometimes she bought a classic she'd always meant to read—*The Custom of the Country, The Portrait of a Lady, The Brothers Karamazov*—even though she knew it made more sense to borrow these books from the library. Once she'd cut out a review of a book about the Scots-Irish and their role in building America. She'd gone right out and bought that one and read it, no stopping, late at night until she was done, suddenly feeling elated about her own heritage, about which she'd previously known so little. Aside from what she knew of her father as a hard worker, she'd never really thought much about what it meant to be Scots-Irish, whereas she'd seen firsthand the real connection of her husband to his people's language and music, to their trials and celebrations. She guessed it had been one of the intangible reasons she'd fallen in love with him.

But who knew why her grandson had gone away to be a soldier? Though she'd hated that decision, she had not told him so, letting him make his own choice. She'd learned from being a mother of two daughters—learned the hard way—that telling a teenage child what to do and what not to do would never work. As the grandmother, Esco tried to raise Jefferson to strength and independence by letting him go out into the world, letting him try, letting him fail. By opening the door when he came back home.

But Jefferson had come back home from war only to leave again on some cockamamie motorcycle trip. She'd been closer than ever to telling Jefferson exactly how stupid she thought his plan was—she'd been less than a day away from spilling her torrent of warnings and admonitions—when he'd explained the details. He'd drive Nigel's Kawasaki down to Mexico City to find Gabriel García Márquez. His hero. The man who had saved his life.

On the surface, Esco expressed a somber tentativeness about Jefferson's decision to leave home again; she fretted and whined to her daughter, Linda, and to Nigel, about the fact that Jefferson knew nothing about motorcycles and nothing about Mexico and very little about highway maps; she endeavored to burn a never-ending series of orange candles on the kitchen table until Jefferson returned safely once again; she gazed in a southerly direction each evening at dusk, offering a prayer of safekeeping. But inside, every deep and ancient part of her said, *Yes*, and she began to experience feelings of wonder and delight at her grandson's decision to find the famous writer. To be so brave. To have such hope. This grandson of hers, if he made it back alive, he would do good things in the world.

When Jefferson had outlined his plan in casual tones as they sat on the back stoop, watching the sunset, Esco had concealed her surprise. He'd begun by talking about a book that had become incredibly important to him, a book, he finally admitted, that had saved his life. Esco had followed his story without a pause. The concept of a book saving one's life was not new to her. She'd had the experience several times, though never on an actual battlefield.

But what was the book? she wondered. Who was the writer? She asked her grandson, trying to predict even as he paused and spoke the words. *Catcher in the Rye? A Separate Peace?*

But then he had told her, "It's Gabriel García Márquez, Esco. *One Hundred Years of Solitude?*"

Ah, she had thought. García Márquez. Of course.

MIDWAY THROUGH HIS second tour, Jefferson began
to feel an imperfect nostalgia for life. He was no longer sad.
He had been surprised so many times that he had become
a believer in the power of abrupt change. He knew without
any doubt that he was meant to live, and with that knowledge
came confidence, and this confidence changed his understanding of himself and the way he lived. GGM was the reason. Good fortune had followed the reading of his words, and
so Jefferson became an evangelist, proclaiming the gospel of
Gabriel García Márquez.

There were those who did not understand, those the text
could not reach, those Jefferson's behavior confused. They
said, on the one hand, that he had lost his mind, and on the
other that none of this ("this" being Jefferson's preaching from
a large book he had strapped to his chest) was funny anymore.
That someone should take that stupid book away from him
so he would stop with the crazy words, the proselytizing, the
rants. So he would focus on his job as a soldier. But there were
others, important others, who were touched. Jefferson believed
in these believers, and his daily work became reaching out to
them with the words he knew would save them, too.

JEFFERSON MADE HIS way south, each day eighty or ninety or a hundred miles closer to the great writer and his city. He and the pup and the bike settled into an easy rhythm, the measured clip of the tires on the pavement below and, up above, in his mind, an exuberant mulling of possibilities. And in every place—town or roadside market—in which he stopped long enough to listen, Jefferson heard tales of wonder and delight.

There was Ocampo, where he met a man who trained snakes to dance, traveling throughout the region with his troupe of venomous serpents, performing in dance clubs and community centers and the courtyards of wealthy families. There was San Miguel de Allende, where he knelt at the altar of the cathedral next to a yellow-toothed, nutmeg-scented woman who gave him a pair of woolen gloves she had knitted, and told him he had to visit the colorful nearby town of Guanajuato. So then there was the diversion to Guanajuato, where he met a man who claimed to have conversed with the devil (dressed in a red leotard and a top hat) while on the way to visit his dead mother in the cemetery of his childhood village. In Comonfort there was the threadbare Vietnam vet who had lived there since 1975, carving wooden toys and drinking black coffee. In Celaya there was Anjali, a woman who fed Jefferson tamarind chicken and claimed to have known his great-grandmother from an earlier lifetime, when she had been a southern belle in Mississippi.

And all the while and every day Jefferson imagined his meeting with Gabriel García Márquez: what Jefferson would say to him, how he would hold his tongue and try to act like neither a second-class citizen nor an intimidated fool. How Jefferson would do his best to remember all he had planned to say.

He guided the motorcycle up and down the curves of the highway, playing with the notions of gravity and the road. Maybe because God knew he'd had enough challenges, or perhaps just because of luck, the Kawasaki did not break down, and he didn't cross paths with any more bandits. At least half the strangers he met did not know anything about a war in Iraq, and a number had never heard of a writer named Gabriel García Márquez. Even when Jefferson said, "Gabo? No comprende, GABO?" often nothing but a layer of fog covered their eyes. Of those whose eyes lit up at the mention of García Márquez, most said Jefferson was crazy, insane, *el loco*, to drive all the way to Mexico City on a motorbike to try to see a famous old writer who was known to be headstrong and slightly paranoid in his old age and, beyond that, sick as a dog with cancer.

Given all of it together, he chose optimism and blind, intuitive, hope-filled faith. He'd skirted so many close encounters with death; who was to say he wouldn't be lucky on top of it? Who was to say he wasn't as lucky as Colonel Aureliano Buendía? What young man who had regularly skirted bullets and shrapnel from all sorts of explosive devices wouldn't believe in the miracle of a simple conversation with a famous old writer?

Over the course of those several days and many hours, driving those Mexican hills and plains, Jefferson whittled away at his hundred favorite quotes so that it was now a compact Forty-One All-Time Best Quotes, at which point it seemed impossible to eliminate a single one. This was the list from which he'd begun creating the collage. Much of the work he did in his head as he drove the Kawasaki, humming and chanting and singing pairs of phrases, moving this phrase in front and that phrase behind until he had what seemed perfect rhythm and syncopation and meaning. Whenever he took a break on the roadside—when he wasn't climbing trees or practicing a handstand or pruning a bush gone wild—he recorded his progress. Using extra paper he'd brought along and scissors and tape, Jefferson cut out the lines or portions of lines or words and rearranged them on the page.

Out there. This had to be the starting place, the opening phrase for the collage. It was followed by the line about all that rain—four years and eleven months and some days, in the novel—and that was followed in turn by *a radiant Wednesday.*

These three lines worked together in sequence, but he needed some words to connect them, some words to make them take on a larger shape. He did not want to call it poetry, or writing, even. In his mind his work was sculptural. He thought of it as trimming an overgrown branch here and encouraging extra growth there. He thought of it as creating in the tradition of carving wood and trimming trees and pruning bushes, only with paper and words. When he referred to it, it was as his collage, but really it was just a poem. He didn't call it a poem, though. He'd never really understood poetry, and had always thought that people who talked about this or that poet were just trying to sound smart.

Jefferson wanted to be able to share the collage with Gabriel once he got to his house, so he had to focus. It needed to be great. It needed to show how much he loved the writer's words and how they had saved so many lives.

On the sixth afternoon of his journey, as Jefferson rested under a broad-leafed bush just outside one of those little towns in the lineup to Mexico City, he worked with those three simple lines—the *out there* line, the one about all that rain, and the one about the radiant Wednesday. He worked to make the lines his own. He struggled with the part about how long the rain had lasted. He'd been in Iraq almost exactly three years, but the truth was, the rain had not stopped the day he came home. If he was honest, he would have to say it was still raining some days. How many years, months, and days was that?

He added a *had* and an *and then* and a *brought*, and he changed *crossed* to *crossing* and *went* to *running*, because each of these changes helped create the connections and the flow that made sense to him. Finally, he worked in the line that had haunted him for so long, the one about the trickle of blood running under the door and out the street, until he felt the unit of four lines worked together like a song.

And then he took a deep breath and connected those four lines with the few additional ones that followed, the ones he'd been working on since he'd left Santa Fe, and he tried it out loud for the first time. He thought of the singing of his collage as a gift to all the birds and the dogs and the donkeys and the children, for all the teachers and painters and contortionists and soldiers and bandits and seamstresses and herbalists and plumbers and massage therapists and tamale makers who might by some small miracle be listening at that moment— any good creature who might reach out and accept a few good words to lighten her load, or perhaps just to help her feel less lonely as she traveled through the day. It went like this:

Out there.

It rained for more than three years and many months and two days.

And then, a radiant Wednesday brought

A trickle of blood out under the door, crossing the living room, running out into the street.

My heart's memory stopped then, replaced by

A viscous and bitter substance,

Someone dead under the ground,

OUT THERE

Dark bedrooms, captured towns, a scorpion in the sheets.
The smell of dry blood,
The bandages of the wounded,
All of it a silent storm,
Me left,
Out there,
Dying of hunger and of love.

Admittedly, it ended on a dark note and was therefore not complete. He had lots of lines left to go. Ultimately, he would overwhelm the darkness with a blast of strong light.

37

JEFFERSON DIDN'T KNOW if this was a common experience for soldiers, but for him—despite his faith, despite his sense of a higher calling—there had come a day when he knew it was time to go home.

He was near the end of his second tour, and he'd been thinking of signing up for a third—life in Santa Fe seemed far away and intangible, and besides, he'd begun to think he'd found his calling as a bard of important words among the troops—not a healer or a minister, but a recognizer of helpful words. He had his book, and he knew to expect the unexpected, to expect miracles amidst the loss. Leaving all that seemed the riskiest move he could make, the one most likely to unmoor him.

He didn't remember the details of where or when, but he'd been there, and there had been lots of blood, and the brilliant screaming had quickly turned to a somber solitary moan. A heavy weight had preyed upon him, and the air turned quiet and slow and gently percussive. Above him a thin translucent presence hovered. He took this to be the barrier between life and death, which though suffocating was not scary. Jefferson had been this close to the barrier many times, and so far he'd suffered nothing more than a few scratches, and gained the insights of light and wonder.

On that day Jefferson had seen a human mass flying through the air at him, propelled by some unseen explosive force. The flying body of a soldier—as Jefferson learned later, a guy named Lincoln from Missouri—pinned Jefferson to the ground, thereby becoming a human shield for Jefferson against any further harm. Jefferson had remained under Lincoln's body as his last blood and breath rushed out.

And he had pulled together the words that seemed to be swirling about in the air, and he had sung,

One Friday at two in the afternoon the world lighted up with a crazed carmine sun, as thirsty as brick dust and almost as cool as water.

Jefferson had gasped to fill his lungs and tried to move his right foot out from under Lincoln's ankles, searching to gain purchase between the hard earth and the dying body, and he filled his lungs and bellowed in search of hope, singing,

A sun as thirsty as brick dust, and
almost as cool as water.
A sun as thirsty as brick dust, and
almost as cool as water.

Jefferson had chanted until the dying Lincoln breathed his last breath, and then he'd been able to slide himself out from under the body to find himself inside a small home of window-less concrete block. The dirt floor had become a great pulsing river of blood. He stood on his own two feet and allowed his eyes to adjust to the darkness, his nose identifying a horrific smoldering, his ears capturing the transition between somber moaning and a symphonic weeping dirge. And then he saw them. The bodies piled up, draped in tragic, grotesque beauty.

He hadn't needed to open the book's cover, even though he stroked it at his chest. He had known precisely the idea called for in that moment. He had sat back down in the dirt and the blood, all quiet, and nestled into the nest of bodies, his arms wrapped around his chest and his chin raised to whoever might be listening in the heavens above, and he had whispered the words inspired by the famous writer who knew exactly what it felt like to go on living in a war-torn world. *It rained for many years and many months and many days. It rained. It rained. It rained and rained and rained.*

Later he learned that in addition to Lincoln, five soldiers had died instantaneously in the blast, and five more had suffered injuries that eventually led them to a slower death or lost limbs. It took a long time for help to arrive, for rescue workers to discover Jefferson alive, though he had no memory of the drive back to Anaconda or what must have been a number of people carrying all those bodies. Later he thought of it as a blessing, all that waiting time, those hours he had hovered in solitude so near to the barrier between life and death.

It was dinnertime several days later when Jefferson took the opportunity to stand at the front of the dining hall and offer his tribute to all that loss in the concrete windowless home. Looking back on it, perhaps it had all been too fresh. Perhaps he should have waited a week or more. But he'd felt a need that evening to express his deepest emotions, the intimacy he'd felt with those young men as death approached and overtook them. He'd thought his fellow soldiers would benefit from just the right words, sung in the holiest of spirits.

He had decided upon a phrase he had recited many times to various members of the Tenth Mountain Division, one of his favorite adaptations. He stood up on the table nearest to him, clapped his hands, and began:

An explosion ricocheted across the land . . .

He was drawing out the one-syllable *land* into multiple syllables in what he felt was an inspired marriage of melody and verse when a soldier from across the room began yelling obscenities as he raced toward the front of the room, toward Jefferson.

It had taken Jefferson several moments to register the other soldier's voice, but when he finally stopped his singing, Jefferson saw the guy and heard him say, "Stop with the blood traveling over the curbs and avoiding the friggin' dining room tables'!"

It was a soldier who did not know Jefferson's name but who had observed him several times in the preceding months and who had studied *One Hundred Years of Solitude* in his freshman English class. The guy's best friend had been among those killed in the windowless concrete home.

He stood ten feet from Jefferson and screamed. "What is your problem, man? You think you're some kind of prophet? You think we want to hear about a pistol shot echoing through the house right now?"

Jefferson, still standing on the table, was trying to figure if the hostility he was sensing in the guy's voice was real. Was he angry? Was the guy going to break down and start crying any minute and apologize to Jefferson, explain that he was just stressed out and sad and confused? Jefferson felt certain the guy did not mean that stuff about pretending to be a prophet. Like Jefferson was crazy or something. The guy hadn't meant that.

Hadn't it been a help all this time, his reading of García Márquez's lifesaving words at just the right time? Hadn't the other guys realized that Jefferson wasn't much of a soldier, and that his role as a chanter, a singer, a *recognizer* of important words was so much more important? Jefferson had assumed the other soldiers knew this about him, that he was sort of like a chaplain but with a different Bible.

The angry soldier's words stung him from across the dining room, the closest thing to a mortal injury Jefferson had suffered. He lifted his eyes to stare into the guy's angry eyes before scanning the faces across the room, searching for at least one person who understood. Up and down the rows of faces he scanned, finding nothing. Nothing but fatigue and sadness and confusion and anger.

"Sit down, you lunatic!" someone else yelled from across the room.

"Yeah, shut the fuck up!" came another.

They might as well have been improvised explosive devices, stinging through the air, killing him anonymously from across the room. He stared at his feet, jumped down to the floor, and found his way out of the building. It was the last time he chanted in the war zone, though his lips continued to move incessantly and to breathe and whisper the words that Jefferson now knew were for his salvation alone.

Several weeks later, Jefferson flew home to New Mexico after a ten-day stopover at Fort Drum. It was mid-spring 2009. When he arrived in Albuquerque, there were Esco and Nigel, just beyond the security doors with a red balloon.

HE MADE HIS way along Autopista 57, through the small towns of Pedro Escobedo, Palmillas, and Tepeji del Río, the December sky snowless and tepid and gray. Midday, early December: he could feel the pulsing capital up ahead. Gabriel was out there somewhere, along with nineteen or twenty or twenty-one million others.

Once he reached Mexico City, Jefferson planned to make his way to the part of the city in which García Márquez was known to live. He did not have any idea what the neighborhood was called or where it was located within the masses, but he figured that Gabriel was famous, and that he would ask around, like they did in the movies. Where did the rich artistic people live? Where were the bookstores and coffee shops? If it was anything like Santa Fe, the rich artistic people with their bookstores and coffee shops lived right in the middle of things.

As for his larger fears, Jefferson began to acknowledge the truth: he was not the only young soldier who, having avoided death, had found himself pacing the planet for answers to unknown questions. Answers to the question *Why?* The fact that García Márquez had been moved to write those scenes in the novel about senseless executions—those firing squads for one man, as well as the massacre of thousands of innocents in the town square—proved to Jefferson that this was not the first time survivors had had to go on living. It also proved that the writer was Jefferson's dear friend—his hero and his friend, the man who had managed to reach out across the ocean and the sandy plains to scream at Jefferson to live despite the death all around him.

Jefferson stood up straight in the shaded ground under the poplar tree in the forlorn little plaza of Ciudad Satélite. He clipped a few unruly sprouts from the tree's otherwise smooth trunk, feeling he'd made a contribution to the overall feel of the place, and he practiced a handstand for several minutes as a tribute to all the good care he had received so far on his journey, for all the specific blessings and, yes, miracles he had been able to witness. It wasn't about luck, or being in the right place at the right time. What Jefferson knew was that he had somehow been equipped with just the right sort of eyes to see a miracle as it occurred. It was as if he had a special playback function in the back of his eye sockets, somewhere near his brain, that slowed real life down and helped him to see an overlay of very bright light on top of all the darkness. Sometimes the special eye function was joined by an added ear function, something that allowed him to hear a chorus of hallelujahs in his head. There were so many beautiful hallelujah songs in the world, and Jefferson had never heard one that failed to bring him to tears, so when his inner ears began to play hallelujah songs, he thought of it as a unique medley of all those songs that had come before. Usually he found himself humming wordless syllables until he got to the hallelujahs.

While upside down, he began to hear a beautiful melody and those simple syllables that went along with it, and he closed his eyes and sang.

Hallelujah!
Hallelujah!
Da, da-duh, da-duh, da-duh, da,
Da, da-duh.

Hallelujah.

Ha, lay.

Loo.

Yah!

Ha, lay, ay.

Looooo.

Yay!

Sometimes there were more words, but those were what came today.

He'd heard that song back behind his eye sockets many times in Iraq when something had exploded nearby. He knew not everyone had these special eye and ear functions, and he was thankful he did. They'd been important along the way, and they were still keeping him going, giving him sustenance. Jefferson wasn't saying they were permanent, but he hoped he'd continue to have them at least until he made it to Gabriel's house. They would help him have the courage to fulfill his larger plan, which he knew now was to say thank you.

Jefferson was in the process of inverting himself, getting his feet back on the ground and allowing the blood to level out within all the parts of his body, when he saw that a group of kids had joined him in the plaza around the base of the little tree. They appeared to range in age from ten to fourteen, and the youngest was missing several teeth and a leg.

"Where did you come from, guy?" the little one-legged one asked in clear English out of his dirty little mouth, his weight leaning into a single crutch.

"Yeah, guy. Where you from?" said another.

Because Jefferson had, in effect, just been musing on this question himself, he had a ready answer for the scruffy and truant and bright-eyed kids, who seemed more curious than threatening. Their question seemed, if nothing else, fair. Here he was, standing in their territory, considering their great capital city.

Who was he and where had he come from?

"Out there," Jefferson said then, and allowed his eyes

and arms to travel in a broad arc, indicating the whole of the universe. "I've come . . . from . . . out there." He repeated it because it was true, and in the moment he felt the weight of his young audience. He was returning from his time as a soldier out in the world. It was less important that he had been a member of a particular army on soil known as Iraq, and more important that he'd journeyed to the birthplace of human civilization and witnessed great loss. Much like Colonel Aureliano Buendía, who had left home for many years, Jefferson was a man trying to find his way back. Trying to find his way back to the world as he had known it before war.

Out there was where he'd been.

The kids shuffled a bit in their dirty shoes and scanned him from his black hair down to his beaded high-tops. The answer did not satisfy them, it seemed, and with their eyes they tried to ascertain more.

"Are you an American?" an older boy on a purple bike asked. And then, continuing as if he already knew the answer, "Are you a sucky American or a nice one?"

Jefferson laughed at the fairness of this question and at its humor. It traveled through his ears to his throat and down beyond his chest, where it burrowed into his rib cage and waited, musing and festering and insisting on a response.

A few quiet minutes passed as Jefferson stared southward toward Mexico City, dreaming of all that still lay ahead. The daydream gave him the voice and courage to say the words that followed, the best answer he could muster for these kids, the answer he believed was as close to the truth as any he could imagine.

"I am Jefferson Long Soldier, and I am doing my best to be a good American."

AS HE FLEW back home across the Atlantic, Jefferson had known it was the end for him, even though the war soldiered on. There would be no third tour. He had not been home in three and a half years, so long in such foreignness that he could not imagine his grandmother's face. He remembered that his cousin was very large, with a good smile and an infectious laugh, but he couldn't remember how Nigel spent his time. He was pretty sure his cousin didn't have a job.

In the bulbous clouds surrounding the plane, Jefferson had tried to see if the rain hitting the wings and thickening in the sky was in fact a rain of yellow flowers, the welcome-home carpet that Jefferson half expected to accompany soldiers everywhere as they returned from war. For the soldiers in García Márquez's world, the yellow flowers had followed the conclusion of twenty years of war, creating a carpet so thick that it had to be cleared with shovels and rakes. And though something told Jefferson there would be no yellow flowers on the ground in Santa Fe, still he looked for them out the window. He could hear that beautiful hallelujah song playing in his head, and the shafts of light through the dark clouds were particularly bright, like from movie camera lights. Colonel Aureliano Buendía had deserved a light-filled, flower-drowned sort of homecoming. He had, after all, devoted almost a quarter century to his cause, whereas soldiers like Jefferson had only missed a few years of what would have been college or a first real job. Maybe it was fair. There was the miraculous thing with his eyes and ears, and if he had to choose, he wouldn't have traded that gift for flowers.

He had closed his eyes as the plane cruised on, 33,000 feet above the black water, trying to dream of the young man he guessed he was supposed to be, now that he was going home. He squeezed his eyelids tight and tried to think of a simple list of qualities about himself. The effort was immediately unsuccessful. He needed to recall the outline of his own face and the shape and color of his own eyes, Jefferson decided, before he could think about internal things. He was fairly certain he had a warm smile, like Esco's, but were his eyes blue or brown?

HE RODE ALL night through the city's sprawl, on toward the core. The going was slow, for there was so much humanity to see, and he stopped a few times to rest, to drink some water, to witness the life of a stranger. Curious and full of questions he found himself, only some of them having to do with his search for GGM.

Have you ever been a soldier?
What is your mother like? Do you know your father?
What's your idea of a miracle?

He made sure he was he headed toward downtown, *el centro*. And more specifically, he made sure he was headed toward Zócalo, the neighborhood a nice woman had mentioned as a possible good place to begin his search. The woman was a housekeeper, she told him, and had once been employed by a diplomat's family there.

By four in the morning, through the growing light and midrises, he began to see patches of green grass. Here poverty was hardly visible, only an occasional lonely wanderer like himself, and there were no more cardboard shacks or free-roaming roosters. There were trees and lawns and buildings designed by architects. Bright umbrellas were being set upon street corners for lattes and, later, lunch.

By mid-morning, after several consultations with snack stand operators, he became fairly certain he'd arrived in either the place called Zócalo or the place called El Distrito Federal. He left the motorbike chained to a pole, whistled for the pup to follow, and together they continued on foot. Five-star hotels and shopping. Beautiful men and women walking with iPhones, parking BMW motorcycles, and getting out of dark sedans.

It was unexpected to him, and posh, and none of it seemed right. Try as he might, Jefferson could not imagine the old writer, that man with the famous wiry eyebrows from the back cover of his paperback, living near any of this hubbub. There were swanky residential side streets, to be sure, all stacked with high-rises. Maybe when García Márquez had been younger, he would have had an apartment in a high-rise to entertain his intellectual friends, but he was an old guy now, and—Jefferson couldn't help it—he didn't believe old guys who wrote novels lived in high-rises.

It was late morning when he came to the bookstore owned by an American named Fernanda, who was obsessed with Latin American literature and who had moved to Mexico City from Brooklyn after 9/11. Fifty-two years old with tight eyes, this Fernanda was nothing like Fernanda del Carpio, the most beautiful of the five thousand most beautiful women in the land, the woman conceived by García Márquez, the Fernanda Jefferson thought of as the real Fernanda. The Fernanda of the bookstore had hair of no true hue, and in the end she proved unable to guide him. She smirked and crossed her arms and warned Jefferson about disappointment. Didn't he know? He'd be lucky to get within a city block of García Márquez. Didn't he know? The old writer did not talk to anyone.

But Jefferson's hope had reached a great height, for it was the hope that comes at the end of a long race. So he thanked the bookstore owner for listening to his story and left her with a smile, practicing a short handstand outside the front door to shake off any negativity that might have attached itself to him because of her lack of faith. Then he made his way to a bench in a nearby plaza. It was a Saturday, early December, and it was raining, and he could think of nothing better than to wait to see who might approach and offer to help him.

He spent the afternoon on the bench watching a photographer snap candids of nearby lovers. He saw a multitude of people pass by, and several times he thought he had identified a person who could help, each time asking the critical question, in his best mix of Spanish and English. "Perdón. Dónde vive el gran autor, Gabo? Mucho famoso?" He began with the name he now understood might be the writer's most familiar nickname, Gabo, and only if that name received a shrug did he move on to the more formal "Dónde está Gabriel García Márquez?"—a sentence that Jefferson knew translated literally to "Where is Gabriel García Márquez?" If the names Gabo and García Márquez got no response, Jefferson did his best to ask where the rich people lived, and the artists. Several times he held out his street map to a kind-looking man or woman, raised his eyebrows, said, "Los ricos?" or "Los artistas?" and hoped for a miracle. After two hours and twenty-three minutes and a lot of sweating, the most common response he had received was still "Who?"

It was getting on toward evening, and he was sure he was as close as he had ever been to GGM. He walked on his hands for a while up and down the sidewalk, Remedios yipping at his side, trying as always to generate some good energy. He trimmed a few stray shoots off the trunks of several lime trees and then returned to his bench, a place he felt sure would eventually attract the right person.

The sun was beginning to set when the old woman arrived, stooped against her cane in front of his bench, her head wrapped in a green towel as if she'd just washed her hair. Jefferson was ready. Here she was, his helper. He could see a shimmer around the outline of her small frame, and the refrain from the hallelujah song began to play way back in his ears. She looked at him, and he spoke the question, slowly, as best he could. "Por favor." *Please.* "Dónde está Gabriel García Márquez?" *Where is Gabriel García Márquez?*

The woman looked at Jefferson and paused, peering up through the branches of the almond trees above, up to the high-rise balconies. She looked behind her with a stern brow, and then she looked ahead, to the left, and to the right, and finally she placed her forehead down into the pocket of her hand as it lay open and propped against her cane. She seemed to be navigating the tangled streets of the metropolis, retracing her steps to a place she had visited long ago. Jefferson waited, hopeful.

When the old woman returned from her mental wanderings, she waved her one free hand in a new direction, what Jefferson guessed was eastward. She spoke in a fierce Spanish he could not follow, but from the vigorous thrashing of her left wrist, he guessed he must still be many miles away from the right neighborhood. As best he could, Jefferson asked her to confirm this fact and she nodded, *Sí*, and thrashed her hand and wrist again in what he interpreted to mean *Get going!* He was thanking her and standing then, preparing to retrieve the Kawasaki and head off in this new direction, when the old woman's language became intelligible, as if she had finally found the words for which she had been searching, nodding and smiling. "San Ángel. San Ángel! No, El Zócalo! San Ángel, señor! Sí, señor."

IT WAS RAINING again, and Jefferson's thoughts had turned
to literature and its embrace, a good story's ability to guide
the reader to a better life, to help him to know himself more
fully. Iraq seemed so far away. Though he continued to kneel
every morning and read the list, seeing each of those names
and faces as clearly as he had ever seen them, Jefferson could
no longer smell the acrid aftermath of each unique explosion.
Try as he might to remember that smell, to recall the singe
of his nostrils, the sensation had fallen into a new category
of memory, the memory recalled with effort rather than the
memory that shrieks in the dark of night.

He had spent the morning walking in the rain and asking many people the same question—*Where is San Ángel?
Nearby, yes?* He continued to trust the words of the old
stooped woman, who had seemed so certain that this was
the neighborhood Jefferson sought. He had left Remedios
the Pup with a kind shopkeeper who said she loved the
name Remedios and loved *One Hundred Years of Solitude*,
but had had no idea that García Márquez lived in Mexico.
Wasn't he Colombian? Still, Jefferson continued to have
great faith in the act of asking for help. So far, it had led
him right.

Again, most people shrugged at his question, or appeared unwilling to stop and talk because of the rain, but there were three who tried their best. A middle-aged woman with a very large bottom shoved into a tight black skirt seemed to want to help, but she also seemed confused, pointing down one street, giving him directions in an English-Spanish hodgepodge, then pausing and pointing in the opposite direction, down a different street. A teenage boy carrying a boom box said he'd played with Gabriel García Márquez's grandsons when they were young—yes, he knew where the boys had lived—but he'd never met the writer, had only heard his grandmother speak of him. Did Jefferson want him to show him where the grandsons, those little boys, had lived all those years ago? A delivery guy unloading several cases of soda for a snack shop was pretty sure about Miércoles Street, or somewhere near that.

In this way, the blind leading the blind, the curious helping the curious, the trustworthy aiding the trustworthy, Jefferson ended up in the place called San Ángel, the place he believed he had been looking for. From a brochure in the lobby of a small inn, he read that it had been an ancient settlement long since enveloped by the metropolis. He sat on the curb across the street from a snack shop and a park, and he waited for what would happen.

It was quiet, a kind of quiet he had not yet experienced in Mexico City, and something about this quiet made him believe he must be in the right place. This was the enclave within the stormy chaos that Jefferson imagined that writers everywhere might seek. It had the feel of gravity and of slow, fluid thinking. It had the feeling of refuge.

He sat on the curb, drinking Cokes and eating peanuts, pretending he belonged and waiting for something to happen. Occasionally he took out the collage and worked on it a little.

At the end of the day a woman and her two young daughters walked to the park from an opposite side street and began playing a game of tag on the small green patch of grass, near a swing and slide. Jefferson watched the children play and enjoyed their quiet company, having no intention of asking the woman for help. She was obviously from this part of the city, a local in this quaint neighborhood; she had packed a snack for her girls in her satchel, and she said a number of times that it would soon be time to go home for dinner.

It was she who spoke to Jefferson, smiling. Was he visiting San Ángel?

Jefferson, tired, told the truth. "I'm trying to find Gabriel García Márquez," he said. "He saved my life, you know?"

She wanted the whole story. What had happened to Jefferson? How had he come to know of the writer? Was he American?

And so he told her. Beginning with Ms. Tolan and Honors English 4 and including the list of losses and ending with the Forty-One All-Time Best Quotes and Nigel's Kawasaki and his great fortune with the bergamot woman and, really, just about everyone he'd met along the way.

"I've got to find him," he said finally. "I've got to tell him."

The woman seemed surprised, as if she'd learned something new about a story she'd thought was already finished.

It turned out that she'd known Gabriel García Márquez since she was a little girl. She'd grown up next door to him, and her parents were friends of his and his wife's. They'd shared meals, celebrated holidays, alternated between homes. Lots of people love him, she said. Lots of people dream of meeting him.

And then she wrote down the famous writer's address—on Calle Miércoles—and a few particulars about his compound on a piece of paper from her purse. He had done most of his own gardening until he grew too ill, she said. Perhaps the old man might have changed his habits, but if it were her, she'd wait on the south side of the wall, just outside the old turquoise garden gate with the symbols of the cosmos carved into its wood. In the past he'd liked to pick up his newspaper there. She knew because as a teen she'd had trouble sleeping, and sometimes she'd sat on the curb outside her compound and visited with him in the wee hours. "He's an insomniac—or used to be," she said.

It was a good bet, she said, though he was older now, and he'd been very sick with cancer for a long time. Though he'd survived, his mind wasn't what it once was. Jefferson could try, though, the woman said. He'd need a miracle, but why not try?

IN ALL, IT rained four days, three hours, two minutes, and a handful of seconds. During that time Jefferson buttressed his courage in the covered walkways and narrow alleyways of San Ángel, Remedios the Pup by his side.

And then the sun came out, and Jefferson followed the woman's instructions to the end of the little street behind the public garden, where it became a cobbled lane. The wall that stood before him, she had explained, would look like posole, a deep ivory with flecks of brown and rust, and it would be draped with a tangled mess of trumpet and wisteria vines. From the other side he would likely hear peacocks screaming. Occasionally one of the more skilled flyers among them might leap momentarily to the top of the wall, just long enough to gawk at the outside world before falling backward into the old man's garden. He loves his peacocks, the woman had said.

When Jefferson arrived, all of the woman's words proved true save the peacock teetering on the wall. Here was the posole-colored wall hung with vines. Here were the proud yelps of birds from the other side. Jefferson wasn't certain, but he guessed they were decades-old almond trees standing in a long line. Spreading out tall and wide and dense, the line of trees said *No* to the heat and to the sun and to anything else that might threaten a man's solitude. On the other side of the narrow cobbled way came the scratch-scratch-scratching of chickens and the intermittent calls of what he guessed must be a lone peacock.

He felt ready to get his bearings, to watch the compound gates, to see the cars pass by, the neighbors walk past and wonder, but nothing else. Now that he stood so near, Jefferson was sure he was not ready to knock on the front door.

He turned to the left and walked until he reached the end of what he believed to be García Márquez's wall and the beginning of the next property, about fifty yards down, and then he turned around and continued back in the other direction. He passed the front entrance, rough-hewn double pine doors with a tarnished lion's-head knocker, and went on until the wall rounded the corner of the modest street, and followed a smaller brick lane until he was out of sight behind fruited trees and overhanging vines. The wall reached another corner at the end of another hundred yards, and around it the lane turned into a two-rutted grass and dirt alleyway.

Jefferson followed the alley as far as his eyes could manage, down into the greenness. In front of him, just before the corner, stood a wooden door, a single wooden door stained turquoise, raised several inches above a bed of fine gravel and carved with the moon and the stars. Just in sight of the main entrance with its driveway, this one looked to be the portal for a housekeeper, a gardener, anyone taking out the trash. It was here, at this spot near the back corner of the property, that Jefferson decided to camp out for the evening. It was possible someone would see him, think he was a bum, ask him to leave, but Jefferson believed in the power of his intentions, and he believed this was the spot where he'd wait until morning.

He had some confidence to build and some remembering to do: Why had he come down here again? And besides all that, a whole lot of reading.

At some point in the trip, somewhere between San Miguel

and Querétaro, Jefferson had realized with great disbelief he that he had never actually read *One Hundred Years of Solitude* in its entirety. Not from beginning to end. If someone had asked him his favorite scene or favorite line, Jefferson would not have paused, for those were questions with lots of easy answers. True, one's favorite line, one's favorite scene even, might change from day to day, but he'd always have an answer ready for a question like that. So many favorite scenes. So many three-page sentences. But if someone had taken him for an expert, if someone had asked him what the novel was *about*, its themes, even its plot, Jefferson would have crossed his eyes and mumbled. The truth was, he had not once read the whole story.

JEFFERSON STAYED AWAKE for the next thirty-six hours, taking breaks for sandwiches and to use the bathroom at the little snack shop down the street, and read *One Hundred Years of Solitude*, making notes in the margin as he went along, Remedios the Pup by his side. During that time no one came in or out of the turquoise gate, though a young woman walked out the front entrance in the early evening and returned again the next morning around nine, and another woman, an older woman, arrived midmorning and stayed until about four, and twice a third woman, scarfed and sunglassed, drove off in an old brown Mercedes, each time returning about an hour later. Jefferson kept track of the comings and goings on a blank piece of notebook paper, folded up with the rest of his important papers and tucked inside the novel's front cover.

Oh, but the reading of that story he thought he knew so well! So many characters to keep track of—all those Aureliano Josés, all those Arcadios, all those gypsies, all those years of war—and the repetition reminded him of that perpetual motion toy the guidance counselor at Santa Fe High had kept on her desk. Thank goodness for the family tree printed just after the title page. He felt he must be an idiot for having to consult it so many times. Was Aureliano José the son of an

Arcadio or of an Aureliano? And who was the father of those identical twins switched at birth?

But when he stopped being so hard on himself, Jefferson discovered something unbelievable—that after all the time he'd spent with the novel, there was still more to be discovered. For instance, how had he never before noticed the idea, in the mind of the youngest Aureliano, that literature was a plaything, a device to make people laugh, something to be enjoyed?

The story involved flying carpets, and it led him through swamplands and highlands and several times past a petrified Spanish galleon. It escorted him into the bedrooms of concubines and the hammocks of nostalgic lovers, and liberated him from any meager ideas he may have had of sex or of family or of home. Oh my God, and the women. Jefferson was swept away by the most beautiful woman among five thousand of the most beautiful women (Fernanda!), as well as the one who could eat more than any man, an award-winning gastronome known as the Elephant. But most of all, the story reminded him of war and all its devastations. At the end of the 436th page, Jefferson was both satisfied and exhausted.

He read by the light of the moon and on into the next day, read until he forgot that the wall upon which he leaned was not the one at the end of Tesuque Street under the shade of ponderosa pines but instead the wall surrounding the compound of GGM. He had never been a fast reader—he decided this was because he enjoyed the sentences too much to hurry—and so it took him all of the following day and night to finish reading, just an hour before the sky began to shift into morning.

Jefferson was considering the beautiful sad end of the story of the Buendía clan—mourning the losses left by those ants and trying to fathom what it all meant—when he heard the shuffle of slippers on the other side of the wall. At first he thought it was just his own mind imagining the shuffle of José Arcadio Buendía's slippers as he made his delirious ghostly rounds of the old family home in the novel, but then he concentrated and took a firm hold of his reality. He could see that this was no dream, that he was most definitely slumped against the posole-colored wall with the novel clutched against his chest, and that he could hear chickens scratching in the gravel on the other side. There was the old turquoise door, carved with visions of the cosmos; there was the faint odor of garbage from the neighbor's cans, just five feet away; and then, an undeniable *cock-a-doodle-doo*. And there it was again, the shuffle of what sounded like slippers on the other side.

Jefferson sat up and dusted himself off, put the novel down next to him, and tried to arouse his brain. Could it be?

Oh, no. He looked down at himself. A mess. But there was no time to try to make himself look prepared or presentable. He was dirty, hungry, and tired. Remedios whimpered the whimper of a neglected pup.

He stood up, dusted off his sweats, and moved toward the turquoise door, trying to plan what he would say to whoever it was, about to discover him there on the sidewalk in the predawn night And then, just as he breathed a hopeful sigh, the heavy handle began to turn, and as he watched—like the sound of distant birds singing unknown arias, like the jangle of the tambourines of gypsies and the accordions of generations of drunken musicians—the gate swung outward and he heard a bass voice, as deep as the ocean, humming a playful melody, one of those Sousa marches Esco liked to play on the CD player in the kitchen when she was cleaning.

A stooped, white-headed figure in pajamas moved out into the moonlight.

A man, yes, very old, shuffling in his robe and slippers, the back of his head shimmery and threadbare, his tilt fixed on something several feet from the gate, down in the street. Jefferson looked—the newspaper. Thrown down there rather than up on the sidewalk where it should have been. Behind the old man, a small guinea hen and a white Pekingese followed, *trit-trot, trit-trot,* anxious improper bodyguards.

The old man's legs did not seem to work so well, and as Jefferson watched, he shuffled the few feet and began to bend down, trying to reach the extra eight inches beyond the sidewalk to the street, where his newspaper lay. Even after he'd bent all the way down, his fingers didn't quite reach, and he mumbled something to the hen and the dog, Jefferson guessed a curse against the paperboy, and slowly raised himself back up to standing and surveyed the scene around him. The dark quiet of night was loosening its hold, and the old man scratched the back of his head and took a deep breath.

Jefferson hated to see an old man, any old man, struggle like this. He wanted to help, but now he was afraid of frightening him, giving him a heart attack. And then, almost worse, if that old guy turned out indeed to be the famous writer—Jefferson could not even bring himself to think the three full words GABRIEL GARCÍA MÁRQUEZ in that moment; it embarrassed him, it seemed so unlikely—he would have no idea how to explain himself. Why was he sitting at the famous writer's back gate? This was not the introduction he had hoped for, although in truth he had not planned an alternative.

On his second attempt, the old man brushed the newspaper with his fingertips, but he still could not grasp the thing. Jefferson hated watching this. For several seconds he considered whether to pretend to have been a passerby and retrieve the newspaper himself and hand it to the old man, but he felt he had been hiding and watching too long, that his position was inexplicable at best, and more likely infuriating. It was too bad he hadn't announced himself at the start, when the gate swung open, but he hadn't, and now he felt as if he should remain only an observer.

The old man began a third try at the paper then, chuckling to himself and the hen and the little dog. You had to be very old to have a chuckling perspective on anything at this time in the morning, Jefferson thought—it must have been around 4:00 a.m. The man reached out and steadied himself against the turquoise gate that, Jefferson had been told, led to the garden of Gabriel García Márquez.

Now the old man was shaking his head, having failed for a third time to grasp the paper. He had wrinkles far deeper than the man Jefferson had imagined from the picture on the novel's back cover. Where were the broad shoulders, the thick, hairy chest, the dense, moist skin he'd guessed went along with those eyebrows? Where was the gangster speaking in incredibly long sentences?

Having failed to reach the paper by stooping, the old man placed his hands on his thighs and folded himself down until he was crouched in a low squat, able to put his palms on the walkway in front of him and his knees on the walkway under him and his toes on the walkway in back. He moved like an old dog toward an old bone, the guinea hen clucking next to his head and the Pekingese standing at attention near his feet.

Jefferson watched all this, trying to reconcile the scene with all his previous expectations.

And then, success. The old man grasped the newspaper with his right hand, pulled it to his chest, and, reversing the process, sat back on his knees and heels and sighed another deep sigh. Jefferson sighed with him, and smiled. It was possible that this old man was just the kind of old man who could have been a younger man once, sitting at a typewriter all day long, smoking cigarettes, writing complicated and beautiful sentences, writing important stories. It was possible.

Concerned that the old man would go back through the gate without noticing him, Jefferson stepped out from against the wall, scuffing his sneakers against the pavement and clearing his throat and freeing Remedios from his tight grip. "Um, excuse me, sir?"

But he and the pup seemed only to have caught the attention of the Pekingese. The dog pranced several paces in their direction and began a low growling as the old man moved methodically from his kneeling position to take a seat on the curb. He proceeded to unwrap the paper from its plastic bag and rubber band as if unaware of any larger commotion. He had just begun humming that Sousa march again when the Pekingese began to bark, moving in a semicircle around Remedios, who had retreated to perch atop Jefferson's feet. But the old man kept reading and humming.

"Excuse me? Mr. García Márquez? Mr. García Márquez?" Jefferson said it as loudly as he felt comfortable speaking at that hour. Someone from the house or a neighbor would hear the commotion soon. When even that didn't rouse the old man, he took the risk of grabbing Remedios in his arms, leaping with her over the little dog, and landing just a few feet from the old man, saying once again, "Excuse me, sir. I'm so sorry to startle you . . . I'm really sorry, but your dog— Habla inglés?" Jefferson said finally, suddenly remembering that he was in Mexico City, and that he didn't have any proof that this old man sitting before him was actually Gabriel García Márquez, and that even if he was the famous writer, his English at four o'clock in the morning was probably not so good.

"Yes, I speak English," the old man said, laying the paper on his knees and turning to face Jefferson. "Where did you come from, anyway? I didn't notice you there."

"Oh, wow, it is you. You're him. You're GGM—I mean, García Márquez. Oh my god, oh my god," Jefferson said as he moved closer to the old man and focused in on those eyes he'd studied so many times from the back cover of his book. The old man had taken the growling Pekingese into his lap, and the guinea hen scratched nearby.

Jefferson was smiling so hard, his head was back in Iraq in his bunk, thinking of the war story he had wanted for so long to tell the famous writer. For a long while he had lumped it all together as one big bad experience, like a mouthful of rotten tomato he had to swallow, but in that predawn moment next to the old man, the little seams Jefferson had used to sew it all up together began to unravel, and the individual stories of war cried out to be remembered individually. He remembered the day he saw Tristan's hand blown off, and the other time he'd thought he'd stepped on a land mine but hadn't, and also about those three little Iraqi girls and how he'd sometimes imagined them as butterflies flying up into heaven. There was so much to share, so many stories García Márquez would appreciate, but Jefferson found himself unable to speak, and so he just sat there next to the old man and smiled, clutching the tattered paperback to his chest and a few times shaking his head and saying it over and over, *Oh my god, oh my god.*

Without fanfare a peacock had joined them on the curb and strutted now to the street, just in front of where they sat. The old man said something to the bird, an endearment, Jefferson thought, and within moments the peacock had swept his tail feathers up and out behind him in a wide arc. "See, I'm the boss," said the old man, pointing to the plumage and laughing out loud at his joke.

This seemed like the invitation for which Jefferson had waited so long. All his hesitation melted away, and as he watched the bird strut, he too gained confidence. He looked into the old man's eyes.

"You see, sir, my name is Jefferson Long Soldier. And your book, *One Hundred Years—One Hundred Years of Solitude,* no?—it saved my life. Literally. I mean it, man." Jefferson took the old man's hands in his own. "It saved my life. I'm telling you the truth, see."

The old man looked into Jefferson's eyes, nodding, saying nothing.

"So that's why I rode down here, no, on my cousin's motorbike to find you, see? I needed to find you so I could tell you how much you mean to me, and so I could thank you. For saving my life, you know? So here I am. . . . Thank you," Jefferson said, looking up at the old man again because his eyes had once again shifted down to the stones. "Thank you,

Mr. García Márquez . . . Mr. Gabriel García Márquez . . . thank
you . . . for saving . . . my life."

Without knowing it, Jefferson had started to cry. His
shoulders were shaking, and his chin was pinned against his
chest, his hands now supporting his head. He was thinking
about all the things he had wanted to say to the old man,
all the quotes he'd memorized and planned to recite just to
pay homage. How he wanted to explain to the writer how
high school students weren't really old enough to read literature like *One Hundred Years*, at least not the high-school-
ers he'd known at Santa Fe High, and that it had, unfortu-
nately, taken Real Live War to make him understand why
great writers write at all. That he thought a really good idea
would be to teach great literature to soldiers in war zones.
But all the questions he'd had—whether GGM had been a
soldier himself (Jefferson guessed he must have been) and
whether he'd had to kill anyone, and whether his real-life
family in Colombia was anything like those bizarre Buendías
in Macondo, and whether he'd ever ridden on a magic carpet
for real—turned to silence as the two of them listened to the
waking of the day. All his emotion, all his praise and sympa-
thy and love, came out only as a muddled mess of tears.

After a few minutes the old man reached out with his right
hand and patted Jefferson on the shoulder. Then he stood up
slowly and motioned for Jefferson to follow. Remedios and the
Pekingese and the guinea hen scampered underfoot as the
two of them began to walk down the narrow street Jefferson
had come to know so well and then turned down a dirt lane
and then another and another until they became lost in the
labyrinth of San Ángel, the light of the moon their guide.

The old man spoke every now and then, pointing out the
blossoms of flowering vines and noting the homes of friends,
the workshop of a favorite potter, a woman who had made him
a set of ice cream bowls, a shrine to Our Lady of Guadalupe,
the tree from which he occasionally swiped mangos. But

mostly he was quiet, peering up into the starry night, clucking his tongue at the moon, chuckling at unspoken jokes.

Jefferson guessed they had rounded the end of a large arc and had begun circling back toward the García Márquez compound when the old man told the story of his own grandmother and grandfather, how they had met on a starry night in the city of Riohacha. "They were wonderful people," the old man said.

They passed a small grass plaza surrounded by smaller, simpler homes before the old man stopped and turned to Jefferson, almost as if he'd just remembered his presence. "Tell me a story now," García Márquez said, and when Jefferson hesitated, the old man said, "Tell me a story about your grandmother." As Jefferson thought what story he might tell, the famous writer explained that he believed that everyone became a natural storyteller when the subject was his own grandparents. "These are the first people we come to know, truly know, as separate from ourselves," he said. "With our parents, we are too close, but with our grandparents, we begin to see the possibility of myth, of magic, of tragedy and of unexpected miracles. With our grandparents we begin to comprehend that the world is very large and forgiving."

Jefferson did not know how this theory related to him, so he said the only thing he knew to say. "When I was nine months old, my mother left me with my grandmother and never came back. I never knew my dad, but I understand he was a hundred percent Lakota."

The old writer had stopped walking and peered into Jefferson's eyes. "Let's sit," he said, and looking around and finding no bench, he motioned toward the curb.

The two sat, and Jefferson continued. He explained that he didn't know any stories about his grandmother, nothing very interesting, at least. That she was the one who had taken care of him as a baby, the one who had cooked his meals, washed his clothes, and run the corner grocery store so that she could buy him clothes at Walmart. He explained that she was half Mexican but had never been to Mexico, and that her mother had died when she was fourteen. Jefferson explained what he knew about his grandmother's father, a German Scots-Irish man who built the corner store and attached home in which he and Esco still lived. And then he remembered the thing that would mean something to the writer.

"She's a whole lot like Úrsula Iguarán. You know Úrsula? In your novel?" He opened his eyes wide in the old man's direction.

"Ah, sí, la abuela. Bueno," said the old man, nodding as if he understood. "A tough old woman."

But at that moment Jefferson had realized a horrible truth. He did not know his own grandmother's story—not much of it. This truth set off a series of rambling thoughts in his mind. The dogs sat on either side of them and the hen and peacock continued their scratchings as Jefferson began again to speak the words as they came to him. It was his grandmother's story, yes, perhaps similar to that of the grandmother in García Márquez's novel, but different. His grandmother's story as he began to imagine it for the first time. A woman living her life, reading books and cooking food and doing a whole lot of things before he'd ever known her. Yes, he had known all along that the two of them were not the same being. He wasn't stupid. But Jefferson had never imagined, before that moment with the old writer on the curb, the secret hopes and dreams and heartaches that must have made up his grandmother's life.

"She was born in Santa Fe on June 16, 19 . . ." He paused because he could never remember the year of Esco's birth, though she had told him many times. "I think it was 1942," he said. "But it may have been '41. One of those two." And then he went on, telling what he knew and what he imagined about her earliest years with both a mother and a father, how she had loved to climb the piñons near the arroyo, how she had loved to lie on her back in the grass and stare deep into the blue sky.

"Her mom was from Chihuahua, I think," Jefferson said, thinking now that he should have asked his grandmother about that before he'd taken off on this journey, about whether she thought they had any relatives living there still, since he'd be traveling through.

"She learned how to read as a kid, but she didn't become a real reader until I went to elementary school and needed help. She helped me learn to read, and that's when she really started loving books." Jefferson thought about this for the first time. It was true. His grandmother was a real reader, the kind of woman who always had a stack of books on her bedside table and fell asleep each night with one facedown on her chest. "If I had to pick one, I'd say her favorite writer is Kurt Vonnegut Jr.," he said. "But she also really, really loves Eudora Welty."

"Ah . . . ," said the old man, his keen eyes on the ground. "Claro."

"But she hasn't read *One Hundred Years of Solitude*," Jefferson said apologetically. "Not that I know of, anyways."

"Ah, sí," said the old man.

"I'm gonna work on her, though. I mean, not that you need any salespeople. Not that you need any help—you know what I mean? But for her, you know? I want her to read *One Hundred Years* for her. Because, you know, it would change her life."

He talked, and the old man listened. At some point his stories about his grandmother turned into something else, and Jefferson found that he was talking about Ms. Tolan and the tears she got in her eyes when speaking the words *Gabriel . . . García . . . García Márquez.* He was telling about RT and the three Iraqi girls and their father, driving away in their little Toyota. About beautiful, plentiful Tajia and their passion among the bags of pancake mix and vats of canola oil. About the angry soldiers yelling at him that last time in the dining hall. All this went on for what must have been hours while the old man listened. He did not interrupt to ask questions or try to get ahead to where he felt the story might be headed. He did not fidget. He did not cross and recross his legs. He did not seem to have to fight off drowsiness. Occasionally he nodded, and a few times he raised his eyebrows.

Until finally the cocks were crowing all over the neighborhood and a man down the block was wheeling his trash cans down to the street, looking at Jefferson and the old man and the dogs and the birds in a funny way. They walked back toward the old man's compound, talking about the grass and the flowers and the sky as they went, and as they neared the street where the old man lived, Jefferson said how much he'd enjoyed meeting him and that he planned to be in town a few more days (the truth was, he had no real plan) and that if it was okay, he would be waiting by the back gate, the turquoise gate carved with the visions of the cosmos, in the wee hours of the next morning, just in case the old man was free to go on another late-night walk with him.

"Sí, bueno," said Gabriel García Márquez. "Perhaps."

And then, because he did not want the moment to end, Jefferson explained that he had one more thing he wanted to share with the old man. Just a little something.

They were standing at the corner of Calle Miércoles and Buena Vista, the turquoise gate in view, when Jefferson began to chant. It seemed the right time to share the collage he'd been working on all that time. If he was honest, he'd begun the collage even before he'd set out on this journey, from the time he had started collecting favorite lines in his mind and in his heart. True, it was the kind of project that could go on a lifetime, forever being refined, but for the moment Jefferson believed it was good enough to share. And besides, here was the great writer standing before him as the first light entered the new day. It was Saturday, mid-December, and the morning had a luminescent mistiness about it that reminded him of the possibility of angels.

OUT THERE

Jefferson took a half step back from the old man, into the middle of the narrow street, and he filled his lungs with hope. He closed his eyes, and lifted his chin to the heavens, and began to chant the words that came to him now as if they'd been imprinted forever on the canvas of his mind.

He began with what was really the title—Out There—and he chanted that a few times to warm up his voice and to make it clear to GGM that he was serious. The old man stood perfectly still, his chin slightly cocked. And then Jefferson launched into what was in that moment his favorite line, revised to fit the collage, among the Forty-One All-Time Best Quotes.

It rained for more than three years, and many months and two days.

This too, Jefferson chanted a number of times before going on.

And then,
A radiant Wednesday brought a trickle of blood,
Out under the door,
Crossing the living room,
Running out into the street.

My heart's memory stopped,
Replaced by a viscous bitter substance.
Someone dead under the ground,
Dark bedrooms,
Captured towns,
A scorpion in my sheets.
Conservatives and Liberals, all of them wearing funny
Underwear.
The smell of dry blood.
The bandages of the wounded.
All of it,
A silent storm.

Sarah Stark

Me, left out there.
Dying of hunger and of love.

He stood in the street, chanting each word as if it were its own unique memory, holding the paper on which he'd written and scratched out and rewritten just in case he forgot a line next to his chest. If he had to say, it was one of his best-ever efforts as an individual, if only because he had worked so hard on the collage, and he felt it was better than trying to explain in normal sentences to Gabriel just how important the words were. One of his favorite stanzas was about the big world Jefferson had experienced "out there," a world he believed was best described by García Márquez's language—parrots reciting Italian arias, hens laying golden eggs to the sound of tambourines, men making gold fishes, children discovering ice. How great it was to sing a collage to the original creator of these ideas.

Although Jefferson knew that he'd taken a few things out of context, he felt as if GGM wouldn't mind. In fact, didn't it prove that the novel was even more universal if Jefferson could read a paragraph about falling in love with a woman and transform it into a tribute to falling in love with a book?

He chanted on, peeking out from under his closed lids to see if the famous writer seemed to be enjoying himself, and more importantly, if he seemed to be understanding all the connections.

Then I found it.
Gigantic and sturdy.
Almost enough to drown me in a cistern.
Its soft whispering,
A mineral savoring
Of love.

I hung my hammock between almond trees and made love to it
in broad daylight.
I gave thanks to it.

He chanted the bit about being too young to see the things he'd seen, about finally being able to hear music again, about the hope of one day being able to smell oregano. He chanted the bit about the blessing of living beyond devastation.

That I would go on living,
Human and nostalgic,
Remembering without bitterness,
Multiplying all that is good,
Softness in my heart.

By the time he had finished, the sun was in Jefferson's eyes, but that did not keep him from seeing the old man's smile or from hearing his words or the heavy clap of his two hands together.

"Bravissimo! Bueno!" the old man said.

"You liked it?"

"Who's the writer, now, huh?"

The two of them stood facing each other a few moments, no words left to say, the day breaking warm in the distance. Jefferson's ears were beginning to play that hallelujah song, and he was considering singing it softly for GGM, just to make the perfect moment that much better, when the old man turned and began shuffling away, offering a quiet but certain "Hasta luego" as he disappeared behind the turquoise gate.

JEFFERSON HAD SPENT the day exploring the sunken gardens and, later, drinking coffee under the umbrella of a café stand, replaying his moonlit walk with the great writer. The idea pulsed all around him—the idea that he, Jefferson Long Soldier, had lived to tell his story to Gabriel García Márquez.

No one else in the whole world knew. He passed laughing children in the park, and he wanted to tell them. He passed old men reading newspapers, and he wanted to interrupt with his news.

Late in the day he began to get excited, eating a messy plate of beans and rice as slowly as he could manage and asking for five refills of iced tea as he began to anticipate his second encounter with Gabriel. He thought the sun might never set.

But.

Eventually.

Night.

Came.

And there Jefferson sat, against the posole-covered wall, giving thanks for a multitude of things, so many people, so many devastatingly beautiful experiences, and waiting. It was just past midnight, probably at least several hours to go before GGM would come for his newspaper through the turquoise gate again, and so Jefferson did his best to organize his thoughts. Sleep would come later. He would sleep once he was back home. For now he had some thinking to do, some prep work for his second visit with Gabriel. The first one had been amazing on many levels, it was true, but Jefferson had realized during the course of the day that he'd failed to mention so many important things to his hero. So many things to remember. And stories. Jefferson began to list the things and the stories he would share on this, his second night with the great writer.

For starters, there was the list. He had alluded to it, but he hadn't read it to Gabriel. Tonight he would read it. He was sure that would make an impact. And then there was his plan to say thank you, which had somehow gotten lost in the first visit. He'd muttered the two words, but they had come out garbled, and so Jefferson felt that after having come so far, it was worth another try. Saying thank you was not a thing that could be overdone. Then there were his favorite lines. He'd sung the collage, but that was different from reading the actual list of Forty-One All-Time Best Quotes, which he planned to do tonight. That was so important. How could he have forgotten it?

The paperboy threw the newspaper short of the sidewalk again, the thing landing in almost exactly the same spot in the street as the previous morning.

Soon enough a hint of light came, and the scratching of birds on the other side of the gate was soon followed by the shuffle of steps Jefferson had been awaiting. Gabriel was coming. Jefferson could hear his footsteps.

Much as on the previous evening, he got up and dusted himself off, but this time he stood out in front of the gate, holding the newspaper he'd picked up, ready to present to his friend. Remedios the Pup waited at attention by his side.

Just as on the previous night, the heavy handle began to turn, and soon the turquoise gate was swinging out to reveal the famous writer in his pajamas, his little dog and the guinea hen at his feet. The old man had a look of disequilibrium about him this time, though, his eyes unnaturally glazed and his gait off-kilter, so Jefferson stepped forward to offer his assistance, telling Gabriel "Good morning" and "How are you doing?" and "Here's your newspaper, sir."

The old man looked at Jefferson anew, as if his old eyes had taken a moment to focus upon the young man standing before him, and then he smiled an old man's smile, saying, "Why, thank you, and how kind of you." He took hold of Jefferson's elbow and proceeded with his shuffle away from the turquoise gate, asking him his name, and whether he'd like to join him in a walk by the light of the moon, and whether he had any stories he'd like to share.

IT WAS THE end of the fifteenth day, and with Mexico City
fading behind him, the climb of the high desert plains ahead
of him, and many miles to go on the tired Kawasaki, Jefferson
began to think of everyone he needed to thank. He started
with the entire country of Iraq, thanking all those citizens of
that distant land for all their sacrifices. And then the US Army,
his Tenth Mountain Division and the men and women who'd
shared his living space. Thank you, Rock Guns, he said in his
mind. He'd met a famous writer, his very own Gabriel, and
while it had not changed everything, it was an accomplishment. How many people could claim it? Some people thought
miracles changed everything, and that was missing the point.
He was grateful for the trip and for the time he'd shared with
the old writer, and he was thankful for all the miracles that had
happened along the way, even for the bergamot woman who
had chosen to spare his life.

Gabriel García Márquez was still Number One, but after
him a long list followed in Jefferson's mind, beginning with
Esco, who he knew was responsible for so much, much of
which he would never know. He guessed he probably would
have died of diaper rash or curdled milk in his bottle or that a
flash flood would have whisked him away in his stroller or that

he would have been devoured by red ants if it hadn't been for her. He needed to find Josephina Maria C de Baca, and he wanted to write to Tajia, and then there was Ms. Tolan and, of course, Nigel. He'd go see Dr. Monika in a few days, tell her some new stories, and later he'd begin a list of a whole lot of other people he needed to thank, some of them teachers, many of them strangers.

Jefferson rode slow and easy on the way back home, taking the time to stop along the way whenever there seemed a good reason. By the time he made it back to that roadside spot near the little town of La Parrita and saw the lone man still standing on the edge of the road, he already knew he would stop. Though their conversation was brief and bare, a mix of Spanish and English, Jefferson learned the story of the man's difficult adolescence, and of his love of nature and his hope for mankind too. Every day, the lone man told Jefferson, he waited on that roadside until one person stopped to say hello. Some days he waited all day. Some days the first passerby stopped.

In the end, it took Jefferson almost eleven full days to reach Santa Fe. It was late afternoon on Christmas Eve—the best day of the year in his hometown, he had always thought—by the time he took the off-ramp onto St. Francis Drive. Even though he imagined his grandmother had been cooking all day, he bought two dozen tamales at Posa's on the way home. When he walked through the front door to surprise his family, there they all sat, playing Scrabble and listening to Nat King Cole, Esco's favorite for the holidays. It was as if he had never left, all over again—only this time the sameness, the coming home, proved to be a comfort.

After all the hugging and a short dance sequence from Nigel over in the corner and a flurry of questions about how his trip had gone and how had it worked out with the famous writer guy, and how Remedios was as a traveler, Esco told him that the C de Bacas would be joining them for dinner, and did he know Josephina'd had a little baby? She'd decided to be a single mom, had moved back home with her mom because the baby's father was good for nothing, and, oh yes, she asked about Jefferson from time to time. Esco had thought it was the nice thing to do to include their family for Christmas Eve. She hoped it would be okay with him—she would have asked him if she'd known he was coming home. Jefferson had no words to answer his grandmother, because everything she was saying struck him as so ordinary and good. His eyes began to be aware of a bright light in the corner of the room, sparkling against the ceiling and letting off a soft, warm glow. He could hear the opening few chords of the hallelujah song. It was a little difficult to have a conversation when his gifts were in full swing like this, so he just let an easy smile wash over him.

After he'd talked a little more and gotten the pup some food in the kitchen, Jefferson went down the hall to the bathroom. He closed the door on the festivities and let the warm quiet pinkness of the space, these old tiles, hold him. Esco had a vanilla votive burning on top of a washcloth on top of the toilet tank, giving off a smell like all the holidays he'd ever had. He ran hot water and washed his hands and looked over his skin in the mirror. It was clear now, though he could see some scarring from before. He felt a slight sadness over this fact, as he'd always worked so hard to have clear skin, but it was Christmas Eve, and he'd made it home on time, and Josephina and her baby would be coming over soon, so he shook away the small vanity and allowed himself to look straight into his own eyes. They looked good, he thought, as he leaned in real close and stared, just a minute. If someone had seen him, they'd misinterpret, think he was studying his own surface. Really Jefferson just wanted to see for sure. Yes, his eyes were brown—just as they'd always been, he guessed. They didn't look so tired, considering all that riding. There was even a little holiday sparkle to them, the part of them that could see extraordinary light overlaid on what might appear as darkness to someone else, this quality he swore showed itself now in the mirror as the best part of wisdom.

"Oh, you look so good," Esco said when he walked back into the kitchen.

And there it was. Finally Jefferson could say what he'd wanted to say for so long.

"It's really good to be home, Esco. It's really so good to be home."

Out There
BY JEFFERSON LONG SOLDIER
IN TRIBUTE TO GABRIEL GARCÍA MÁRQUEZ

It rained more than three years, and many months and
    two days.
And then
A radiant Wednesday brought a trickle of blood,
Out under the door,
Crossing the living room,
Running out into the street.

My heart's memory stopped,
Replaced by a viscous bitter substance.
Someone dead under the ground,
Dark bedrooms,
Captured towns,
A scorpion in my sheets.
Conservatives and liberals, all of them wearing funny
    underwear.
The smell of dry blood.
The bandages of the wounded.
All of it,
A silent storm.

Me, left out there.
Dying of hunger and of love.

Out there,
Everything, even music, reminded me of beauty, and
That literature was the best plaything of all.

Out there, a big world:
I didn't know why we were fighting.
Parrots painted all colors,
A hen scratching to the beat of a tambourine,
Men making fish,
Women replacing buttons,
Children discovering ice.

Out there,
I could not find what I was looking for.
Every house a madhouse.
Daily habits nonsense.
The eggplant patch of my memories,
Nothing but mourning and exile and dust.

Then I found it,
Gigantic and sturdy,
Almost enough to drown me in a cistern.
Its soft whispering,
A mineral savoring
Of love.

I hung my hammock between almond trees and made love
    to it in broad daylight.
I gave thanks to it.
Why?

OUT THERE

It opened my eyes.
I saw a light rain of tiny yellow flowers falling.
Yellow flowers falling on the town,
Covering the roofs and blocking the doors.
Yellow flowers opening up the most hidden passageways
    of my heart,
Lifting me up into the air.
I saw a new day breaking out on the horizon,
A sediment of peace filling me.

It had never occurred to me until then to think
I was too young to know
That I would hear music again,
That I would smell the whiff of oregano,
Roses at dusk.

That I would go on living,
Human and nostalgic,
Remembering without bitterness,
Multiplying all that is good,
Softness in my heart.

CPSIA information can be obtained at www.ICGtesting.com
Printed in the USA
LVOW12s1402060414

380520LV00003B/3/P